DEAD MAN'S HAND

A Calvin Watters Mystery #1

LUKE MURPHY

DEAD MAN'S HAND
A Calvin Watters Mystery #1

www.authorlukemurphy.com

SECOND EDITION trade paperback

May 25, 2018

ISBN: 978-1-7753759-1-3

Cover designed by Ryan Doan - www.ryandoan.com & Casey Snyder Design – www.caseysnyderdesign.com

Praise for *Dead Man's Hand*

"Luke Murphy's *Dead Man's Hand* is a pleasure, a debut novel that doesn't read like one, but still presents original characters and a fresh new voice." —Thomas Perry, New York Times bestselling author of *Poison Flower*

"It's always a pleasure to welcome a new voice to the ranks of mystery-thriller authors. So welcome Luke Murphy, who delivers plenty of both in his debut novel, *Dead Man's Hand*. Give it an evening and you may want to give it the whole night, just to see how it turns out." —William Martin, New York Times bestselling author of *Back Bay* and *The Lincoln Letter*

"Part police procedural, part crime fiction, *Dead Man's Hand* is a fast, gritty ride." —Anne Frasier, USA Today bestselling author of *Hush*

"Luke Murphy writes in a clean, mean style, as compelling as a switchblade to your throat. Murphy's the real deal." —Rick Mofina, award-winning author of *Six Seconds*

"*Dead Man's Hand* is a pedal-to-the-metal thriller. Luke Murphy pours a load of talent into his first novel, and it takes off on the first page. Vivid characters and wire-taut plotting make Murphy's novel a five star read. Don't begin *Dead Man's Hand* if you need to do anything else today." — James Thayer, author of *White Star*

"What happens in Vegas, stays in Vegas? Be glad. Be very glad. Luke Murphy puts on display the seedy underbelly of Sin City, where deceit, treachery, vengeance and the double cross are practiced like an art form. For a tight taut thriller, bet on a *Dead Man's Hand*." —Anthony Bidulka, award-winning author of *Dos Equis*

"Calvin Watters is an anti-hero you will cheer in this solid debut that poses twisted questions about crime and punishment." —Julie Kramer, award-winning author of *Shunning Sarah*

"*Dead Man's Hand* gripped me with terror from the first sentence. Tense! Thrilling! Terrifying! Luke Murphy is a great mood-builder on the order of Dean Koontz!" —Betty Dravis, award-winning author of *Six-Pack of Blood*

For Mélanie, Addison and Nève—the girls who keep me going.

Acknowledgements

The most important people in my life: my wife Mélanie, my rock and number one supporter. My daughters, Addison and Nève, who didn't always realize that Daddy had to write, but took my mind off things with frequent games of Ring-Around-The-Rosie.

I'm the first to admit that this novel was not a solo effort. I've relied on many generous and intelligent people to turn this book into a reality. I'd like to thank the following people who had a hand in making this novel what it is today. I'm indebted to you all.

(The Conception) I need to thank the creative and very brilliant:
Mrs. Joan Conrod
Mr. John Stevens
Professor Paul McCarthy

(The Touch-ups) A special thanks for those last minute edits and details, as well as the final nod to:
My agent, Ms. Jennifer Lyons
Dr. Robert Clark

(The Research) For their professional expertise, knowledge in their field and valuable information, thanks to:
Ms. Joanna Pozzulo (Institute of Criminology and Criminal Justice)
Keith MacLellan, M.D.
Officer Laura Meltzer (Las Vegas Metropolitan Police Department)
Constable Keith Cummings (Ottawa Police Department)
Employees of Treasure Island Hotel in Las Vegas

Any procedural, geographical, or other errors pertaining to this story are of no fault to the names mentioned above, but entirely my own, as at times I took many creative liberties.

And last but not least, I'd like to thank you, the readers. You make it all worthwhile.

PROLOGUE

At exactly 6:15 p.m. on a Sunday, Calvin Watters parked his rusted Ford Taurus across the street from a vacant house. Climbing out, he put on a pair of sunglasses and scanned the neighborhood for any movement or potential hazards.

He moved to the back of the car and opened the dented trunk. It creaked in the still night as it slowly swung up. He pulled out a worn black leather case and slid it under his vest. Then he closed the trunk and headed for the door.

He'd been using the rundown house in the red-light district of Las Vegas as his workshop for three years. It suited his purpose. No interruptions, no inquisitive neighbors. Even the local police avoided the area.

He checked the perimeter again. At six-five and 220 pounds, with tattooed arms and gold chains dangling around his thick, muscular neck, a black man like him just didn't go unnoticed in Las Vegas.

The street was silent as he approached the house. Weeds sprang from cracks in the sidewalk and shattered liquor bottles blocked the entrance. The barred windows were broken and the screen door had been ripped off its hinges. His sense of smell no longer reacted to the stench of urine and vomit.

Calvin surveyed the area one last time. Extreme caution was one of the reasons he had succeeded in the business for so long. His habits had kept him alive. Satisfied no one had seen him, he trudged his way up the walk.

Even though he was the best in the business and had once enjoyed the adrenaline rush that came with the trade, the next part of the job made his skin crawl. His goal was to save the money he needed to get away, start over, but he didn't know if he could last on the job long enough. That uncertainty made his life even harder.

He unlocked the door, stepped inside and shut it behind him. Heading for the basement, he took a narrow set of wooden stairs that creaked as he descended into darkness. His dreadlocks scraped cobwebs along the rough ceiling. He flicked the switch and a low-watt bulb cast dim light.

The tiny room had almost no furniture. The bare concrete floor was dirty and stained with dried blood. In the middle of the room, a lone wooden chair—double nailed to the floor—was occupied.

"Hello, James," Calvin said, his face expressionless.

James Pierce stared at him through bulging, fear-filled eyes.

"Sorry about the bump on the head, but I couldn't have you conscious when I moved you here."

When Calvin removed the case from his vest, he saw Pierce's pant leg moisten.

"I'm sure you're wondering why your shoes and socks are off and your pant legs rolled up. We'll get to that."

He laid the case on a small table, strategically placed next to the chair. "There's only one way out," he said, snapping open the lid. He knew his hostage saw one thing when he looked at him—professionally trained brutality.

He checked his watch. Pierce had been there for four hours. The waiting and anticipation alone were more than most men could handle. They often begged for their lives. It was a very effective method.

He stared at Pierce for a long moment and then turned away, his stomach churning.

Get a grip, Calvin! Hurry up and get it over with before you change your mind.

And lose the reputation he'd spent three years building.

He ripped the duct tape from the man's mouth and pulled out the old rag. "Time for me to collect."

Pierce gasped, breathing in air greedily. "Please, Calvin. I beg you. Don't do this."

"You're a degenerate gambler, James. Your expensive hobby and inability to pay has put you here. You knew the rules. They were laid out well in advance."

"No! Please..."

Calvin tried to block out the man's cries. A sudden dizziness overwhelmed him and he grabbed the chair to steady himself. *Finish the job.* "You know how this works." He stared at Pierce.

"I promise I'll pay. Just give me one more day. Please."

"You knew the rules. You've already had an extra week, James. You're lucky Mr. Pitt is a forgiving man, more forgiving than I am. He's only counting that week as one day late. But if you aren't in his office tomorrow morning with all the money, you'll be seeing me again. Every late day will count as two. And I won't be so nice next time."

"I'll pay." Pierce sobbed.

Calvin heaved a sigh. "Relax. It'll all be over soon."

He leaned over the table. For effect, he took his time as he opened the leather case and removed the tools of his trade. "One day, one joint."

This was when most of them broke down all the way. And Pierce didn't disappoint him. A scream boiled from the man's belly and erupted like a relentless siren.

Calvin ignored Pierce as best he could. There were 206 bones in the human skeleton. A pro had trained him to use them all.

"Hammer or pipe cutter?"

"God, no!"

"Hammer or pipe cutter?" He threw a punch at Pierce's jaw, sending bloody spit into the air.

"Hammer!" Pierce screamed.

"Finger or toe?"

Pierce squeezed his eyes shut. "Toe."

Calvin stuffed the dirty rag back into the man's mouth. He turned and pressed play on the radio resting on the table, turning the volume up a few notches, careful not to bring attention to the house. The pounding, vibrating beat from Metallica not only drowned out his prey's moans of pain, but the sound took him back to his glory days. He removed a ball-peen hammer from the pouch and moved in on his quarry's bare feet.

"Toe it is then."

He got down on one knee and lifted the hammer above his head.

After Pierce had passed out from the pain, Calvin checked the man's breathing and then entered an adjoining room that could be locked from the inside. On one side, the shelves were piled with canned or packaged food and beverage containers. He had stored several months' worth of supplies in case he ever came under siege and was trapped.

His complete arsenal hung on the other side. He'd been collecting weapons for three years, purchasing them where he could when he had saved some money. Now the arsenal was almost complete and in his mind, quite impressive. The arsenal had been developed for defensive purposes only.

He had never carried a gun as a collector, but now he selected a weapon for his trip. Something small enough to conceal, but at his ready in case he ran into a nosy cop or former client.

He checked on Pierce again as he left the bomb shelter and moved upstairs to his computer. Once the computer booted up, he hacked into a couple of restricted sites, trying to find any mention of his name by a babbling client or angry competitor. Seeing nothing, he switched over to the LVMPD site to make sure Rachel was staying clean. He checked up on her three times a week. He wouldn't let her slip up.

He logged off and documented his latest collection, noting the methods that worked with Pierce, as well as times and techniques. All of the information was added to a file that spanned three years.

Shutting down the computer, he returned to the basement. He transported Pierce to the gambler's blood-red sedan, which Calvin had parked by the river. He knew that within the hour James would wake up and drive home. What would he tell his wife? There was no worry about Pierce ever relaying this incident to anyone else. Calvin was sure of that.

As he drove back to his workshop, he let out a soft groan. "I need out."

Book One: The Set Up

CHAPTER 1

"Set, three eighty-five, three eighty-five."

As was the custom, the rowdy hometown crowd grew quiet in anticipation.

Calvin—USC's All-American running back—stood behind his quarterback, waiting. His number had been called for a play he'd executed hundreds of times. Most teams were prepared for the play, but none could stop him when he had his eye on a target.

The Trojans were up by four points with less than three minutes left. All they had to do was eat the clock—kill time—and they would be Sugar Bowl champs again.

The Nebraska Cornhuskers were ranked #1 in the nation on defense, but on this day they had been unable to stop Calvin. He already had 118 yards rushing, but another 42 would give him the new school record, beating the record he had set last year.

If I can turn the corner and get a block, I can spring it for a touchdown.

As the center was about to snap the ball, Calvin saw the captain of the Nebraska defense call an audible and change the defensive positioning.

He scanned the field. His quarterback had missed the change. None of his teammates had seen the audible call. They were frozen, awaiting the snap of the ball. If they went ahead and ran the play, there was a chance that he would not only be tackled immediately, but the whole design of the play would be blown.

The smart move would be to receive the ball, fall to the ground and keep the clock running, giving his team an opportunity to run out the clock. Or he could try to run the play on his own and carry the team on his shoulders.

"Hike!" The quarterback grabbed the ball, turned and held it out.

Calvin received the handoff, securing the ball with both hands. But his fullback missed the critical first block.

Everything after that happened in slow motion.

The Husker defense roared full throttle toward him. He was able to dodge the first defender on natural instinct, but as he was avoiding that player, two Cornhuskers struck him at the same time. One caught him high while the other dove low, cutting him at the knees. The sudden impact twisted his legs into a position the human body was not meant to be in. The excruciating pain, combined with the force of the hit, jarred the ball loose from his numb fingers.

Fueled only by adrenaline, he twisted on the ground and reached for the ball against the football-hungry attackers. When the dust cleared, a Nebraska linebacker held the ball up in victory.

Calvin grabbed his knee and screamed, but that was lost in the clamor of the crowd.

In a pool of sweat, he shot up in bed. *"Jesus!"*

Pain bolted through his swollen right knee, but the emotional pain from a shattered ego hurt even worse. It was the same pain and nightmare that had visited him many nights over the last four years. He was the only one to blame for USC's humiliating loss and his own humiliating personal downfall.

Removing the sweat-soaked sheets, he hobbled across the room, dodged the strewn clothes on the floor, stepped into the bathroom and quietly closed the door behind him. He flicked on the light and squinted as the sudden brightness blinded him. Then he reached for the bottle of Percocet, his loyal companion in these isolated, agonizing nights.

He shook three of the blue painkillers into his hand, his steady diet of Percs. When he couldn't get enough from his doctor, he bought extras from a dealer. He downed the pills, chasing them with a mouthful of water. They would take some time to kick in, but relief was on its way. The drugs, along with his secret hopes and plans, were all that kept him from slipping over the edge.

He used his hands on the vanity to hold his weight and stared into the mirror. At twenty-six, he already had the hair and face of a stranger.

"You should let your dreadlocks grow long," his boss suggested. "More intimidating."

The patchy facial hair was Calvin's decision. The overall effect was menacing—just right for his line of work.

His sharp brown eyes, which at one time had won him glances from beautiful women in college, were usually hidden behind dark sunglasses. Unseen eyes were intimidating too and when he took them off to stare at a victim, he could use his eyes to look like a madman

He closed them now and shook his head in disgust. "You look like shit. Hell, you *are* shit."

The press had certainly thought that, four years ago. Always ready to tear down a hero, they had shown no restraint in attacking him for his egotistic, selfish decision and *obvious* desire to break his own school record. One minute he was touted as the next Walter Payton, the next he was a door mat for local media.

Looking at him now, no one would believe that back then he was a thousand-yard rusher in the NCAA and welcomed with open arms in every established club in Southern California. Hell, he had been bigger than the mayor of LA.

The sports pages of the various newspapers in the USC area had indeed printed headline stories about him the day after the game, but not the kind he'd imagined when he'd decided to run with the ball.

That the resulting injury had ended his college football career and most importantly, any chances of a pro career didn't matter to them. By making the wrong, selfish, prideful decision, he'd made himself a target for the press and all USC fans.

"No one to blame but yourself," he muttered to his haggard reflection.

If he'd just fallen on the ball, taken a knee and stopped the play without trying to be the hero, his life would be different.

The devastating, career-ending knee injury wasn't the quarterback's fault for missing the audible, or the fullback's fault for missing the key block. It was his and it had taken him some time to understand and accept responsibility for it. In the end, Calvin Watters, an unstoppable force, had been brought down by his own foolish pride.

He splashed cold water on his face, took a step back and turned sideways, assessing his body, proud that he'd been able to maintain his well-sculpted physique through hard work, discipline and the right diet.

Three months after his last surgery, when the doctors said they'd done all they could, he had set up a home gym in his apartment.

"Everything okay, Calvin?"

He looked at her in the mirror, her eyes barely open from the sudden light.

"How long you been standing there?" he asked.

"Only a minute." Rachel approached him and wrapped her arms around his midsection, rubbing his abdomen. "How long have I known you?"

He smiled. "A few years."

She pinched his minimal fat and squeezed his bulging pectorals. "In all that time, your body continues to get harder and more muscular. What a six-pack. A guy in your line of work, with everything you've been through, shouldn't be able to keep up like this."

He turned and pulled her to him. Her hair smelled of sweet jasmine and her body felt warm and soft.

"Go back to bed, Rachel. I'll only be a minute."

"Okay, but hurry up. I'm in the mood." She winked and smiled as she closed the door.

She was right. His abs were still smooth and rock solid and although his legs had lost some of their bulk, focusing his exercise around a permanently disabled knee had made them more lean and muscular.

He grunted. *I could keep up with any twenty-year-old on the field.*

He was now aerobically in the best shape of his life, even with the long hours and emotionally exhausting nature of his work.

My work.

After he spent three years building a reputation as the toughest collector in Vegas, no one even knew he'd been one of the greatest college running backs ever. To them, he was just "The Collector."

He knew Rachel would feel his misery and he didn't want to bring her down. Not tonight. He shut off the light.

When he tiptoed from the bathroom, he saw that Rachel had already fallen asleep.

"So much for being in the mood," he whispered, smiling to himself.

He limped across the room and sat next to her, careful not to wake the sleeping beauty.

When he'd run into her three years ago, just legal at eighteen, he'd wondered how she'd reached that point, how she'd fallen into a life on the streets. He didn't know much about her back then, didn't even know her name or even how prostitution worked. He'd seen a lot and learned not to be taken in by a sad story and a pretty face.

A blonde, blue-eyed angel.

He slid beneath the sheets, growing numb and weary as the Percocet kicked in and the pain began to subside. A strand of hair covered Rachel's mouth and he inched it away from her face.

He marveled at her. She'd survived years of abuse from her stepfather. How such a petite woman had escaped and recovered—for the most part—inspired Calvin. And he had taken it upon himself to pay her stepfather back, even though Rachel knew nothing about it. The man now knew what pain was all about.

Calvin had to collect enough to take her with him when he got out.

He was well paid for his gruesome work and he spent only the bare minimum to cover basic expenses and bills. And to cover those special purchases spread out over the last three years that were his investment for the future. His cheap, rundown apartment and dilapidated workshop, as sparsely furnished as a prison cell, were all ways to reduce costs.

He stared at the ceiling and thought about how he'd had to force himself to do the job on Pierce. How much longer could he take it?

He shook his head against the pillow. *I just want a life.*

The Percocet sank in deeper and he drifted into unconsciousness. He fell asleep with his leg hanging over the edge of the bed, dreaming about one more chance.

CHAPTER 2

"Dale, we need to talk."

Dale Dayton bounded down the staircase still wet from his shower. He thought he knew what his wife wanted, but he'd give anything to avoid the discussion.

"I'll be back in a minute," he said, kissing Betty on the cheek.

He noticed the coffee pot half-filled and realized his wife must have been up early drinking coffee and waiting for him. He poured a cup and went outside to retrieve the morning paper, delaying facing her a moment more.

"Dale," she hollered from the doorway.

He had thought a baby might help "the problem," though he'd always known his job was the real issue.

But Betty knew what she was getting into marrying a cop, didn't she?

Dale had always been a cop and always would be. And he was a damn good one at that. What he found more difficult was being a good husband and father.

When he came back into the house, she was waiting. Without making eye contact with her, he picked up Sammie and gave him a hug and kiss before settling his son back into his highchair.

Betty's mouth turned down in a pout. "I'm serious. This is

important."

"Okay, okay. What is it?"

"I think that—"

His beeper went off.

"Don't take it," Betty said, her voice rising.

Ignoring her, he checked the number. "I have to, honey."

He picked up the phone and dialed the number. He listened for a long moment and then hung up. Grabbing his jacket and holster, he threw Betty an apologetic look. "Sorry, I gotta go. Jimmy's on his way. I promise we'll talk tonight when I get home. Love you."

He kissed her on the cheek and ran down the hall.

"I won't be here when you get back."

His backbone stiffened. Her words stopped him, frozen, his hand still on the doorknob. His insides tightened. He turned around. Betty stood right behind him now, an intense gaze in her eyes. The ambush was premeditated and even though he was a gifted investigator, he had never seen it coming.

"What do you mean?"

"You know what I mean, Dale. This isn't coming out of the blue."

A car horn honked.

He glanced toward the door and then back to his wife. "Damn it. Let's talk about this tonight."

She slid a white envelope out of her housecoat pocket. "Here. Like usual, I knew you wouldn't have *time* to talk. So I took the liberty of writing it all down." She handed him the letter.

"Don't do this, Betty."

"This is a long time coming. We both know it. It's all there." She pointed to the letter in his hand. "Read it whenever you want. But you're not changing my mind."

"What about Sammie?"

"He's coming with me."

A gloomy silence ensued. He hoped the silence would tempt her to say more, but she didn't. His throat was dry, as if he'd just drunk a glass of desert sand. Unsure of his next move, he knew what he should do, but didn't have the words.

Betty's anger was warranted, but he was caught off guard nonetheless. She was right. This was overdue.

He took her hand. "Please, Betty. Just stay. I'll make it right." His voice lacked conviction and he knew it.

The horn honked again.

Betty sighed. "Just go. I know that's where you'd rather be anyway."

He moved in a trance-like state.

"What the hell took so long?" his long-time partner asked as Dale slid into the passenger seat. "Did Betty want to have one of her *talks* again?"

Dale still didn't say anything. Grief consumed him. He felt the bulge in his inside breast pocket, where Betty's note was lodged.

"What the hell's wrong with you?"

"Just drive, Jimmy."

His partner pulled the car out of the driveway.

"What do we have?" Dale asked, still dazed.

"David called it in—a possible match to the Black Orchid case. The boys have him in a silver-and-black '69 Camaro on Highway 15."

Dale felt the adrenaline start pumping. *A high-speed chase. Just what I need.*

The Black Orchid case involved six prostitutes killed within a three-week span. The killer had brutalized and sexually assaulted his victims. As of now, the only real lead was a local tattoo parlor owner.

Dale unholstered his weapon and checked the clip.

"How do you like your new Kimber Custom Stainless?" Jimmy asked.

"I love it. Better than that old revolver you still carry."

Jimmy smiled. "Smith & Wesson, baby. But that's my alternate duty weapon. I have a semi-automatic for my primary handgun, just like the department says we *have* to. But the S&W is the gun I chose as a recruit over thirty years ago. I trust that gun with my life, literally. It hasn't let me down yet."

"That's true of everything until the first time it lets you down." Dale thought of the talk he'd just had with Betty. "This isn't the Wild West, Jimmy. I know they allow us to choose our own firearm, as long as they're standard factory production, but you need to upgrade, man. An allowance is issued each year to replace our equipment."

"Hey, it's been approved by the Firearms Training and Tactical Unit and qualified quarterly."

Dale laughed at his old-school partner.

"There they are," Jimmy said, pointing to a row of black and whites following a Camaro. "Hang on."

With the red-and-blue dome lights rotating on top of the cruiser, he pressed the gas pedal to the floor and they edged to the front of the pack, avoiding the dense morning traffic. Dale saw that the sheriff and FBI had vehicles in the chase too.

Without warning the Camaro veered off the Las Vegas freeway, taking West Flamingo Avenue and heading toward Spring Valley.

Jimmy cursed. "Where's he going?"

"Turn here. We can cut him off at Palms Casino."

They took a sharp left and sped down Hotel Rio Drive, breaking off from the pack, the sound of sirens fading.

Dale rubbed his face, trying to recall the shortcut. "Go here." He pointed.

"Got it!"

Dale picked up the car radio. "Angela, I need the 592 blocked off at South Valley Boulevard heading east."

As the hotel came into view, Jimmy had the accelerator to the floor. "Come on, you bastard," he muttered.

Dale grabbed the dashboard. "Let's not play chicken with this guy."

The Camaro came to a screeching halt.

Jimmy braked and brought the cruiser face-to-face with the Camaro. The three black and whites had parked behind it, barricading the highway.

Dale let out a grunt. "We got him. Let's go."

The smell of burnt rubber filled the dry Nevada air.

Dale drew his gun and aimed at the Camaro's driver-side window as he approached with caution. He could see the shadow of a man through the tinted windshield.

The engine revved.

"Get out of the car," he ordered. "We have you surrounded."

Without warning, the Camaro took off, heading straight toward them.

Dale and Jimmy opened fire. Bullets ricocheted off the grill and shattered the windshield. Dale aimed low, taking out the front passenger tire. The car flipped into a tailspin, end-over-end. They hit the ground as the car continued to roll, landing roof-to-roof on top of their own cruiser.

Dale clambered to his feet and dusted off his pants. With his gun still aimed at the car, he advanced with ease, his partner right behind him. "Cover me, Jimmy."

He holstered his weapon and pried open the car door, now upside down. The killer hung from the seatbelt, his face bloodied, a deep gash across the top of his head.

Dale bent down and checked for a pulse.

"I'll call the EMTs," Jimmy said.

"Forget the EMTs. This guy's gone." Dale sprung up and took a deep breath in and out. "Now that's the way to start a day."

For a brief moment, he almost forgot his whole world was crumbling around him.

CHAPTER 3

Doug Grant sat in his private office and rubbed his temples. He hadn't expected everything to come to a head. He just wanted to be happy, free from the constraints, able to live a normal life. But what would be the consequences?

He went through the usual morning paperwork, feeling older and more alone than he had in years. He was proud of being thorough, a trait learned from his father. At sixty-three, Doug was still very much a working boss. His son, Shawn, now thirty-five and Vice President of Operations, was learning the business from him.

He marveled at how far he'd come: the Greek Hotel and Casino—the second largest and most profitable casino in Las Vegas. He had taken it over when his father, Sherman, had passed away eight years ago. Doug had turned the casino into a multibillion-dollar business and he looked forward to turning over full control to Shawn at the right time. Recent events had moved up his planned date for semi-retirement by years.

He heard the front door to the suite swing open, but he was sure he'd locked it so he wouldn't be disturbed. He wasn't expecting visitors and his first appointment downtown wasn't until this afternoon. He rose to investigate, but before he could, Ace Sanders strode into his office.

The rival casino owner wore a fake tan and cocky grin. Sanders owned and operated two casinos, the Golden Horseshoe and the Midas.

Neither was as successful as Doug's.

Doug frowned. "How did you get in here? That door was locked."

"Magic."

Sanders offered his hand, but Doug ignored it.

The man sat on the leather sofa and put his feet up. He had a languid smile. "You know, I really wish you would use your home or casino offices more. It's a bitch to get down here."

"That's the point. Privacy. No interruptions. Obviously it isn't working."

Sanders said nothing.

"What the hell are you doing here?" Doug asked with malevolence in his voice.

Sanders studied the office before answering. "I just stopped by for a chat. I think you should listen this time and consider what I have to say."

Doug stayed seated in his desk chair. *Not again!* "How did you get up here without an appointment?"

Sanders' chuckle was thick with sarcasm. "Same way I got through the front door. Please, Douglas. I'm Ace Sanders. I can do whatever I want in this city. Enough small talk. I want your casino and I'm willing to up my price."

"We've been over this before—too many times. I won't have this discussion with you again. I'll never sell this casino. Ever! Most of all not to you. This place was my father's, now it's mine and it will be Shawn's. And I hope that when he has children, one of them will want to be a fourth-generation owner."

"$250 million!" Sanders shouted the number as if it were a revelation. "Which is $50 million more than my last offer."

"No."

"You're making a mistake, old man. At least think about the offer." Sanders' voice remained even and calm.

Doug looked at him through tired eyes. Sanders kept increasing the offer and was wearing him down.

"No!" Doug's heart was beginning to race. "Listen to me. Don't ever come back here again. You hear me? Now *get out.*"

"This is a mistake." Sanders got up. He reached inside his coat and pulled something out.

Doug froze for an instant. But it wasn't a gun.

Sanders had pulled out a round plastic piece and he flipped it onto Doug's desk. The coin spun on edge before falling. Doug picked up the poker chip and studied it.

"That is a ten-thousand-dollar Golden Horseshoe betting chip," Sanders said. "A token of my kindness. Come by some time and have some fun. On me, of course. What do you have to lose?"

Sanders headed for the door, shaking his head and grinning the whole way. Before exiting, he turned. "And Douglas, this is far from over."

Doug rose and pointed a crooked finger. "Get out. Now!"

As Sanders left, Doug felt a sharp pain in his chest. He sat down, clutching his left pectoral. He took a few deep breaths and regained his composure as the pain subsided.

Studying the casino chip, he thought he might just take Sanders up on his offer. But that would be another time. He slipped the chip into his desk drawer and went back to his usual routine. He was not going to let Sanders ruin his day.

CHAPTER 4

The dream woke him again. Why was it tormenting him?

He opened his eyes and a dim light across the room caught his attention. He saw Rachel seated at the little table, writing vigorously in a notebook, her face a mask of concentration. Books, pens and paper were scattered across the tabletop.

"What are you doing?"

She jumped at his voice. "You startled me."

"Sorry." He slid off the bed and crossed the room, his eyes still adjusting to the light.

With the speed of a high-school student hearing the bell, Rachel threw a few items into her knapsack and closed it.

"What are those?"

"Nothing."

Calvin grabbed the bag. "What are you hiding from me?"

He opened the knapsack and removed a stack of textbooks. "What are these?" He picked up the top one. "*Understanding Human Behavior.* Where'd these come from?"

"They're for school." Her face reddened. She pulled the books from his hands and shoved them in the bag.

"School?"

"Yeah, school. That big brick building where you gain knowledge.

Ever hear of it?"

"Why are you getting so defensive?"

"I didn't want anyone to know about it."

"About what?"

She exhaled out loud. "I'm taking online courses at CSN. Okay?"

"Since when are you a student at the College of Southern Nevada?"

"This is my second year in a two-year psychology program." She pursed her lips. "I want more for my life, Calvin. So far, it hasn't been like I dreamed."

He wrapped his arms around her. "I think that's great. I'm so proud of you."

She rolled her eyes and pulled him closer. "I want more."

He took her by the hand and led her back to bed. "Me too, Rachel. Me too."

Calvin woke up squinting at the blinding sun shining through the window. The curtains had been pulled back and tied with the strings. He took a moment to shake the cobwebs and then reached across the bed. Rachel was gone.

He swung his legs over the side of the bed and sat up on the edge. He tested his knee for stability and flexibility. It would never get any stronger. He had severely torn the anterior cruciate ligament in his right knee. Reconstructive surgery had replaced the ligament and two arthroscopic surgeries were necessary before he could walk. Even with the plates and rods, he was thankful when he made it through a day without agonizing pain.

He used the muscles in his arms to heave himself off the bed, rising to his feet and stretching his long, muscular body. He began his ritual knee workout, easing into each exercise, holding at the first point of discomfort. Using light enough resistance, he performed three sets of twenty repetitions of the various exercises. This was the most important time of the day for his knee and he couldn't overdo it.

First, he lay on the floor, raising his leg up and down doing hamstring stretches. Placing a hand against the wall, he performed some quadriceps stretches, then moved to strengthening exercises—leg extensions, straight leg raises, buttock tucks, quarter squats (both single and double leg) and forward and lateral step-ups.

For three straight years at college, he'd been awarded the 'Hard Hat' award for the team's hardest worker on and off the field. The amount of time and hard work he had put into preparing for football was still paying off now.

After twenty-five minutes, he was satisfied, though perspiration ran down the back of his neck. He showered and dressed, then strolled across the street to Ed's Breakfast Grill. He'd wait until he had returned to his apartment to run the stairs, first walking and then progressing into a quick jog. His weightlifting was done at night before bed.

It was past the morning breakfast rush, so he sat down at a booth in the half- empty diner. A scowling, uniformed waitress set a fresh mug of coffee in front of him and slid the morning paper across the table.

"Good morning, Calvin. What'll you have today, honey?" Her pen hovered over a notepad.

"The usual, I guess." He tossed the menu down on the table.

She snatched up the menu and headed back to the counter. Calvin was no longer alarmed by how she screamed his order out through the window into the kitchen.

"Hey, Calvin!" Ed, owner and cook, nodded in Calvin's direction.

He was a big man who sweated a lot, but Calvin thought of him as a friend, not just someone who was good to his steady customers.

Calvin gave a quick salute and turned to the morning paper. As he always did, he skimmed the news to the sports section first. He enjoyed keeping up with some of the players that he'd once played against and dominated in college. He couldn't believe the money that players made in the NFL. Players with half his talent were making millions.

Should be me.

The slamming of a plate brought him back from the past. The waitress pulled some silverware from her apron and handed it to him.

"Thanks," Calvin said. He always felt that eating was wasting time, so he gobbled it, paid his bill and left a modest tip.

He checked out of the motel, paying cash. He was part of the cash-only economy—no banks, no government and underreported income. To keep the IRS off his back, he did file taxes for a third of what he made and listed himself as a "freelance messenger." Close enough.

He headed to work.

Donald Pitt sat at the desk in his tiny office eating an egg sandwich. As he bit into it, a clump of melted cheese dripped and landed on files that were scattered across his desk.

"For fuck's sake! Dixie, get in here!" Pitt called out for his secretary.

"Hello, Donald."

The voice that came from the doorway wasn't Dixie's and he dropped half the sandwich into his lap.

"Ace," Don said. "I wasn't expecting you until later."

"Having trouble with the sandwich?"

Don used a napkin to wipe the egg from his pants. Never one to waste time on hygiene, he finger-combed what hair was left on his balding head, parting it to the side. He rushed to the door, greeting his best-paying and most frequent client, his arm extended the whole way.

He pulled a chair out for the casino owner.

"You called?" Don's young secretary came to the doorway, one finger twirling a piece of gum in her mouth.

"Never mind, Dixie." He waved the secretary away, who left rolling her eyes.

He shut the door and turned back to his visitor. "Please come in, Ace."

Sanders entered but didn't sit. They had met seven years ago and Don still didn't trust him, but he'd already made a small fortune handling most of Sanders' dirty work. He just needed to keep Ace happy for a little while longer.

"So…is everything set?" Sanders asked.

"Pretty much," he replied, sitting back behind the desk.

"What about Watters ?"

"He won't be a problem. I can handle him." He smiled, but his partner didn't return it. He thought that Ace probably didn't like that Don was in control of this part.

"You just make sure that he's in Grant's private office by 9:30 tomorrow morning." Sanders' tone was hard.

Don leaned forward. "Tomorrow morning? Why so soon?"

"It needs to be done ASAP. Time is running out and I can't wait any longer."

"Will everything be ready?"

"Of course. You just take care of Watters. It'll be perfect. It has to be. You better hope it is."

"I don't know. Sounds risky."

Sanders pulled a brochure from his jacket. He opened it to the centerfold and set it on the desk. "A piece of this will be all yours." He pointed to the layout of the new Greek Hotel and Casino.

Don's eyes widened. The place would make millions. He tried to touch the paper, but Sanders grabbed it and stuck it inside his jacket.

"How about a deal memo for a sense of security?" Don said. "I would feel better knowing I have some documentation for my share."

Grinning, Sanders slapped him on the back. "You'll just have to trust me, Donald."

He frowned. *I have no choice.*

When Sanders left, he relaxed back into his chair. All he could think about was that Sanders could no doubt pull this off and would be a real power in Vegas.

CHAPTER 5

Calvin didn't get to work until after eleven, a good time for an impromptu visit. He walked into the little shop and the odor of cigarette smoke and sweat assaulted him. The noise he had grown accustomed to the last three years—fingers tapping keyboards, phones ringing and sports games from around the world on the televisions—greeted him like a punch in the gut. A couple of heads shot up from behind newspapers, but seeing a big black man, they returned to their reading.

The lines for the day were already posted on the board and he scanned them as he nodded to the secretary, who was busy painting red-lacquered nails. "You got something for me, Dixie?"

She opened a drawer and searched it. "Nothing here."

His pulse quickened, but he said nothing. He headed to the back.

"Hey, Don." Calvin nodded at his boss.

Pitt looked up from his computer. "Where the hell have you been?"

"What? I never punched a clock before."

"Sorry. Tough morning. I have nothing for you yet today."

"What about my cut on Pierce? I know he paid you in full this morning."

"What? No, he hasn't. Well…he paid part of it."

Calvin put out his hand. "Stop there. I don't want to hear it. I got his attention the other night, told him to pay you this morning and I know he did, so stop trying to hold on to my money."

Pitt started protesting and he cut him off. "Now." Calvin leaned forward and glared into Pitt's piggy eyes. "He owed you $20,000 and I want $4,000 in my hands within the next minute."

Pitt sighed. "Not you too. What a morning."

"Me too? What do you mean? Who else was in here?"

"No one. Never mind. I'm too tired to argue with you. You're right anyway. Dixie said Pierce limped in this morning before I arrived and paid it all." Pitt smiled. "I guess he got the message."

"My money, Don."

"All right. Calm down. I'll get your money." Pitt disappeared into the back of his office and returned with a large envelope. "Here's your $4,000. Count it if you want. You finished?"

"No. You still owe me $6,000 from the job before that. Harry Walker. Five days ago. I know he paid too, because if he hadn't, you'd have already sent me back to see him. I want everything settled before I leave the office this morning, so don't even waste your breath. Just get my money."

Pitt sighed and raised his hands, then dropped them to his side. He went into the back again and brought Calvin a larger envelope and sat down.

Calvin stuffed both envelopes into the deep pockets of his jacket. "I'm not counting now. I'll do that later. If anything's missing, I'm coming back to collect from you. And what Pierce received will seem like a slap on the wrist."

"What's gotten you in such a bad mood? You forget to take your meds?"

Calvin lunged across the desk as Pitt sprung back, his chair striking the wall hard.

Pitt raised his hands in a defensive posture. "Whoa! Just kidding. Loosen up. You got your money. Go. I'll call you when I need you for the next job."

"That's what we have to talk about."

"I'm tired of talking. Let's do that another time." Pitt turned his back to Calvin and began typing on the computer keyboard. But Calvin stood still and stared, thinking about when he and Pitt had first met.

After his humiliating injury, he'd moved to Vegas to start over. He had no contacts, no money and no prospects. He was feeling sorry for himself and blamed everyone else for his situation.

His first night in the new city, Calvin had gotten drunk in a local pub, started a fight and beat up two customers, a bartender and two bouncers. Pitt saw the fight and even went to court to vouch for Calvin, saying he acted in self-defense—a total lie. One of the bouncers had gone to the local ER. A severe concussion, Calvin had heard. He could have gone to jail.

"I like your style," Pitt had said.

When the man asked Calvin to collect for him and showed him the money, Calvin figured he owed the bookie. Besides, no other offers were that good. And even though he hated the collecting job now, he was still somewhat proud to be the best. Pitt's rate of return had been 100 percent since Calvin had taken over.

"I thought you were leaving." Pitt scowled. "What's your problem today?"

"I want out."

"What do you mean, *out*?" Pitt said in an icy tone.

"That's it. I'm done."

"Oh, really?" Pitt got up, walked around the desk and sat on the edge of it, folding his arms across his chest. "Tell me, what is it you plan to do?"

"I don't know yet." He thought about the ways he could hurt Pitt. But that would be a bad move.

"Of course you don't, because you can't do anything else. You don't have a degree, you have one knee and you look like a bum."

He took deep breaths and did a slow mental count to calm down.

Pitt continued. "Remember when I found you? You had nothing. No job. No money. No home. Nobody! I saved you. I was the only one there for you. I saved your ass from the slammer. You *owe* me."

"I don't owe you shit. I paid that debt off long ago."

"Don't give me that bullshit. When you had nothing else, I offered you twenty percent of every collection, in cash. More money than you could ever dream of, with the shape you were in. I turned you into the perfect collecting machine, an intimidating giant with a psychopath's lack of emotion and the capacity to be a madman when the job required that kind of terror. Did you forget that?"

Calvin shook his head. "You came to *me*."

"That's right. I did. I thought that an angry football star was perfect for the job and I was right."

"I should have listened to my brother when he tried to talk me out of it."

Pitt grunted. "Your brother. A lousy L.A. detective. I hate cops. I don't trust 'em."

"Josh just made detective first grade—a *real* job. He tried to warn me, but I was too stubborn to listen. I'm sick of this."

"Tell me..." Pitt smiled and Calvin would have liked to remove it. "Just how much money has Joshua made over the last three years?"

"Not everything is about money."

"Maybe so, but I haven't seen much that money can't buy."

"There's more to life." Calvin shrugged. "Like being happy."

Pitt wiped his eyes in mock sympathy. "Ah, gee. The leg breaker isn't happy. I'm all choked up."

"I want out now. We're all square on what you owe me. I'm finished."

"Well, you can't just walk out, Calvin. You've been torturing people for years and they put people in jail for that. When I wanted deadbeats terrified of you that was one thing. But let's say that now I decide to get some of the deadbeats to go to the police and press charges against you. At first you were an asset, but maybe now you've gotten out of control."

Calvin lost it. With both hands, he grabbed Pitt by the collar and slammed him against the wall, which cracked behind Pitt's shoulders.

"Listen to me, you son of a bitch," he said between gritted teeth. "I'm leaving this business. Understand?"

The Adam's apple in Pitt's throat shifted when he swallowed. He raised both hands in surrender. "But what am I going to do? You're my only collector. Where will I find another one?"

"I don't care. It's not my concern." Calvin loosened his hold, but only a little.

"Okay, okay."

Calvin let him go.

"But I need you for just one more pickup," Pitt said. "It'll be soon. I won't have time to find a replacement, so you'll have to do it."

"I've already said I quit. It's over."

Pitt sighed. "After this one, you're done with me. You'll be a free agent. I promise."

Calvin thought for a moment. One more pickup—one more payday—and he could take Rachel along with few worries.

"What's the job?"

"Douglas Grant owes me some money. A lot of money, in fact."

Calvin's eyebrows shot up. Grant was one of the richest, most powerful men in Vegas. Why would anyone like Grant have anything to do with Donald Pitt? And why would he borrow, or even have to borrow, money from Pitt when Grant's estimated net worth was over $300 million dollars? "Why would Grant be doing business with you?"

"None of your business. Are you in or should I have someone else collect the $40,000 commission?"

"It's $40,000? How much does he owe you?"

"Exactly $200,000. He borrowed $150,000. Now the interest is $50,000." "And you've waited this long to collect? Even at your rates, it takes a long time to get the interest up to fifty grand."

"I thought lending to Grant would lead to business with his friends. You know how many dealings I've had with Sanders? Hoped to start with him, work up to Grant and then move around."

"How'd that work out for you?" Calvin asked dryly.

"Not good. But it was worth the try. Also you don't push a man as powerful as Grant. I know he's good for it, but if I put pressure on him, I'd lose him all the way—*and* the two hundred grand. So I've waited. He called last week. Said he wanted to get this matter settled and he'd have the money in cash sometime this week."

The job didn't make any sense, but it wasn't up to Calvin to figure out all the whys. His job was simple. He was the collector and the only collector who could pull this task off because of Grant's status and power. In that sense, Pitt did have a point.

And the extra $40,000 would make taking Rachel with him a lot more affordable.

"I'll do it. But for a job this tough, I want $10,000 cash up front now. And $30,000 more when I bring you Grant's money." When he saw Pitt gearing up to protest, he added, "No one else could do this one and you know it."

"You want my blood too?" Pitt screamed. "I've already paid you the $10,000 I owe you and now you want me to pay you $10,000 more before I get paid? That's crazy."

"No. Those are my non-negotiable terms for this last job. Take 'em or leave 'em. If you don't give me the $10,000 now, good luck finding another collector who can get that much from Grant."

Pitt made strange sounds in the back of his throat and his face reddened. It looked as though he was trying to pull his hair out by the roots.

Calvin chuckled. "I think you're losing it."

"I am. And it's your fault."

"Yes or no. I've got better things to do than stand around waiting for you to decide."

After a couple of shallow breaths, Pitt said, "I'll get you another $10,000. But never again."

"I think that's the one thing we do agree on."

Pitt mumbled his way to the back offices for the third time and returned with a fat envelope. "Take it and get out of here. I'll call when it's time."

"Good afternoon, Mr. Watters. Right on time as usual."

"Hey, Chet." Calvin slung his duffel bag onto the front counter. It landed with a thud.

"What are you using today?" The young man unzipped the bag and rummaged through the contents, pulling out weapons. "SIG P 210-6, Smith & Wesson Model 940, Beretta PX4 Storm, Colt Government and a Browning High-Power. Nice selection." Chet checked each gun to verify they were unloaded.

Calvin smiled. "Thanks. Just handguns today. Give me two 50-round boxes of nine millimeters."

"Paper or plastic targets?"

"Paper."

The man handed Calvin ten pieces of paper of solid black circles with scoring rings on a white background. "Do you have your own eye and ear protection?"

He showed the man his glasses and ear plugs and muffs. He always doubled-up on ear protection to fight the increased noise pressure level inside the shooting range.

"Did you want to renew your annual membership today? Since this is your third year in a row, there's a discount."

"Nah," Calvin said. "I'll do that another time."

"You know the regular rules." The man snickered. "No holster drawing, cowboy action shooting or combat-style shooting." Chet put his fingers in the form of a gun and imitated a cowboy. "Just sign this waiver and that's $19.99 for the ammo. You know where the handgun range is. Markus is already down there."

He signed the waiver, paid, placed his guns and targets back in the bag and left the lobby.

He moved straight to the handgun range and entered the soundproof air-locked corridor. Markus, the head Range Safety Officer, smiled and waved when he saw Calvin. Markus had also been Calvin's teacher for the concealed-carry license course he had taken when he'd first joined the club.

"Hey, Calvin."

"Markus." Calvin nodded.

"We're hot right now. But in a few minutes you should be good to go."

Calvin stood back and watched through a Plexiglas window. A row of lanes were occupied and clients fired their weapons at targets, each at a different range length.

The lanes were covered by absorbing foam material on the floors, walls and ceilings for noise reduction. The bullets struck targets and then passed through a rubber curtain before hitting the metal backstop and falling safely into angle-plated collectors.

Markus walked over and stood beside Calvin.

"Are you entering the members' tournament next month? If you win it for a second year in a row, it's a free membership."

He grunted. "I'll think about it."

He waited as each shooter, one by one, raised their hand to indicate they were done. When the last person raised his hand, they placed their guns on the firing line table with their actions open.

Markus said, "We're cold. Go ahead in, Calvin."

He donned his eye and ear protection and made his way to lane six, dropping his duffel bag on the table. He hung a paper target on the target holder positioned on a slide and hit the electrical switch. The motorized assembly withdrew the target and he stopped it about thirty yards away. He then hit another switch and the lane's ventilation system started. It would pull smoke and lead particles away from the shooting line to reduce the risk of lead poisoning.

He loaded his Browning High-Power and took aim. His face was a mask of concentration. He steadied the weapon with his right hand, used his left for support and then squeezed the trigger.

CHAPTER 6

When the phone rang, she felt a chill and checked caller ID before answering. "Hello?"

"Is Ace there yet?"

"No." Her body trembled as it always did when they spoke. She never knew if it was from excitement or fear. Maybe both.

"When are you expecting him?" His tone was brisk, like always.

"Soon." She pulled the curtain aside a few inches and watched the back yard. "Most of the time he parks on a side street and comes in through the back."

"You know what to do?"

"Of course. I'm not an idiot. You've told me enough times."

"Don't get smart, Linda. You know how important this is."

She knew not to mess with his hair-trigger temper. But when he got this way, it only excited her more.

She spotted Ace rounding the corner of the house, using his key to unlock the back door. "I see him coming."

"Good. Don't let me down. Call me when he leaves. And like always, make it look real."

"Those acting lessons are coming in handy after all."

She smiled, but the call was disconnected without a goodbye. She jogged down the hall, stripping off layers of clothing along the way to the back door. She took a deep breath and prepared herself. She sat on the edge of the table, spread her legs and hoisted her feet in the air—showing off her double-jointed, dancer flexibility—as the door opened.

"We have twenty minutes," she whispered in a sexy, raspy voice.

Ace and Linda Grant lay naked, bathed in sweat on top of the bed sheets.

He let out a breath. "You're gonna kill me. Do you see what you do to me?"

"Come on, baby." Linda stroked the tuft of hair on his chest. "Poor Linda needs to have her fun too." When his penis stirred, she gave it a teasing stroke with her fingertips.

"You're a bad girl, Linda." He grabbed her hips to turn her around, but she pushed him away.

"We don't have time. Doug will be home soon."

"Why did you marry him, anyway? Did you ever love him?"

"Oh, I loved him. I loved his money and the thought of owning the Greek. I knew that if I danced at the club I would land him."

"You do have a way of catching a man's attention."

She arched her brows. "I caught yours."

"What would I do if we hadn't met at that conference?"

"I don't know," she whispered.

"The sex has been amazing." He tried to kiss her, but she moved away again and headed toward the walk-in closet. She disappeared inside. A minute later she emerged wearing a Victoria's Secret floral silk kimono.

He thought Linda's body was still as tight and firm as it had been when she'd first moved to Vegas to become a show dancer.

"We need to stop meeting here," he said. "It's getting too risky. Especially now, being so close."

"Doug knows." She cinched the belt around her waist, but left it opened a bit to reveal just enough skin.

"What?" This wasn't what he was expecting.

"The other day he showed me pictures. Of you and me. Then he asked for a divorce."

He sat down to think.

"A divorce, Ace," she reiterated. "That would leave me with millions." She pouted her lips and in a child's voice added, "But I want a lot more."

"You're evil." He smiled again.

"You know that I signed a prenuptial agreement. I had to prove I wasn't marrying Doug for his money. His family and friends never trusted me. If we divorce, I'm only entitled to ten percent of Doug's estate and I'm immediately taken out of his will, which alone is worth twelve percent non-voting stock of the casino. I'd be losing my part ownership and stock worth multi-millions. After everything I have done for that man. Is that fair?"

"What did you say to him?"

"I had to cry, kneel and then give him the best blow job he's ever had. He says he forgives me and we need to get things straightened out with a counselor, but I don't quite believe him."

"He bought it?"

She chuckled. "I'm not divorced yet, am I? But we both know that as stubborn as Doug is, once he makes up his mind, he won't change it."

"I know. The damn fool won't sell the Greek! Did you search his office yet?"

"No, I'll do it tonight while he's at work."

She approached him and wrapped a muscled leg around his waist. When she opened her kimono, her nipples were hard. "You do have a plan, don't you, Ace?"

"You know I do."

"Good, because he barely speaks to me now and he's getting colder and more distant. I can't do more to reach his heart than I'm already doing."

"Shit!"he snapped, pushing her away.

"I know." She approached him again and started massaging his shoulders. Then she reached around and grabbed his midsection, kneading it like dough. "I could get those divorce papers at anytime and then all of our plans are ruined."

"Why didn't you tell me this before?"

"I've got it under control, but we have to move fast. Doug is coming to harm soon, isn't he?" Her lips curled in a smile that could melt a man's heart.

He nodded.

"Fatal harm?"

"Well, yes."

"I thought so." She walked across the room. "You know I'm not just in his prenup. I'm in his will and at his death I get three times as much as I would after a divorce."

He grinned. "You are evil beyond a doubt."

"When does the *sad* event take place?"

"Soon, baby. Very soon."

He tried to grab her one more time, but again she brushed him off. "No time, Ace."

"Right."

He put on his sports jacket and took his time walking toward the door, wondering exactly how much he could trust Linda. *That* could be calculated to the dollar and penny. He liked that kind of clear understanding. How long had Linda been counting on Doug's death, rather than just a divorce?

She was ice to the core and he'd have to watch her. He didn't want to think about not having sex with her. It was amazing that he had not gotten bored yet.

When I have the Greek, I'll think about what to do with Linda.

As soon as Ace was gone, Linda dialed a number. It was answered on the first ring.

"So?"

She grinned. "He bought it."

"Is he suspicious?"

"Give me some credit, will you? Ace thinks *he's* calling the shots."

"Good. When will it happen?"

"Ace says soon."

"Good. I gotta go and get some work done."

"Me too. I need to take a shower and wash this filth off. That man is disgusting. I have to close my eyes and think of you just to get through it."

"I don't know how you do it."

She pouted. "Hey, this was your plan, pimping me out. It's getting to be a strain to play the repentant unfaithful wife and the superfreak lover at the same time."

"I know you better than anyone, Linda, and you have to admit that deep down you love this. But we'll be together soon."

"I'll do it for you."

"No, you'll do it for *you* and that's why I love you. Go have a shower and I hope you think of me when you do."

"I've already started."

CHAPTER 7

Doug Grant was mentally and emotionally drained.

That little slut Linda.

He had to admit that it felt right to think of her that way. She thought he was fooled. But he didn't get to run the second-largest, highest-earning casino in town, or deal with the mob, or deal with the new Vegas as a Disney World and retirement theme park by being stupid or rigid. He did fall for her, but at the back of his mind, he had no illusions about the nature of his appeal to a woman like her.

Divorced for almost fifteen years, he'd met Linda when he decided to upgrade the casino entertainment. Linda had been one of the dancers.

They'd been married for six years, with no children. He was too old and Linda had never shown any interest in being a mother. Linda was always too concerned about keeping her dancer body trim and fit. Doug's fatherly love remained focused on Shawn and his other child, Shawn's younger sister, Melanie.

The shock and unexpectedness of Linda's infidelity had almost caused a heart attack. He'd never been the same since.

Shawn was almost ready. Doug had been training his son and showing him the ropes for the last fifteen years. As the Vice President of Operations, he had the respect and loyalty of the key staff at the casino. He was all business, but fair and hands-on without being a micromanager. Shawn was smart and could be ruthless. Retirement was near and he'd turn almost everything over to him. Shawn would be a great CEO. Doug could chair the board, with veto power over only a few essential matters. That suited him fine.

Shawn would receive an additional thirty-six percent of voting stock, giving him fifty-six percent majority ownership and voting control of the company.

Melanie would not feel slighted. Doug's only daughter was in med school and headed for a career as a top surgeon. Non-voting shares plus a stock and cash inheritance would almost equal Doug's bequest in value, so neither child would feel that the other was favored.

The remaining twenty-four percent of non-voting shares were divided in half between his ex-wife Beth and Linda. He didn't want to give Linda a dime, but as his wife she was contractually privileged, even if she had been "stepping out." That was more than enough for two women who, he had to admit, had never interested him as much as his business did. What was wrong with him? Too late for that. Making the best arrangements and having easy years seemed like the best he could expect.

Because his ex-wives both had nonvoting shares, Shawn in the end would have one-hundred percent voting control, with certain decisions that would have to be approved by Doug, for as long as he was chairman. He still hadn't told Shawn that yet.

Linda was about to lose her entire part-owner share of the Greek stock, because Doug was meeting with his attorney to discuss the processing, filing and serving of the divorce papers. It was her own fault, because Linda had known from the time she signed the prenup that divorce would lead immediately to that loss of ownership. However, she'd found that "car salesman," Ace Sanders, more attractive and important than all the love and everything else that Doug had given her.

He should have acted sooner, but filing for divorce required too much energy. Now, he was forcing himself, tired as he was, to finalize the divorce, get it over with and get his life and emotions in order again.

He slumped deeper in his chair. He was done for the night. He'd already spent too much time thinking about his personal problems.

There was a rap on the door.

"Mr. Grant, have you signed off on those papers?"

He looked up to find one of his night-shift pit bosses standing just outside the door.

"Darryl, come in."

The casino employee entered and Doug handed him the papers.

Doug walked toward the big office window that looked down on the casino main floor.

"How does it look tonight?" he asked.

"Philip called in sick, so I moved Joey to table games supervisor and Nancy is the stickman tonight."

Doug nodded but didn't speak.

"Is everything all right, boss?"

He sighed. "I watched my father build this building with his own hands. It has grown from a small, nickel and dime outfit to what it was now, an operation that generates hundreds of millions of dollars annually and is still growing. I just don't know how much I have left."

He saw the employee's reflection in the window, shuffling his feet uncomfortably.

"What can I do?"

He turned around and smiled at his employee. He wasn't going to burden this young man with his troubles.

"I'm done for the night, Darryl."

"Yes, sir."

He said his goodbyes on his way out of his casino as he did every night, making sure every employee at the Greek felt appreciated. He gave Shawn last-minute instructions.

"Have you thought anymore about our expansion idea?" Shawn asked.

Doug nodded. "I'm going to look at some properties tomorrow. See you in the morning."

"Bye, Dad."

He left the casino thinking about his appointment with the lawyer tomorrow afternoon.

There was an outside chance that Linda knew he was playing her, but it was all about the money—even if she knew. She'd be on the way out of his life by nightfall tomorrow.

Ace Sanders sat in his trademark black Ferrari outside the Greek Casino, a few blocks from his destination. He couldn't believe the long hours that the sixty-three-year-old Grant still put in at work. Everyone knew the man was a grind.

Not a big-picture guy like me.

Ace let his staff do the dirty work. Everyone reported to him daily at eleven and unless there were problems or decisions that needed his direct involvement, their reports were enough. He'd always paid well to recruit top casino executives and for years had left the management of his casinos up to them.

Once done with details, Ace spent the rest of the day roaming the floors of both casinos, talking to the high rollers and charming them into bringing in new, rich customers. He loved the games, the women and the house's guaranteed wins.

Ace watched the front of the casino. No movement.

As he waited, he shuffled a deck of cards and dealt four poker hands. He dealt the last card and set the remaining cards on the passenger seat between the hands. He picked up his five cards and smiled.

Three queens.

He checked the other dealt hands. "This really isn't your night, Douglas," he muttered.

He opened the glove compartment and pulled out the weapon, a smooth, seven-inch, high-carbon hunting knife, a beautiful, shining tool that left almost no evidence at the scene, except for whatever the police could learn from knife wounds. They might figure out the kind of knife that had been used and the cuts would tell them a bit about who used it, but he was sure that nothing would tie him to this. He'd bought the knife from a famous German knife maker who had personally made it for him, so it would never be traced.

He was about to exchange two cards when he saw his target exit the building. Ace checked his watch. It was after ten. Grant was a classic creature of habit, someone who *deserved* to fall behind as times changed.

Grant waited as the valet retrieved his car, then hopped in and moved into traffic.

Ace waited a moment before turning on his headlights and following Grant's vintage Jaguar. He remained a good distance behind—he already knew the route the man would take home.

The two cars turned off the main road without another car in sight. There were no streetlights, but he could see Grant's Jag approaching a vacated strip mall that had been closed down for years.

Ah, the perfect spot.

A deep thrill climbed Ace's body.

Doug had just turned onto the back road, less than fifteen miles from his place, when he noticed the car behind him. It moved quickly, lights flashing.

What now? A cop?

He shook his head but pulled the Jaguar into the deserted parking lot of an abandoned strip mall.

A Ferrari pulled beside him on the right side.

Shit. Ace Sanders.

Sanders was the last person Doug wanted to see.

Nothing moved in the Ferrari. The windows were blacked out, so he couldn't see the driver's face.

It has to be Sanders. What's he doing? Is he fucking nuts or just arrogant beyond recall?

The window of the Ferrari moved down. It was Sanders. Did he want a confrontation?

Doug rolled down the passenger-side window. "You need something?"

"I was hoping I'd catch you before you got home," Sanders said. "We need to talk."

"About what?"

"Linda."

Doug was shocked that Sanders would bring up her name so boldly. He watched Sanders climb out of his car and walk around, moving between the two vehicles. Sanders leaned back against the Ferrari's passenger door and raised his hands in the air. "Truce."

Truce?

Sanders' eyes softened. "Look, Doug, I know we've had our differences in the past. But I think that if we leave the past where it belongs, in the past, and move on, then there is a mega opportunity for us to make some real money in this city."

Doug had no idea what Sanders was talking about. What opportunity?

"If you just hear me out," Sanders went on. "Then what I have to show you will be very beneficial."

"You said something about Linda." Doug said.

"So you'll hear me out?"

Speechless, Doug stared out the front windshield, refusing to look in the man's direction. What could Sanders possibly say about Linda? Was this some last-minute attempt to try to save her in some way, somehow persuade him to think better of her, take her back? That wasn't Sanders' way at all. And what was this opportunity?

Maybe I'll learn something I can use to fight Sanders. Some slip-up.

He finally looked at Sanders and nodded slightly. Doug heard Sanders' car door open and then slam and then Sanders got into the passenger seat of the Jaguar. He set a leather bag on his lap

The tension in the car was palpable, the quiet haunting.

"What about Linda?" Doug asked finally.

Sanders shook his head. "I don't want to talk here. I don't want anyone to see or know that we're having this conversation. There's a lot of competition out there. There's a place where we can talk. It's only a few minutes away. I'll give you directions as you drive."

Something in Sanders voice told Doug he didn't have much of a choice.

He was more than a little hesitant to accommodate Sanders. But if there was a possibility that he could learn something new, possibly important enough to change his feelings, then he had to take the chance.

What was he thinking? Did he still have feelings for Linda? This was insane. He should flat out refuse and leave Sanders in the parking lot staring at the Jaguar's taillights. But he couldn't.

Except for Sanders' occasional directions, the drive was quiet. He had yet to look his way and Doug was beginning to panic. He couldn't sit still any longer. The silence was unnerving him. "So what's up?"

Sanders twitched, as though Doug's question had startled him out of a trance. He stared at Doug as if he hadn't known the man was in the car with him.

"There's something you need to see," Sanders said.

"What's in the bag?"

"After I show you something, we'll talk about what's in my bag."

Five minutes later they were driving through a heavily forested area.

"It's in there," Sanders said, pointing to the woods that surrounded the region.

Doug balked. This was idiotic. What was Sanders going to show him—bleached bones from a murder? Or was this really some sort of truce, Sanders thinking about a partnership with a prime piece of real estate to invest in. Doug knew Sanders always had a motive for money. This area could work for a casino/hotel.

He didn't like it, but his curiosity was overwhelming and stronger at the moment than his fear. He had to know what was so important to see or discuss about his wife that Ace would drive him out to the middle of nowhere. Ignoring his every gut instinct, he slowly got out of the car.

Ace sat in the idling car and watched as Grant got out and looked around. He had worried that Grant would refuse to go along and felt for the knife in his jacket.

Then he joined Grant. "This way," Ace said, motioning.

They moved past scrub and over thick grass. It was hard to see more than a few feet ahead.

"Why didn't you bring a flashlight?" Grant asked, a tremor in his voice.

"I know where we're going." After a few more steps, he said, "It's right in there."

Grant slipped past him, parted the shaggy branches and leaned forward.

Ace took a step closer. *Perfect.*

He yanked Grant's head against his shoulder, thrust the knife deep into one side of Grant's throat, then sliced all the way across with such force he could feel the knife's edge slide along Grant's spinal cord. Masses of blood gushed and spurted from the wound.

When the trailing tip of the hunting knife left Grant's throat, Ace let the limp body drop to the ground. Looking into his victim's dead eyes, he smiled with intoxicating pleasure and wiped most of the blood from the blade, using Grant's expensive suit as a towel.

With the calmness of a seasoned veteran, he walked back to Grant's car, opened the passenger door and took out his leather bag, careful not to leave any bloodstains on or inside the car. He opened the bag, pulled out a couple of towels, a shirt and a pair of pants, and set them to the side.

Unbuttoning his shirt, he removed the bloody garments and gloves and threw everything into the leather bag, including the knife and its sheath. With the towels, he wiped all the blood off his body that he could see. He put on a fresh shirt and pants, closed the leather bag, made sure it had no blood on it anywhere and put it back in the passenger seat. Then he pulled on a new pair of clean gloves, eliminating any possibility of prints on the steering wheel.

He needed to go back to the mall, pick up his Ferrari and leave Grant's vehicle abandoned there. The only tread marks the police would ever find at the murder site would come from the tires on Grant's own car.

Ace glanced at the body in the bushes and frowned. Pitt wouldn't be happy. Pitt had told him to leave the body in Grant's office, but that had never been Ace's intention. It would have been too risky.

It just wasn't in the cards.

CHAPTER 8

Calvin was jolted from an uneasy sleep by the phone. He reached across the bed and answered with a hoarse voice. "Yeah."

"Get your ass out of bed," Pitt said.

"What is it?"

"The Grant job. Come to the office for the info."

Calvin glanced at the bedroom clock. Seven o'clock was way too early for Pitt and he had not gotten over his improbable story about the loan, or his worry about collecting from someone so prominent in Las Vegas. The closest Pitt had come to a big shot was Sanders, who Calvin thought didn't count.

What was so important that it couldn't wait until the afternoon?

Calvin hung up without saying goodbye. He'd been through the drill enough times that he knew what to expect. There was no need to panic or rush.

This is it!

He rolled over and sat on the edge of the bed, testing his knee. He looked around the rundown apartment and shook his head. Soon he'd be gone, so the state of the apartment mattered less than ever.

He climbed out of bed, noticing that Rachel was gone already, as usual. Most of the time he kept her away from his apartment because it wasn't a pleasant place and it put Rachel at risk if someone tried to collect from the collector. But last night, knowing that this would be his last job, he was floating on air. He had been careless.

Still groggy from the painkillers, he walked to the bathroom and stubbed his toe on a fifty-pound dumbbell. "Shit."

He rolled the dumbbell under the bed and proceeded to the bathroom to splash cold water on his face. He took a quick shower, then dressed in jeans and a tight-fitting T-shirt that exposed the intimidating size of his chest and well-defined biceps.

He smiled at his reflection. Before the morning was over, Calvin would be starting his new life.

He reached the office before eight. It was rare that Calvin got there before the secretary, but the room was quiet and empty, except for Pitt, who was sitting at his desk. In front of him sat a half-empty bottle of cognac beside Pitt's coffee mug.

Pitt gave a wide grin and shook Calvin's hand.

Very un-Pitt-like. Unshaven and smelling bad, the man had bloodshot eyes.

"This is it, Calvin, your last one. We sure are gonna miss you around here."

Pitt seemed unusually chipper. Where did the belligerent man go, the one who lectured him yesterday?

"Well, I ain't gonna miss you." Unsmiling, Calvin stuck his hand out. "The info?"

"Don't be in such a rush. There are some things I have to explain to you first."

"Like what?"

"I don't have to tell you that everything I say is confidential, as always."

"How many times have I done this? You're treating me like a rookie."

Pitt held his arms up in surrender. "Fine. No more chitchat." He grabbed a file on his desk. "I didn't tell you yesterday because you didn't need to know. Now you do. The $200,000 you're collecting from Grant isn't a gambling debt. It's payment for some jobs I did for him over the last couple of months. He had some work he didn't want anyone to know about."

"Like what?"

"You don't need to know that."

"Why would he come to a scumbag like you when he can afford the best and trust them?"

"That's the point. He researched me, found out I wasn't only a bookie but could do other things too, or arrange for them to happen. And he knew that no one would ever think that we'd do business together. Opposite ends of the social scale. Even I have to admit that."

"What does all that have to do with my collecting this morning? Get to the real point."

Pitt sighed. "Maybe I won't miss you so much after all, Calvin. The point is that this whole situation is already very embarrassing for Grant, even though no one knows about it."

"Sounds like he *has* to keep the whole thing secret."

"He doesn't want to drive to a meeting with two hundred grand in cash. That's why the meeting is at his private office. He doesn't have a secretary, so it'll just be the two of you."

Calvin said nothing.

"He needs you to be discreet in that building and seem more like a rich associate than the collector you are." Pitt strode to the closet, opened the door and stepped inside. "Here's his plan. You're going to be disguised. He's added you at the front desk to his appointment list, but not as Calvin Watters."

Great. This was getting weirder by the minute.

"The cover story is that you're Winston Coburn III, an heir who owns three casinos in Atlantic City and is thinking of expanding his operations to Vegas." Pitt came back out of the closet holding two shopping bags. "Coburn is only in town for two days to check out available properties—small casinos. Start small and build. He's meeting with Grant to get his advice about which casinos he should take an interest in and discuss the possibility of a joint venture, if not with Grant himself, then with his son, Shawn."

"So I just walk in?"

"Yes. You'll go in, flash a business card that states you're the CEO of three casinos in Jersey and the security guards will confirm that you're on the appointment list. Then you go up to Grant's penthouse office on the twenty-fifth floor."

Calvin scowled. "Do I look like I own three casinos?"

"You'll have everything you need to complete the image. Besides, it doesn't matter what the guards think about your appearance. They'll assume you're eccentric. You wouldn't be the only one from New Jersey like that."

He still didn't like it. "Why the disguise exactly?"

"People know you, know what you do. You'd stand out anywhere unless we disguise you. And Grant doesn't want you identified." From one of the bags, he pulled a Panama hat with an encircling wide brim. "Here. Put this on. It should fit."

Calvin donned the hat and tugged the brim down over his brow. He glanced over one shoulder and caught his reflection in the mirror by the bar. *Shit...I look like a fool.* Pitt was right, though. The hat distracted attention from his face and hair.

"Good," Pitt said. "Now put on these glasses." He handed Calvin a pair of large-framed sunglasses, which hid a good deal of his face.

"Last but not least..." Pitt reached into the second bag and pulled out a long, tan overcoat.

Without a word, Calvin put on the coat. It was roomy, even on him, with a loose neckline that he could tuck his woven dreadlocks into. The cuffs reached past his wrists and covered his body tattoos. The coat, which extended past his knees, was long and baggy enough to conceal his physique. "I look ridiculous. Is all of this really necessary?"

A black man with no distinguishing features.

Pitt shrugged. "I've seen worse...maybe. It's an odd combination, but as a partial disguise, it's great."

"Well, I'm taking this off now." Calvin removed the hat, glasses and coat. "I'll put them back on when I get to the parking lot of Grant's building."

"Fine. Here's your Winston Coburn III business card, engraved, embossed and on special paper."

He studied the card. It was impressive and not something Pitt would have thought of or paid for. *What the hell am I walking into? And who else is in on it? Grant?* "Anything else?"

"In case there's a problem with your listed appointment, you should know that Dixie called the front desk yesterday afternoon as your secretary. She said Grant was very interested in meeting you on your brief trip here and he's agreed to your request for an early-morning appointment."

"How early?"

"Nine thirty. The front desk isn't going to disturb a man like Grant to confirm an appointment until you show up. Then they'll call him to confirm. If he doesn't answer, they'll assume he stepped out for a minute because he's intrigued by this unexpected opportunity to talk business with Mr. Coburn."

Calvin chewed on this information for a moment. "Why are you giving me so many details? You've never done that with any jobs before."

"This is the *big* one," Pitt said. "Whatever you have to do to get in to that office, do it. Make sure you're there by nine thirty. Wait for his return if you have to. If you don't make this meeting, I don't know how long it'll be before he's ready to try again." Pitt stared at him. "You want this to be your last job? Then get it done right the first time. Once you get the money, come straight back here. I'll give you the $30,000 balance on the spot and it's *adios, amigo*."

Calvin gave a nod. *Adios, amigo* sounded good to him.

He turned his thoughts to Grant. The man was often in the local papers and he knew he'd recognize him anywhere. "Give me the address."

While driving to Grant's office, Calvin tried to still the uneasy thoughts that flickered through his mind. He had known Pitt for three years and the man wasn't acting normal. He was nervous about something. And that didn't sit well with Calvin.

Something's up, or maybe it's the size of the payoff.

Calvin didn't buy into Pitt's story about Grant owing him $200,000. Not completely. Most casino owners in Vegas hired men like Pitt to do the dirty work and keep quiet, but Grant hiring Pitt for various illegal jobs was inconsistent with the character and reputation of the casino owner. Through the decades that Grant had run the Greek with his father and in the last fifteen years with his son, he'd had a good reputation as a somewhat honest man. To Calvin, Grant was a man who wouldn't get near such jobs.

So why does Pitt want me to see Grant?

If there was something going on here—and Calvin was sure there was—he was going to have to improvise and be careful too. His instincts had never failed him before. Calvin wanted to talk to Grant himself and find out what was really going on.

With most jobs, he only knew his target by name. It was easier if he didn't know the person. This time he had no personal connection, but almost too much information.

He remembered when the rich had welcomed him into their group as a promising, clean-cut athlete bound for glory. Now he was just an outsider looking in. Just another thug.

The upscale building was located in downtown Las Vegas, the city's central business district. It was originally the town site and gambling district located in the center of Las Vegas Valley, but it had taken a backseat to the Strip, which was located just south.

When he arrived at the expensive office complex, he ignored the valet parking and parked on the street. He put on the hat and sunglasses, stepped from the car and donned the coat.

Surveying the crowded sidewalk, he zigzagged through pedestrians hurrying to work. He strode through the rotating door into a bustling lobby, where men and women in tailored suits hustled to meetings.

It was 9:12 a.m. He was a bit early.

Oh well. Better to be early than late.

He entered the building and approached the counter, where a short, stocky security guard held a clipboard.

"Winston Coburn III to see Douglas Grant." Calvin handed his business card to the guard.

The guard scanned the clipboard. "Yes, Mr. Coburn. I have you down for a nine-thirty appointment. I'll notify Mr. Grant that you're here and see if it's okay to send you up."

"No problem."

The guard called Grant's office. He listened for a minute, then hung up. "Mr. Grant isn't in his office. He probably stepped out for a few minutes. You *are* a bit early. Would you mind waiting until I'm able to reach him?"

Calvin's smile disappeared. He remembered his boss's words.

"Listen, uh…" he read the man's name tag, "Gus. Yes, I mind waiting. Grant knows that I'm flying back to Atlantic City this afternoon, which is why we made an early appointment. I don't care if he's there now or not. I'll wait for him in his office, but absolutely not in this miserable lobby."

"But Mr. Coburn," the man stuttered, looking at his partner. "Do you think Mr. Grant would mind?"

The partner shook his head. "Nah, he's okayed it before, plus he made the appointment so he is expecting him."

Gus still looked uncertain when Calvin jumped in. "If you don't get me to an elevator in the next thirty seconds, I'm leaving. And when Grant calls to ask why I missed such an important meeting, I'll tell him that *Gus* wouldn't let me go up."

"Fred," Gus called to another guard who'd just joined him. He explained the issue to the man.

"Right this way, Mr. Coburn."

They took Calvin through the metal detector and used the manual detector to scan his body as fast as they could, without a word. He was probably the only collector in Vegas who had never carried a weapon.

They escorted him to the nearest open elevator.

"Please don't say anything about the delay to Mr. Grant," Fred mumbled. "We could lose our jobs."

"I'll think about it." Calvin stepped into the elevator. "Penthouse," he said to the elevator operator. "Doug Grant's office."

He was pleased with how he'd gotten in. He might be only a bill collector, but he knew how to act with the arrogance of the very wealthy.

Ace was parked in a modest rental car. He'd been waiting for half an hour in a distant corner of the parking lot where no one would recognize him, but where he could see everyone leaving or entering the building.

He'd called Pitt twenty minutes before and had confirmed that Watters was on his way and that he'd agreed to wear the hat, sunglasses and coat before he went into the lobby.

Ace had spotted Watters as soon as he walked down the sidewalk to the front entrance and entered the building. He was impossible to miss and would not be forgotten.

Killing Grant in his office or transporting him there after his death would have been too risky and probably impossible with the state of the art security system in the complex. Watters was the perfect fall guy, but Ace had to link Watters and Grant somehow and that was the challenge. A guy like Grant wouldn't be caught a hundred yards from Watters. This was the only way Ace could see connecting Watters and Grant and it could also potentially implicate Pitt. There was no other way to associate Watters with Grant and still lead the cops to connect the dots.

Earlier, Ace had an informant get him all the information he needed on the LVMPD, because once the Grant homicide investigation began, he'd be following it with interest. He could have dialed the Homicide Division directly, but he wanted to play the concerned, frightened, *innocent* citizen, one who only knew to call 911 in case of an emergency.

He waited ten minutes after Watters had entered the building before picking up his untraceable cell phone and dialing the three digits.

"Hello, 911 emergency."

"I need to speak to someone right away," he said. "A murder is about to occur and the police need to stop it."

Ace could tell by the sound of the police officer's voice that the man was concerned, but the officer remained composed. "Would you repeat that, please?"

He did.

"I'm going to transfer you to Homicide. Please hold."

The call was picked up in ten seconds. "Detective Hartford, Homicide. You're claiming someone's about to be murdered. Who? And where?"

Ace grinned. "I have reason to believe that Doug Grant is going to be murdered."

"Doug Grant, the casino owner? When and by whom?"

Hartford sounded shocked. That was the reaction Ace wanted. It would make the detective more likely to act than stop to think about the credibility of the call.

"Just listen," he said, forcing his voice to sound scared. "I'm risking my life by making this call. If people involved find out I've reported this information to the police, I'll be the next dead man." He didn't wait for a response. "I have solid information that a man named Calvin Watters is going to murder Doug Grant in his private office in the next few minutes. You need to get patrol cars over there right away."

He gave Hartford the address even though he knew he didn't need to.

"Watters entered the building three minutes ago. He made an appointment with Grant for nine thirty this morning under false pretenses. He's using the alias Winston Coburn III and he'll have a phony business card to show the guards at the front desk. He's wearing a Panama hat, black sunglasses and a long tan coat. By now, he may already be on the elevator. If you don't get officers there in time to stop Grant's murder, I'll let it be known anonymously that you received this call and because of your delay, you're to blame for Grant's death."

"Okay. But you have to tell me your—"

Ace hung up. Then he drove away, smiling.

Grant's suite was the only one on the penthouse floor. When Calvin strode out of the elevator, he approached the double front doors and knocked.

No one answered.

He tried the doorknob and found the door unlocked.

Hmmm...I guess Grant really did step out.

He pushed the doors open and walked in. "Hello? Grant?"

Silence.

Since Grant had left the doors unlocked, Calvin could only surmise the man had planned to return soon. Besides, Pitt always had good information as to where the target would be.

Maybe Grant left the money for me to pick up, to avoid meeting me.

He passed through a secretary's room, which connected to a larger carpeted office with a bathroom off to one side. Grant's office. The aroma of expensive leather and the scent of pipe tobacco filled the air.

This was the first time that Calvin's boss had ever been wrong about where a prospect would be. Also, from what he had seen, Grant hadn't left the money in a package to be picked up. He would have put it near the front door or somewhere else where Calvin could easily spot it.

He jumped when the phone rang, then ignored it as he made a beeline toward the mahogany desk. He studied the papers on top— memos, documents, bills, the usual stuff. There was also a framed picture of Grant and his wife from their wedding day. Nothing with Calvin's or Pitt's name.

He searched around again and saw no indication of the money. The last thing he wanted was to be caught snooping around in Grant's office.

The phone continued to ring.

Obviously, no one is here. Hang up already.

No Grant, no money. This last job was getting more suspicious by the minute. And Calvin's finely tuned sense of danger from his years on the streets was buzzing.

Something's off here.

Riffling through the papers on Grant's desk, he heard police sirens in the distance. He jerked upright. They were getting closer.

The phone finally stopped ringing but the sirens grew louder.

Proper procedure he'd been taught was to call immediately when a job failed and await instructions. As badly as he wanted to get out of there, he still had the reputation he'd built.

"Calm down, Calvin," he told himself. "This is your last job. Do it right and you're done."

Using Grant's desk phone, he dialed an outside line. "Grant's not here and neither is the money."

"What do you mean he's not there?" Pitt sounded worried.

"I'll tell you again. Grant's not in his office. You were wrong."

"He has to be there!"

"Nope. I'm leaving. And I've just finished my last job. You're going to have to get someone else to try to collect. I'm coming back to give you this stupid disguise and pick up a few things."

"No, wait!" There was a slight pause. "Grant may show up any—"

Calvin hung up. Sirens shrilled outside as though they were maybe a block away. He peered out the window. Sure enough, four police cars were pulling up to the curb, lights flashing. The sirens were cut off in mid-wail.

Okay, this is all too weird. I'm getting out of here. Fuck this.

He headed to the elevator, but hesitated. Were the cops heading up or taking care of business in the lobby? If he took the elevator down to the first floor, some of the officers might be heading up in the elevator, while a couple would take the stairs. He made it a general policy to be invisible to cops as much as he could. Whatever was going in this building, he didn't want to be a part of.

"Shit!" he muttered.

It would take too long to climb down twenty-five flights of stairs. And it would kill his knee, not to mention that he'd eventually be greeted by the officers.

There was only one thing to do. He'd take the elevator to the third floor. The officers going up the stairs should be well past that point. He'd then get off the elevator and take the back stairs down three flights. He could manage that much.

When he reached the third floor, he got off the elevator and searched for the exit sign. Sunlight filtered in through windows at both ends of the hall as he found the emergency exit and started sprinting down the steps, taking two at a time.

At the bottom floor, his breathing had quickened slightly, his shirt was damp with sweat and his knee throbbed. Cops would be in the lobby, so he went straight to the emergency exit at the back of the building.

Damn.

The door was wired to set off an alarm if opened from the inside. He took less than a minute to disconnect the wires from the alarm, then ran down the back alley without looking back.

CHAPTER 9

When Dale Dayton arrived at the murder site, nosy spectators were being ringed back by the police, while others drove past, stirring up dust clouds of dry Nevada air. Dozens of police cruisers, along with the emergency medical teams, had responded to the emergency call.

He accelerated past the road block and pulled up to the curb, grabbing his Styrofoam spit cup and exiting the car. As he badged his way past the cops at the front, he noticed four road flares placed around fresh tread marks on the gravel at the side of the road.

He found a junior officer standing nearby and said, "Make sure this area is secured."

The officer said, "Yeah, thanks. I know how to do my job." Then he walked away.

Dale scanned the crowd of bystanders herded behind yellow police tape. News traveled fast in Vegas. Angry and scared citizens, as well as the meddlesome media, were always drawn to the scene of a crime.

A familiar group awaited him. *Suits*.

The lieutenant, Dale's sergeant, the Clark County sheriff and the mayor huddled behind a strand of tape. It was rare when the lieutenant made an appearance at a crime scene. And Dale had *never* seen the mayor at one. But this time, the victim was Doug Grant. High profile cases wake up all the supervisors. They would want to talk to him as the lead detective.

Dale frowned. *Gotta avoid them if I want to get real police work done.*

He followed the recently trampled tracks into the woods and weaved through the thick brush to where Jimmy was waiting, scribbling in a notepad. Slipping a pair of latex gloves over his hands, he knelt down next to the body.

"He's been identified twice," Jimmy said. "The deceased is Douglas Grant."

"Anything else?"

"Chargers lost last night," Jimmy added with a sarcastic grin.

Dale gave a brief nod, ignoring his partner's poor attempt at humor. He put his cup on the ground. "Let's have a look-see, shall we? Larry, did you get a picture? I wanna roll him over."

"I have ten from this side, all angles," the crime scene photographer said. "I also got a sketch of the crime scene and some overalls. I'll go get a couple of angle shots of the roadside tread marks that we can keep on record for any comparisons. Also, I'll have Eddie craft some molds of the marks."

Larry left.

Dale rolled Grant onto his back. He let his breath out when he saw the man's face. Gray eyes stared blankly back at him, the thin face pale and gaunt. Even with slight bruising, there was no mistaking Doug Grant.

He glanced at Jimmy. "Time of death established?"

"Between ten o'clock and midnight last night."

He studied the gaping slash in the victim's throat. Smooth edges and sides, plus depth of cut, indicated a very sharp knife pulled hard and fast by a righty.

Vicious.

He lifted Grant's hands and analyzed the wrinkled palms. "No defensive hand wounds. Grant knew his killer or got jumped. Who the hell would jump him out here?"

He scanned the surrounding area, mentally cataloging everything in view.

He looked up at Jimmy. "Who called it in?"

"Woman jogger."

Jimmy nudged his head in the direction of an ebony-toned woman in her early twenties. She was clearly shaken and sat on the tailgate of the ambulance while an EMT watched her. Wearing a tight body suit, she had the physique of a seasoned runner.

"Not bad, huh?"

Dale ignored his partner's remark. "Take him away, guys."

He had served twelve years, but this was the most prominent murder case he'd been assigned to. He was used to killings in Vegas for drugs or money. This one seemed very personal.

Jimmy studied him, scrunched his eyes and frowned. "Didn't you wear that suit yesterday? You slept in it, right?"

"Fuck off."

Jimmy chuckled. "I told you that you were too old to have a kid."

"I'm forty-six. That's not too old."

"It doesn't seem like such a good idea now, does it? Trying to placate Betty."

Dale didn't respond. It had been two days since Betty's announcement and he hadn't told anyone, not even his partner, that his wife had left him.

After inserting a fresh wad of Copenhagen snuff between his lip and gums, he moved out of the way as two uniformed men moved in with a gurney. They secured the body on the stretcher and hauled it away.

Dale walked around the crime scene, ignoring everyone in his path.

Jimmy turned to a young, uniformed patrolman. "Watch this."

As if on cue, Dale said, "The murder happened here."

"What makes you say that?" Jimmy asked.

He pulled out the pen that had been resting behind his ear, using it as a pointer. "The clumps of blood and the spatter." He indicated the blotches of red on the ground. "There is no trace of blood anywhere else. No indication of a body being dragged. Grant walked out here on his own volition."

"He could have been carried?"

"No chance. If he were carried, the extra weight would've forced the footprints farther into the ground." He slipped the pen back behind his ear. "We know where the footsteps ended. Let's find out where they began."

He picked up his cup and spit into it.

Dale was glad he had a case like this to take his mind off his personal life. He thought of Betty. She had given up on his round-the-clock work routine.

Right now, that's all he had to keep him sane.

With Doug Grant a victim, Dale would be conducting a homicide investigation bigger than any he'd experienced before. With the mayor and the sergeant watching, he'd have to run it by the book.

He was looking forward to the challenge but not the supervision. There would be pressure on the department and that meant his boss would be looking for quick answers. He'd have to prioritize this case over his other assignments.

Dale had never met Grant personally, but as so many others had, he'd heard many stories about him and his father and son over the years.

He turned to his partner. "Let's get to work."

Calvin was sweating when he made it back to Pitt's office. He mopped his face and neck with his T-shirt.

Dixie smirked. "Hey, a black Elton John."

He whipped off the sunglasses and hat and shrugged out of the coat. With a nod, he said, "You can have these."

The office door was open, so Calvin quietly stepped inside. Pitt was sitting in his chair, facing away from the door. He leaned back in the chair and interlocked his fingers behind his head.

"Hey," Calvin said.

Startled, Pitt unclasped his hands and spun the chair around. His eyes flared when he saw Calvin leaning against the doorway, but he said nothing. .

Staring, he clambered to his feet. "H-how could you…how could Grant not have been there?"

It was obvious he'd wanted to say something else.

"Why are you so surprised?" Calvin asked.

"He was supposed to be there." Pitt sat back down, a faraway look in his eyes. "I want my money."

"Money always is your first priority." He watched the man, suspicion growing with every minute. "I told you, Don. You're gonna have to find someone else to get it. We agreed that my last job was collecting from Grant. I went there. When I left without finding Grant or the money, I'd finished the job. It's over now. I'm walking outta here."

"Not without giving me back that $10,000 I paid you in advance yesterday."

"I consider that final payment for the work I did today. You don't like it, try to collect from me." He widened his stance.

With a groan, Pitt sat back in his chair. "I'm too tired to fight with you. Keep the money. Just go."

Without so much as a handshake, Calvin strode out of the office. He was free. Finally.

Now I can start my new life.

And whatever was wrong with the Grant situation, it was Pitt's problem now.

CHAPTER 10

Dale was used to working with Jimmy. He and his partner had developed a pattern for their searches. They walked about three feet apart, searching the ground for clues.

"You've been on the force four years longer than me," Dale said.

"Yeah. Thirty-one years, why?"

"You ever see a case of this magnitude?"

"Never."

He smiled. "How long we been partners?"

"Nine years."

Dale grunted. Nine years was more than most marriages lasted. "I remember when we were first paired together," he said.

"Yeah, everyone called us the odd couple, like Lemmon and Mathau."

"Yeah, the black-white thing wasn't said back then, but everyone was thinking it. All I heard about was how Jimmy Mason was experienced, conservative, a real by-the-book man."

"Yeah." Jimmy smiled. "And all I heard was that Dale Dayton was a cowboy—instincts and no rules."

"I guess I'll have to be more like you on this investigation." He nodded toward the supervisors huddled at the scene.

"They said we would never make it. Even our age difference would come between us."

"But it didn't. I trust you with my life."

"What, you gettin' all sentimental on me, Dayton?"

"Just sayin', partner. I can't figure it out."

"What?"

"You have four years on me on the force and yet I'm the lead for all of the major cases."

"You think it's a color thing?" Jimmy smiled wide. "You think, just maybe?"

"Yeah, but I don't have time to listen to your whining about persecution right now. For most senior officers, taking a back seat would cause some problems. But not you."

Jimmy stopped walking and turned toward Dale. "Dale, I'm not okay with racism, but I know you do the lead drill better than I would and it has nothing to do with the color of my skin. But as you know, I am tougher and smarter than you."

"Fuck you very much, Jimmy."

"Okay, enough sentimental bullshit. What do you think?"

He knew the stats. The list of possible motives for any murder was profit, jealousy, revenge, concealment of a crime, or the killer was a homicidal maniac.

"Could be a crime of passion," Dale stated. "A passion for near decapitation."

He thought sex was probably involved somehow, but he had no idea how yet.

"Wife?" Jimmy inquired.

"Think about it. Who benefits the most from Grant's death? Linda Grant is now a wealthy woman."

"She was already a wealthy woman," Jimmy stated.

"Come on, that was her husband's money. But now she has no one to share it with. It's all hers."

"You think Linda Grant did this?"

"I don't think Linda committed the murder, or any woman for that matter. Sure, she could have lured her husband out here, but she's much too small and weak to slice his head nearly off. But could be hired work."

"We better tell her first that she's a widow and gauge from there." Jimmy wore a big smile.

"What are you so excited about?"

"Meeting Linda Grant."

"Your wife know you're a perv?"

Jimmy smiled again. "Of course, but she likes it. How do you think we've made it through twenty-five happily married years? I just always appreciate a beautiful woman."

The search was going nowhere. Dale snapped off his gloves, the rubber smacking loudly. He dialed the police station.

"Henry, it's Dale."

"You in the field?"

"Yeah. I need you to find a judge. Tell him that I need two search warrants sworn out ASAP on probable cause. Doug Grant's home and casino, the Greek."

"The casino owner?"

"Yeah, the same one."

"What did he do?"

"I'll add that in myself. Have them ready by the time I get back. Wait. Rephrase that. Get me one unspecified search warrant for Doug Grant."

Dale hung up without saying goodbye. The search would have to be fast, deep and wide.

"Unspecified?" Jimmy asked.

Dale shrugged. "Who knows what Grant owns?"

As he was walking away, Jimmy put his hand on Dale's shoulder. "Dale, be careful whose toes you step on with this one."

After almost two hours of thorough searching, all they had were the tire tread marks.

"Let's go see the widow."

As he and Jimmy turned to leave, Dale felt a sharp tug on his coat sleeve. The detectives turned to face their sergeant standing beside the mayor.

"Dayton, Mason, we need to talk."

Dale spit into his cup.

"Jesus Christ, Dayton, you know I hate that shit!" He turned to the man beside him. "You know Mayor Casey. He wants a few words with you boys before you get going. I'm heading back now. I'll meet you at the precinct."

The men shook hands as the sergeant left. This was the first time that Dale had been this close to Paul Casey. Casey was tall and slender, a bit cocky. Dale couldn't believe he was standing in this heat in a pin-striped double-breasted suit, with not a drop of sweat on him.

"What do you think?" the mayor asked.

"It's still too soon in the case to tell, sir. There is little evidence to go on right now."

"Detectives, I don't want to slow you down. I just wanted you to know that this case takes precedence. This case should be treated with your utmost professionalism and speed. I am depending on you gentlemen to bring me swift justice. Doug Grant was a friend of mine and I don't have to tell you the impact that he and his family have had on this city. I would consider it a personal favor if you brought down the son of a bitch who did this. The city would be in your debt."

It might have been Casey's shifty eyes or trite words but something didn't feel right.

"We'll get him," Dale said.

"That's all I wanted to hear. Get to work, gentlemen." The mayor marched off.

Something wasn't kosher about the whole deal.

Jimmy's face showed he agreed.

"Wait here, I'll be back in a minute."

Dale hopped out as Jimmy pulled up to the police station. As he entered the precinct, the attendant at the front desk shrugged at him. "They just found the judge at the club, rubbing elbows with Vegas's elite. The papers should be here soon."

He thought about running outside to tell Jimmy it would take a while, but then he heard his name called. Detective Joe Hartford rushed toward him.

"Dale, I'm glad I caught you."

"What's up, Joe?"

"The sergeant said you're working the Grant case?"

"That's right."

"I think you should hear this."

Dale looked back outside toward Jimmy, but he followed Hartford across the lobby and into the tech room.

"We recorded this 911 call earlier this morning. Didn't think much of it at the time. Thought it was just some prank."

The lab tech started the recording.

Dale scratched his salt and pepper crew cut as he listened.

When it was done, Hartford said, "After we got the call, we phoned over to the building lobby, but there was no answer. We had to call a second time, a few minutes later, before a security guard responded. We told him the situation and stayed on the line as they tried to locate Grant. There was no answer at his office, and when they finally got upstairs, no one was there. That Coburn character, or Calvin Watters, was nowhere to be found."

"They didn't lock down the building?"

Hartford shrugged. "Amateurs. We sent a couple of patrol cars to the private office, but by the time they got there, there was nothing to see."

"So Grant has a private office in addition to his house and casino offices?"

Hartford nodded.

Dale was relieved that he had asked for an unspecified search warrant that would include all of Grant's offices. It could have taken a day for more than one.

Dale was thinking about how some of the anonymous caller's information had been correct, but some wrong. The rest he could check out himself.

The caller was wrong about the time of death. Grant had already been dead for almost twelve hours when the call had been placed. Was the caller aware of the time of Grant's murder and just trying to confuse the cops? Was the caller attempting to set Calvin Watters up? Was Watters really in the building? He knew who Calvin Watters was and what his involvement meant.

The caller was also wrong about the murder site—the woods, not the office. Could the caller have been aware of a plot to assassinate Grant, but been too slow to respond and didn't know the exact details? How much did the caller know and what might he by lying about?

"No chance of a trace or identification, Joe?"

"Not a chance. The phone had a good scrambler."

"Why would a Samaritan use a scrambler?"

"There are all sorts of whack jobs out there. Maybe that's his usual phone. The techs are busy analyzing the recording for background noises, but that's a long shot."

"Thanks, Joe. Give me a full written report and leave it on my desk."

"Sure thing."

He headed back to the front desk, but the papers still weren't there. Henry shook his head so Dale turned and headed across the lobby to the sergeant's office.

"What is it, Dayton?" The sergeant kept his eyes on his paperwork.

"I want to put a surveillance team on Linda Grant."

"I suppose you want phone taps too?" He didn't wait for Dale to respond. "Do it. I'll get the warrant for it."

Dale nodded and then asked for another favor. After a brief moment to think it over, the sergeant replied.

"Okay, you got it. But be careful. Linda Grant is a pretty powerful person herself in this community."

Dale would track Linda with a GPS mounted secretly on the rear bumper of her car. He rushed back to his desk to get her phone records pulled and the lines tapped.

The search warrants had arrived when he made it back to the front desk. Without further discussion, he hurried outside. When he jumped into the car, Jimmy gave him a doubtful grin.

"Back in a minute, huh?"

Dale was looking forward to questioning Linda Grant for different reasons than his partner who, a married-man of twenty-five years with a sex-drive of a teenager, probably took a little adolescent delight in talking to someone everyone knew was a knockout.

A forest of trees hid the Grant house and a wrought-iron gate secured it. Jimmy said their names into the speakerphone and as the gate swung open, a patrol car followed the detectives' cruiser inside. A gardener, tending a flowerbed, glanced up as they passed by. The front lawn resembled a putting green.

The house was a castle—a six-thousand-square-foot Tudor-style mansion with five bedrooms, marble mantels, antique moldings and a gym.

The house had been on an edition of *Las Vegas Celebrity Mansions* as one of the top-ten visited houses in the city.

Dale was expecting a maid but Linda Grant opened the door. She lived up to her pictures—a beautiful woman with a super-model body, at least twenty-five years younger than her late husband. She wore a formfitting, high-waistline dress in a lavender floral print and black ankle-wraparound heels. She had a simple tassel necklace. Her brown hair cascaded over her shoulders. She threw the detectives an amiable smile.

"Good morning, Detectives."

"Good morning, Mrs. Grant."

"Ma'am." Jimmy nodded.

As they stepped inside, Dale thought her eyes were dark and unreadable. She seemed much more composed for someone who was facing a surprise police visit.

"How can I help you, officers?"

"I'm Detective Dayton. This is my partner, Detective Mason." They both showed their badges. "We have some news about your husband."

"Doug didn't come home last night. He often spends the night at the casino."

"We know, ma'am. That's why we're here."

Now she seemed a little worried. "Please come in."

They stepped into a grand oak-paneled entrance hall. She led them past a front room filled with oil paintings and Persian carpets and into a cozy back room, where the warm sun shone through walls of windows. They all sat down around a glass coffee table.

"Mrs. Grant, your husband's body was discovered this morning in the woods just off highway 515. He'd been murdered."

Linda brought her hand to her mouth and her body started to tremble.

Jimmy pulled a handkerchief from his coat. "Here."

She received the offer and dabbed her eyes and sculpted nose.

Dale continued. "He was killed quickly and didn't suffer."

"He didn't come home last night," she admitted between sniffles. "I just assumed that he'd slept at the office." She wept louder.

"Get her a drink, Jimmy."

Jimmy headed toward a wet bar in the corner of the room. Dale watched Linda. She kept her eyes on her lap and twisted a gaudy-sized diamond on her ring finger.

After pouring three fingers of expensive scotch, Jimmy returned with the glass. Linda sipped it.

Dale went on. "Mrs. Grant, everyone with your husband's prominence has enemies. Can you think of who might have wanted to harm him?"

She shook her head.

"Please, Mrs. Grant. Anything you can tell us would help."

"You're right, we all have enemies, but I can't think of anyone who would have killed him!" Linda said shaking her head. "He was the kindest, gentlest man I have ever known. Just about everyone he knew loved him."

"What would he be doing in the woods?"

"I don't know. Doug hadn't mentioned any new real estate plans. He often looked at property to expand, but he hadn't said."

"I know this is a tough question, Mrs. Grant, but one I have to get out of the way. Where were you last night between the hours of ten and twelve?"

Linda held the tissue to her nose and stared at the detective. "Well, I was home, where I always am." Her hand dropped and her eyes were fixed with rage. "Wait a minute, Detective." She jumped to her feet and raised her voice. "Are you insinuating that I had something to do with my husband's murder? Do you think that I could do that?"

Jimmy stood up and spoke in a calm voice. "Easy, Mrs. Grant. We're not saying that. Please, sit down. We have to ask these questions."

Linda sat back down and Dale studied her. At least part of what he saw was an act. He was sure of it.

"Was anyone here with you, Mrs. Grant?"

"Just the servants doing their regular prep for the following day. We're preparing a wonderful birthday party for my stepson, Shawn, next week, so my helpers have been working overtime and did last night, not finishing until after midnight. I was supervising, so all three can confirm that I was here during those hours. They sleep in the other wing." She pointed to the far side of the house.

That would be easy enough to verify.

"Dale, can I speak with you in the other room?" Jimmy asked.

Dale nodded. "Excuse us, Mrs. Grant."

When Linda was out of earshot, Jimmy whispered, "Dale, this isn't an interrogation. We're just here to make next of kin notification, not start a war. If we piss her off, she has the connections to make our lives miserable."

"I know, Jimmy, but we don't get a second chance to watch her first reaction or hear her side. You know that. So let's see what we can see—don't be a wimp."

"Dale, stop jumping to conclusions. We need to do real investigating, not chase theories."

"I know, you're right. But let's at least look around."

"Is the warrant good for that?"

"Yeah."

"Okay then, but let's be respectful and professional."

They returned to find that Linda had moved from the couch and was standing by the window. She gazed into the backyard at the Grecian-style, in-ground swimming pool. A separate spa was nestled into a large deck that allowed an expansive view of the grounds.

"Mrs. Grant, we need to search the house for anything that could help us identify your husband's killer. There might be something significant here."

She turned and hesitated, "Detectives, I don't think that would be appropriate. I—"

Dale showed her the search warrant. Linda grabbed the paper and read.

"I think I'll call my attorney now."

CHAPTER 11

"Rudy, Danny, please escort Mrs. Grant outside." Dale acknowledged his officers.

"I'm not going anywhere!" Linda snapped.

"Please, Mrs. Grant. It would be a lot easier on everyone if you just cooperated. We might discover something vital to help catch your husband's killer."

"Fine." Linda grabbed the phone and started dialing as she was led outside.

Without hesitation, the detectives went in separate directions, searching each room before Dale discovered a small business office. "Down here, Jimmy."

Grant's home workplace was twice the size of the lieutenant's office at the precinct. A large white bookcase filled with hardbacks covered the back wall. A dustless, new-edition laptop sat on top of a small, gleaming desk. The room smelled of fresh varnish. The desk was cluttered with equipment needed for any businessman to work at home. A beige filing cabinet had been pushed into the corner and a print copy of Rembrandt's "The Abduction of Europa" hung on the wall behind the desk.

Dale looked down at the two-inch-thick carpet, which was stain-free and dustless. "Does this room look recently cleaned to you, Jimmy?"

Jimmy nodded. "I'd say. To a tee."

But forensics could still find something.

"Okay, I'll take the desk. You check the rest of the room," Dale said.

First, he checked the call list on the phone, but it showed mostly calls to the casino. Then he read each item on the papers stacked on top. "Hey, these pages are out of order, like someone rifled them and hurried to straighten them."

"What are they?"

He shrugged. "Bills and accounts. We'll just take it all in." He opened the desk drawers and thumbed through the contents. There was very little.

"Something's not right, Jimmy."

"What do you mean?"

"You've heard about Grant. He was obsessive with his work and a conscientious man to the point that he didn't even have a CFO or business manager. He only trusted himself and his son. There should be boxes full of bills, receipts or documents from the casino around here. This was swept clean."

"Maybe he does all that somewhere else?"

"Like the office where Watters was supposed to have been this morning. You find anything?"

Jimmy removed the Rembrandt painting. "There's a safe back here."

He pulled out his cell phone and flipped it open. "Glen, it's Dale. Send a forensics team over to the Grant home. I need a full sweep of the office plus a safe cracked. Pull it all into the station. The search warrant we have covers repeat searches. Hurry!" Dale hung up. "Let's go."

The detectives walked outside and joined Linda Grant and the two officers, who were standing near the edge of the flower garden.

Linda had the phone pressed to her ear and dropped it when the detectives arrived. "Find anything?"

"I don't know. Thank you for your time, Mrs. Grant. Some people will be coming over. Please cooperate with them. Again, our deepest sympathies for your loss."

When Linda had entered the house, Dale turned to his patrol officers. "You guys wait here until Glen arrives. I don't want our number-one suspect to destroy any evidence."

The cops nodded.

Jimmy backed out of the driveway and through the gate opening. They drove thirty feet before stopping next to a car parked across the street. Dale rolled down his window and spoke to the man sitting in the driver's seat. "All right, Johnny, you and Stan are up. Don't let that woman out of your sight and report anything unusual. You have your thick soles on just in case the pursuit ends up on foot?"

"You got it, Dale."

He handed his colleague a GPS unit. He was hoping that Linda Grant was not as cool as she looked and would contact whoever killed Doug Grant. That was all he could do for now.

As they headed back to the station, Jimmy was silent. Finally he said, "Ace Sanders and Doug Grant weren't best friends."

Dale nodded. "For more reasons than one. We know he kept bugging Grant to buy the casino. But do you think the rumors are true that he slept with his wife too?"

Jimmy smiled. "This is Vegas, right?"

"I deliberately didn't mention Sanders to see how Mrs. Grant would respond to my line of questioning, what there was. We know that Sanders and Grant have been feuding over the years. The hatred between the two is well documented and we also have heard rumors about Sanders and Linda."

"How did she do?"

They traded a look, but Dale didn't answer. He only smiled. Linda had acted exactly as he had thought she would. Linda Grant was at the top of his current suspect list, but Ace Sanders was a very close second.

Linda slipped into the master bedroom with her cell.

"That son of a bitch! The nerve of that man to keep me on hold for this long. I'll have him disbarred before he can even say the word *lawsuit*." She slammed the phone down. Her first order of business was to fire her attorney.

She opened the entertainment unit, which was just a TV monitor feed from the hidden camera at the front of the property. A parked car sat across the street from the gate.

She turned off the screen and got down on her knees, reaching under the bed. Opening up a trap door, she removed a cell phone box and carried it into the separate dressing area of the master suite. She locked the door. Unwrapping the box, she dialed a number.

"What?"

"It's me."

"I know who it is. You better be using the phone I bought you."

"I am."

"What do you want?"

"The cops were just here."

"So?"

"So? You told me I'd be protected. You said nothing would happen to me as long as I followed the plan. Now I have cops here asking me where I was when Doug was killed."

"Is this the Linda I know? Take a deep breath and calm down. This is like a cop show. Suspect the wife, immediate family, blah, blah, blah. As long as you don't do anything stupid, they have nothing. The LVMPD is on a fishing expedition."

"What should I do?"

"Call Ace."

"What?"

"Call Ace and tell him you're worried because the cops were there. Go hysterical. And Linda?"

"What?"

"Make sure to call him from your landline."

She disconnected the call when there was a rap on the door. "Mrs. Grant, we need you to come out."

"Hold on, I'm not dressed," she called back.

She picked up the portable phone. She closed her eyes, took a deep breath and thought about what she would say. She punched the number to the direct private phone line in his office at the Golden Horseshoe Hotel and Casino.

"Ace, it's me. Two homicide detectives were just here. They questioned me for half an hour before searching the entire house. But I don't think they found anything. The lead detective grilled me. He thinks I killed Doug. Cops are sitting outside now watching the house. They..." Her words were fast and her breathing rapid.

He cut her off before she could say more. "Listen, Linda. I can't talk now. I will contact you when I can. Don't call me. Hang up now and wait for my call."

The call was disconnected and another knock came on the bathroom door.

"Mrs. Grant, we're supposed to keep you in sight at all times."

She applied lipstick and mascara, rolled the top of her dress down, exposing just enough cleavage to draw attention, then whirled and opened the door.

"Here I am, boys."

CHAPTER 12

The detectives arrived back after three to a buzzing station. The room was noisier than usual with gossip and unanswered questions.

Dale threw down his fast-food lunch and sat at his messy desk. He opened a drawer and swept every piece of paper inside. The new case files had been stacked on the filing cabinet. He grabbed the files and tossed them onto his clean desk. The forensics, coroner, crime scene and street police all had completed their reports. There was a crime scene analysis and a crime scene sketch as well as Grant's bio. But other than the tread marks found on the side of the road, nothing else had yet been discovered. The reports offered little cause for optimism. He had already issued an APB for Grant's missing car.

The phone call was the only promising lead. It just didn't make sense.

"Hey, Dale." One of his officers approached his desk. "Linda Grant has already placed a call to Ace Sanders. Sanders didn't let Linda speak long enough to say anything incriminating." He started to walk away and then stopped. "Oh yeah, the tracking device has been planted on Linda's chauffeured limo and is operational."

Dale thanked his officer, took a long gulp of coffee, powered up his computer and grabbed the first file. Then he heard his sergeant storm out of his office.

"Has anyone seen Dayton?" The sergeant yelled into the crowd at no one in particular.

The detective waited for his name to be called.

"Dayton, get in here!"

He took his time walking toward his sergeant's office, picking up Jimmy on the way.

The sarge was sitting at his desk watching the television when the detectives walked in. An unlit cigar hung from the side of his mouth. "Sit down, you two!"

Then he grabbed the remote control and turned up the volume on the television. Dale and Jimmy sat back and watched the full report on the Grant murder. The news crew did "man on the street" spots with scared citizens.

Then Dale watched as the mayor was interviewed and said they'd have an answer soon.

The sergeant hit mute. "Personally I don't like the conniving little prick, but I'll kiss his ass any chance I get. We're in the middle of a political disaster. Grant was a major contributor to the mayor's political campaigns and a close friend. The Greek was great PR for Vegas." He was making his point by tapping his finger hard on the desk.

"I've assigned you twelve officers, Dayton. Here."

The sergeant passed Dale a piece of paper. Dale recognized the names on the list. All of the officers were capable investigators. The latitude and assistance that was being given to him re-emphasized how big this case really was.

"Now get outta here and find somethin'."

As he was walking out, his boss called him back.

"Dayton, don't screw this up. And get that fuckin' thing off my desk!" The sergeant pointed at the spit cup as Dale smirked and grabbed it.

Outside the office, ten of the twelve-man investigative team members caucused around Dale's desk.

This was it—bumped up to top-grade detective, or proof positive he couldn't handle a big case or higher ranking. This case would be either a career-maker or a career-killer.

He refocused. "Jimmy, let's fill in everyone. First, nobody talks to anyone about this case. Duncan and Parker, take Grant's son, daughter and ex-wife. His son, Shawn, has been running the Greek, so he should be a good source. What was Grant's *relationship* like with his ex-wife and daughter? Don't be shy, gentlemen."

The officers nodded and left the huddle.

He turned to the next two in line. "Harper and Elliot, take Grant's friends and pricey lawyer, although attorney/client privilege may stop him from saying anything at all. But seeing as how Grant was murdered, the lawyer might be authorized, or feel a moral obligation that most lawyers don't, to say something. But I'm assuming this guy is both Grant's and his wife's lawyer."

The team wrote down their assignment and departed.

Dale gestured toward two officers. "Smith and Ramirez, you take all employees, from pit bosses to cocktail waitresses."

He paused for a moment and then continued. "Sanchez and Lucas." The two stepped forward. "Rival casino owners."

He turned to his two remaining officers. Edwards and Morris were Dale's two most experienced members of his team. "I need you guys to go to Grant's casino office and strip it to the walls. Go into the walls if needed. All of it comes back here. He'll have a safe so take Mark with you. Here, take this." Dale handed over the search warrant. "You'll probably have to push Shawn Grant hard with the warrant to get into Grant's office."

"What are we gonna do?" Jimmy asked when the room was empty.

"We, my friend, are going to Grant's private office."

"Hunch?"

"Yeah. Hunch." He picked up the phone and dialed his sergeant's office. "I need phone records."

Before they left, Dale turned to his youngest officer. "Craig, get me phone records from Doug, Linda and Shawn Grant, as well as Calvin Watters and Ace Sanders. I need local and long distance from their home, work and cell phones."

CHAPTER 13

To save time, Dale brought a couple of members of the LVMPD forensic team. Having twice as many pros working the same office at the same time would expedite everything.

Dale flashed his badge at the guards, displayed the search warrant for Grant's office and made his request. After carefully scanning the warrant and examining the badge, Dale, Jimmy and the two forensic experts were asked to sign in as the security guard fumbled for his keys.

"You two go ahead." Dale indicated to the forensic unit.

The two men followed the security guard across the lobby floor and toward the elevators.

Dale checked the name tags on the security guards' shirts. "Gus, Fred, I was wondering if my partner and I could ask you guys a few questions?"

The guards fidgeted.

"Just relax, fellas. We're all on the same side here. Who was on duty this morning?"

The chubby one swallowed hard and answered. "We were, sir." A drip of perspiration leaked from the guard's forehead. The man looked as if he were going to blow a blood vessel.

"We want to know if a Winston Coburn III had a nine-thirty appointment with Grant this morning and if he had gone up to the private office."

"He sure did."

Quick answer.

The taller guard handed the guest list to Dale, who noticed the perfect penmanship. He gave the clipboard to Jimmy and continued with his questions.

"Do you remember what this guy looked like?"

"I sure do."

He sighed. Evidently, the men had been trained to say as little as possible. He could tell that Jimmy was getting impatient too.

"We knew you'd be coming, so we prepared the video footage. Just come around."

The detectives rounded the counter and joined the security guards behind the desk. The monitors, six in total, were mounted on the inside shelf.

"This monitor is from the front desk camera." The guard used a remote to start the playback. He continued to speak as the footage ran. "He never looks directly into the camera, but as you can see, he's big, maybe six-four or six-five. He was black." The guard looked at Jimmy. "No offense."

Jimmy shrugged. "That's the color of his skin. Why would I be offended?"

The guard shook his head as Dale smiled.

"What's with the clothes?" Dale pointed at the screen.

"Yeah, odd. He wore this big hat and dark sunglasses that covered up pretty much his entire face. Even with that long, thin coat, it was easy to tell he was built like a bulldozer. He must have been close to two-fifty. Couldn't see his hair under the hat."

Dale turned to Jimmy. "What do you think? Could be Calvin Watters?"

"It's hard to tell. Like the guy says, he never looks into the camera or stands at an angle that would give us a good shot."

"Calvin who?" The younger guard asked.

"Never mind. Did this guy show you any identification?"

"Of course. He showed us a pretty elaborate business card. He had a scheduled appointment and passed the security check. Did Coburn kill Mr. Grant?"

He ignored the guard's question, thinking instead of Calvin Watters. He knew of Watters and this situation didn't fit the collector's profile. Watters had always remained under the radar, even with his job.

"Wait a minute. You said that Coburn was in here this morning. Doug Grant was killed last night. Why would you let a guy go upstairs when Grant wasn't in his office?"

"Well, we called up and there was no answer. Just assumed since he had an appointment scheduled, that Mr. Grant had stepped out."

Jimmy cut in. "I can't hear the words, but it seems like Coburn kind of bullied his way up to Grant's office."

The guards looked at each other.

"But you didn't see Grant go up." Dale let them off the hook.

"Never do."

"How's that?"

"Office owners in this complex have privileged parking passes to the basement. They also purchase special elevator keys for the garage elevator that takes them straight to their offices. It's a back way. We never see 'em comin' or goin'."

"So then anyone could sneak in here without being noticed?"

"If they have the special key and parking pass."

"How did this Winston Coburn III elude you guys after?"

"Don't know for sure, but we found the security wires to the back exit disconnected. Someone had snuck out. Could've been him."

"Any video feed in the upstairs offices or this 'privileged' basement elevator?" Dale made air-quotes with his fingers.

"Afraid not. Our clients like their privacy."

"Of course they do."

"Has anyone been in Grant's office since our guys left this morning?" Jimmy asked.

"No, sir."

Dale smiled. "Unless they had the special key and parking pass you didn't know about." When the guards didn't respond, he said, "Thanks, guys."

The detectives took the elevator to the top floor, where their colleagues were already busy.

With no furniture in the first room, Dale understood that Grant had wanted privacy and had no need for a secretary. Without a secretary, witnesses would be hard to come by.

Jimmy whistled. "This is huge!"

"Yeah," Dale agreed. "A lot of expensive and wasted space."

The detectives moved their toolkits into the office, where they would focus their search. Without saying a word, they each pulled on a pair of latex gloves, set the large metal cases on the floor and opened them. They removed their contents and began.

Starting with the double front doors and doorknobs, they moved on to a complete sweep of the entire office, dusting for prints and vacuuming for hair and fibers.

While Jimmy was dusting, Dale searched Grant's personal

belongings. Grant's desk was meticulously organized—papers stacked in a neat pile, drawers conveniently tidied—and the computer had been recently wiped. Linda Grant smiled at Dale from the wedding photo on Grant's desk and he couldn't help but smirk.

Jimmy stood by the filing cabinet with all four drawers pulled open. "These books are in perfect order. Everything is up to date and thorough."

"Does it look like Grant owed money?"

Jimmy shook his head.

Dale scanned the numerous books from the floor-to-ceiling bookshelves, but since Grant's computer was password protected, they would have to take it back to the precinct and have it hacked.

He explored the contents of the desk drawers. Using a pair of stainless steel tweezers, he lifted a blue poker chip from the drawer. "Look at this, Jimmy. Property of the Golden Horseshoe Hotel and Casino. That's one of Sanders' casinos."

Jimmy took the tweezers. "Why would a $10,000 poker chip from Sanders' casino be here?"

Dale shrugged and dropped the chip into a plastic ziplock bag. He knew that plastic held fingerprints better than paper.

As he attempted to close the drawer, something obstructed its sliding movement. He got onto his knees.

"Now what are you doing?" Jimmy asked.

"The drawer won't close." He reached underneath the desk and felt the obstruction. "Something is here. Give me your flashlight."

Jimmy handed Dale the tiny penlight and he squirmed underneath the desk. He flashed the beam across the carpeted floor and then in the direction of the inside of the desk. "Something is taped to the side of the drawer."

"What is it?"

He tore off the strip of tape and a silver key dangled from it. "It's a key," he announced, getting up and then handing it to Jimmy. "I also noticed something else when I was down there." Dale shone the light at the finely sculptured carpet. "Notice anything?"

"You mean the expensive, perfectly maintained carpet?"

Dale returned to his knees and pointed the light at the carpet. "Now do you see?"

"Why don't you just tell me?"

"See the indentations in the rug? Someone moved this chair recently. I didn't touch it and Grant's been dead for almost twenty-four hours. That means that since his death, someone other than Grant has been in here. We know that a Winston Coburn III did come up here this morning, but since Grant was already dead and not here, Coburn must have left."

He paused for a moment. "We also know that the caller said the name Coburn was an alias used by Calvin Watters. We'll find out easy by calling the Atlantic City PD whether there is such a casino owner. If not, that leaves Watters as a potential suspect at least for potential theft and maybe for murder. Did he move the chair, or did someone else sneak in here after he left? We've got a lot of checking to do."

Dale asked the question that had bugged him. "If Coburn is an alias for Calvin Watters, why would he come to Grant's office after the man had been killed?"

"With Grant dead, Watters could freely search the office for whatever he was looking for," Jimmy responded.

But Dale had already formed his own opinion. "Maybe he didn't know the man was dead. What do you make of the key?"

"It's for a safe deposit box at Sun West Bank."

"Tina's bank? Do you think your wife can get us in?"

Jimmy shrugged. "What about the safe?"

He followed Jimmy's finger. He had missed the false wall behind the desk chair where a safe had been hidden. "We'll have to come back for that with Mark and have him open it."

He was quiet and still for a long while.

"What are you thinking, partner?"

"We know a person was in the office and tried to find something. But we're not sure if they found it. We just need to find out how many visitors there were and if one of them was looking for something besides the meeting with Grant, which may or may not have been real, depending on whether there is a Winston Coburn III."

Jimmy replied, "That's a bit complex."

"Well, you better hold on to something, because it's just beginning."

Dale sat at his desk reviewing Grant's bio while the database searched for a match to any of the fingerprints lifted from Grant's private office.

Grant owned and operated the second largest and most profitable casino in Las Vegas, was sixty-three years old and married to his second wife. He had no criminal record and a clean bill of health. The man was a millionaire many times over and his wallet had been full of hundred-dollar bills, which means this wasn't a petty theft gone bad. Grant didn't owe anyone money and had no real rival except for Ace Sanders. Sanders and Linda were currently the only suspects. Other than Dale's suspicions and the tread marks, they had no leads.

He could see a clear motive for Linda, but none for Sanders. Sure, the rumored affair with Grant's wife, but Sanders didn't seem to gain anything by killing Grant. Shawn Grant was ready to step up and run the Greek. And the word was that he was as tough and uncompromising as his father.

He rubbed his eyes and shut the file.

Jimmy waved a piece of paper in the air. "We've got him!" he said with a grin.

Dale pursed his lips. "What do we have?"

"We found three definite sets of prints. Of course Grant's, but the system also identified Calvin Watters. Watters' prints were on the doorknobs, the telephone in Grant's office and the emergency exit alarm. We were able to match them because Watters was arrested a couple of times, more than three years ago, before he became Donald Pitt's number one collector. That seems to confirm what the caller said about Watters using an alias to get into the building. Also, I called the ACPD."

"You've been busy."

"They have no record of any Winston Coburn III, II, or I and certainly not as the owner of any casinos there." Jimmy tossed two papers on Dale's desk.

"What about the other set?" Dale asked.

"The fingerprint we pulled off the poker chip belongs to Ace Sanders. His fingerprints were also in the office on the table next to the guest chair and the doorknob."

"Sanders' fingerprints are on file?" He was surprised.

"His fingerprints were required for municipal records when he bought his first casino, a small one called the Midas, years ago." Jimmy said

At last there was a direct link between Sanders and Grant. If his fingerprints were fresh enough to be lifted, then he'd visited Grant not too long ago.

This opened the case up. In Dale's mind, Sanders was now on the radar screen as an official suspect for Grant's murder. That made three. Watters and Sanders now joined Linda Grant.

Jimmy's voice rose in an excited pitch. "Who cares about Sanders? We have Watters. We have his fingerprints at Grant's office and let's face it, Calvin Watters is as lethal as they come."

"Think about it, Jimmy. Watters' fingerprints in Grant's office are just too easy. If he's committed what's currently the perfect murder, why would he be so sloppy about leaving his fingerprints in Grant's office? The real killer would have worn gloves."

"Sanders didn't."

"No. But he had the justification of meeting with Grant as a rival casino owner." He was about to continue when an officer called from across the room.

"Detectives, Grant's car was found parked at the deserted strip mall off the 592. We searched and dusted the front, back and trunk. The only prints pulled belonged to Grant and there wasn't a trace of evidence inside or out." The cop emphasized his last sentence as if he couldn't believe it.

Dale could believe it though. With each passing second, this murderer seemed more efficient.

"The 592?" He turned to Jimmy. "That's pretty far from where his body was found." He faced the officer again. "What about the tread marks at the murder site? Do they match the tires on Grant's car?"

"Forensics thinks they'll match."

"Let me know as soon as you get a final report."

The officer nodded and left.

"What do you wanna do?" Jimmy asked.

"Run Watters' social to get an address. How does he look in the arrest files?"

"About the same as when he was a football star, but that was almost four years ago. Not at all like the man that the security guards described to us or what we saw on the video."

"He's the only suspect we can move on now. So let's act on the basis that the man who was arrested after he destroyed his football career is the same man who came to see Grant this morning. Get an address. I need to make a call."

When Jimmy left, Dale checked the team list and dialed an outside line.

"Elliot," the voice answered.

"It's Dale. What have you and Harper found out?"

"Not much, sir." His voice sounded frustrated. "Grant had a number of acquaintances but no one very close. The few good friends he did have don't know of any enemies, except for Sanders. His name keeps coming up. Grant was well liked and respected. The friends that we talked to all have solid alibis."

"What happened when you called his attorney?"

"We had a brief discussion with him. Grant had made an appointment to see him this morning, but the attorney wouldn't say what the purpose of the meeting was."

"Stop what you're doing. I need you to stake out a possible suspect."

As if on cue, Jimmy came into the office and dropped a paper on Dale's desk.

He read the address over the phone. He told the officers to proceed as if Watters was armed and to check in on a regular basis.

Dale hung up. "Let's go." He jumped up and grabbed the coat from the back of his chair. "We're going back to the office complex to check that safe. Call Mark and tell him we'll pick him up on the way. And let's keep Watters' name out of the papers. We don't want to scare him off. He's our only fresh lead."

"Lead? Dale, he's our killer."

Dale smiled at Jimmy. "Now who's jumping to conclusions?"

CHAPTER 14

Late in the evening, Calvin took his car downtown for a bite to eat. He hadn't felt this good, this free, in a long time. The prospect of starting a new life had put a jump in his stride. He parked at the curb, dropped coins in the meter and crossed the street to where a blind African American street vendor sat on a stool.

"Hey, Jarvis!"

The man smiled around his toothpick. "Hey, Calvin, how's my football star?"

"Not shining," he replied with a grin.

"Calvin, you been sayin' that same thing for the past two years. Somethin' good must be gonna happen to you soon."

"Actually, Jarvis, my old friend. Things are starting to look up."

Jarvis took out the toothpick from pearly white teeth. "That's what I like to hear. You're a good friend, Calvin."

"You're easy to talk to, Jarvis, and always the first with rational advice. You also know a lot of people and came through for me when I needed you. What's with the new facial hair?"

The man rubbed the tuft of hair under his lower lip and above his chin. "Are you mocking my soul patch?"

Calvin chuckled. "I'll miss you, Jarvis."

"You leavin' us, Calvin?"

"That's the plan."

"Well, good luck, my friend."

Calvin grabbed a USA Today and tucked it under his arm. He pulled two singles from his pocket and stuffed them inside the blind man's pocket. "Keep the change, old man."

"Much obliged."

He entered Ed's Diner.

"Hey, Calvin!" The cook and owner nodded to Calvin from the back.

"Evenin', Ed."

He ordered a cheeseburger with the works. Skipping the front page of the paper, he went straight to the sports section. He sipped at his coffee, enjoying the quiet.

He saw a picture of Toby Jenkins, his former roommate at college, on the front sports page. Jenkins had been Calvin's USC teammate and his backup. The only time Jenkins had seen the field was when the Trojans had a big lead and wanted to rest Calvin. Jenkins, half the player that Calvin had been, had just signed a three-year contract for twenty-four million.

If Calvin had done what was best for his team, he would have been the one to sign that contract.

He was thumbing through the rest of the section when he heard the news on the TV. He glanced up. "Can you turn that up, Doris?"

He approached the counter.

The newscaster did a stand-up on the edge of a wooded area. "Doug Grant, owner and operator of the Greek Hotel and Casino in Las Vegas, was brutally killed and left for dead in the backwoods of Las Vegas late last night. Local police will not offer any details now and say this is an ongoing investigation they cannot compromise."

Next came a short clip of the mayor, praising Grant as a model citizen and pledging that the killer would be brought to justice.

Calvin returned to his booth in a trance. Maybe the police were already at his apartment. He had opened the doors, used the phone and searched the papers on Grant's desk. His prints were all over the office. He'd be the primary suspect—tailor-made as a violent killer and an African American one to boot.

The waitress dropped his meal in front of him.

"I've lost my appetite, Doris."

The waitress laughed. "Yeah, right. Calvin Watters will not inhale his food in three minutes."

"Just bring me the bill, please."

Her smile disappeared. "What's wrong? Are you okay?"

He dropped a twenty-dollar bill on the table and walked out like a zombie.

The sky had darkened. He pulled the hood over his head, jammed his hands into his pockets and hurried toward his car. He'd taken only ten steps when he was stopped by a voice at his back.

"Hey, Calvin, wait up."

He saw Ed jogging down the sidewalk toward him.

"What's up?" Calvin asked.

Ed handed him a twenty. "This one's on the house."

A freebie from Ed wasn't rare. It was inconceivable. "What gives, Ed?"

Ed took him by the arm and led him around the corner to an open space between two buildings. Glancing around, he whispered, "Listen, I know your story and I think you're a good guy. So I have to tell you this."

Calvin was silent. Ed did not say much and he never wasted words.

"I have a friend who works down at the police station. He overheard two homicide detectives talking and your name came up. You know that casino owner who was murdered?"

Calvin nodded and said nothing.

"Your fingerprints were found at his office."

"Hey…" His mouth went dry. "I didn't kill anyone!"

Ed nodded. "But they know you were there. This is where, in the movies, the pal says, 'Go to the cops. That's your best choice.' But I know the Vegas cops. So all I can say is that I'll help you if I can."

"Thanks."

The restaurant owner left him standing in the alley alone.

Things had heated up. He'd gone from free to hunted in ten minutes. He was now on the run, but he didn't know in which direction and he hadn't anticipated or prepared for it at all.

Book Two: The House Always Wins

CHAPTER 15

During the car ride to Grant's private office, Dale read Watters' bio.

His mother was deceased, his father unknown and his brother was a detective with the LAPD. Now that was interesting. Dale didn't automatically love every cop family, but it showed the Watters brothers were not both thugs.

There was little about his past before college, when he'd been clean. Since leaving college, he'd spent some local jail time before Pitt discovered him. That was over three years ago. Since that time, he'd been clean as a whistle, on paper anyway.

Jimmy knew from the street that Calvin was considered terrifying. But he couldn't be dumb to have stayed so low profile.

Dale looked at his partner. "Big fucker isn't he?"

Mark McAllister was waiting on the side of the road when the detectives pulled up.

Dale turned to Jimmy. "This guy? He's the 'Vegas safe cracker'? He looks more like an aging hippie. What's his story?"

"The department found him on the streets. He was just a kid in his twenties who had become a successful criminal and was looking at hard time. The cops spent so much time tracking him, they made him an offer. Go to prison, or join the team. McAllister took the deal. He *is* one of the best at what he does."

McAllister had a bald dome but a long ponytail. He jumped into the patrol car and seemed spaced out, a little bored.

The office was already unlocked and had been stripped clean, so they showed McAllister where the safe was hidden. It took him only seconds to get inside.

On top of a stack of papers, banded together and stacked in a pyramid, was $100,000 in cash. Dale removed the money along with a sheaf of papers and spread the papers across Grant's empty desktop.

"Make sure you mark that money before we get into trouble," Jimmy warned.

"You do it. I hate all this paperwork."

Jimmy took the money and started filling out the papers.

Dale again found it hard to believe the amount of money that Grant had been worth. He lived a Spartan life. If the casino owner had owed Pitt funds, he would not be someone who had trouble paying the debt. All his records were in order.

"Hey, Jimmy." Dale looked up from the small pile of documents in the safe. "Have you heard of Nick Trump?"

"The ex-cop?" Jimmy paused. "Not liked very well in the department. Had a reputation of being a rat. Quit the force a while back. I heard he opened a private investigation operation across town. Another ambulance chaser. That same guy? Why?"

"A receipt from Nick Trump and Associates. What would Grant need a PI for?"

He put the receipt to the side and continued sorting through the papers.

"This is interesting," Jimmy said, holding up a photocopied piece of paper. "The prenup."

They weren't lawyers, but both detectives got the gist. Linda had to be married to Grant for the real payoff.

The will was next.

"Look at the date," Jimmy said. "That was right after Grant's marriage to Linda."

Now they knew that Linda would get a good share there—but that Shawn also had a reason to benefit.

"You think he killed his own father?" Jimmy asked.

"As I said, he has the motive. I'm not counting anyone out."

He opened his cell phone and placed an urgent call. "Hey, Duncan, it's Dale. Have you talked to Grant's son and daughter yet?"

"Not yet."

"Good. Listen..." Dale asked them to see what Shawn knew about the will and those arrangements—judge his reaction. Then he hung up.

Nothing else held their interest, so they took the money and the documents with them and let themselves out.

They got into the car. When Jimmy was seated, Dale said, "Tomorrow morning, early as possible, we've got to go to the bank and open that safe deposit box."

"I'll call Tina to set it up."

"No, Jimmy. By the book. We'll have to get one more warrant today. We are really pressing—but the mayor will help us out if need be, on the quiet."

CHAPTER 16

From a highly touted NFL prospect to a Vegas murder suspect.

Calvin was on edge, his nerves strung tight when he got home, but he saw no sign that the cops had already been by. At least that was good.

He went to his small desk and booted up his computer. It was only a laptop. He kept his *real* computer system at the safe house.

That was the other thing that had kept him sane for three years. Daily knee rehab and weights, and daily online study of what his computer could do. Calvin had never been a computer nerd, but in the last three years he'd learned enough to do most of what the stereotypical flannel-shirted overweight geek could do. Establishing and keeping his computer system state of the art had been his only major expense since arriving in Las Vegas. He saved the rest of his earnings for use in his new life whenever it began.

He had created a psychological profile database of a wide range of people in Vegas, particularly clients, so he could break them down in his collecting work.

At the back of his mind he'd always thought his gift with computers would be his ticket to his new life. He could show most prospective employers what he'd managed to compile about people and how efficiently he'd used the information. Marketing firms, security businesses—both could use him.

Now the computer would have to substitute for friends. Although he knew a lot of people on the streets, he only had a handful of true friends who would even consider touching him right now.

Who could he call?

He hadn't spoken to his brother in years, not since he had taken the job with Pitt. His own brother would simply tell Calvin to turn himself in—if he were innocent, he'd be okay. He was not a naïve cop, but he was straight as an arrow.

The only time Calvin had seen his father since he was little was when Calvin's name had been mentioned in *Sports Illustrated* as a possible Heisman Trophy candidate and a sure top draft choice. His money-hungry father surfaced. Calvin told him to get lost again.

He had three options. One, he could turn himself into authorities. Not promising. Two, he could flee the city, never to return. That meant dumping Rachel, whom he loved. He hated his life in Vegas—but he liked the town itself. Three, he could find out who had tried to frame him and who the real murderer was.

He grabbed a black duffel bag and filled it with clothing. Except for cash for immediate expenses, he had all his savings locked and stored inside his fortified computer room. The $20,000 he'd gotten from Pitt this morning—that would come with him now.

With a fresh dip in his mouth, Dale followed the directions his partner had laid out. Jimmy wanted to get home to his family and he didn't blame him.

He decided to surprise Pitt at his office and catch him off guard. A personal visit from a homicide detective made an impact, even on street scum like Pitt. He wasn't even sure that Pitt would still be there. If he was, it would have nothing to do with business.

He found the office, which was off a crappy alleyway. Neither hinted at the sizeable cash flow Pitt generated.

He walked in and approached the front desk. No one around. Dale yelled, "Donald Pitt. I'm Detective Dayton, Homicide. I need to talk to you." He heard nothing, but headed to the back.

Pitt was seated at a table with someone, eating a late dinner. A rancid odor filled the air.

The man sitting beside Pitt looked huge, even sitting down.

"Wow, a real-life detective," the bookie said, mouth full of food. Pitt chuckled arrogantly and the goon with him joined in. Pitt started to stand.

Dale extended his hand. "Please, don't get up. I won't keep you long."

Part of the detective would have liked to grab the bookie by the collar and slam him against the wall. But the steroid freak next to him kept Dale at bay.

Pitt must have seen Dale eyeing the other man in the room.

"This is my associate, Randall."

Randall had a thick neck and wide jaw. His muscle shirt showed massive welts on his swollen deltoids. He also had a zipper of stitches down the side of his face.

Dale looked at Randall and then back at Pitt. "I was wondering if we could talk business."

With a quick nod from his boss, the bodyguard took the hint. Randall dropped two meaty hands on the desk and lifted from the chair, his triceps looking like horseshoes when flexed. He stood and stared at Dale, his eyes shining with anger, playing the role to perfection, then turned and left.

"What do you want, Detective Dayton? As you can see, we're very busy around here."

Dale glanced at the empty fast-food wrappers on the desk and smirked. "Have you seen Calvin Watters today?"

Pitt picked at some food in his teeth before responding. "Maybe."

He was the classic liar.

"Do I really look that stupid to you?"

"Save the bullshit. He ain't here and I ain't seen him." His smarmy grin broadened.

Dale moistened his finger and turned to a fresh page in his notebook. "When was the last time you did?"

Pitt thought about his answer for only a few seconds. "Well, I seen him early this mornin' when I sent him on a job, but he didn't return. I ain't seen or heard from him since."

"Where was this job?"

"I sent him over to Doug Grant's personal office. Doug owed me some money and I sent Calvin to collect. But the bastard never came back. He probably took the loot and disappeared. Never should have trusted him for a job that big."

Dale laughed at the thought of Pitt calling Grant by his first name, like they were acquaintances.

Did Pitt make the anonymous call? If he'd set up Watters for murder, then he'd have a cover story already prepared to innocently explain his collector's presence at the office. Now he knew that Pitt's cover story was "just a collection."

Dale wouldn't mention the call just yet. He wanted to see how this played out. "Did Grant have a gambling problem?"

"I'm not saying that."

"How much did he owe you?"

"I'm sorry, Detective, that information is confidential."

"I can get a search warrant and go through your papers if that's what it takes."

"Do what you have to do."

Dale frowned. "Do you have a recent photo of Watters?"

The bookie opened up a desk drawer and took out the picture. He handed it over.

How convenient that Pitt had a current photo of Watters to give him. Dale studied it. He recognized the man in the image, but he actually recalled Calvin in his USC days. "Handsome fella."

"We like our collectors to be intimidating. I had Calvin start developing that new, scary look when he began working for me."

"I'm gonna keep this."

"Sure, help yourself."

Dale reached into his jacket pocket and pulled out his business card. "Here's my card. If you hear from Watters, let me know."

Pitt took the card, though he didn't seem too eager to do so. "Don't worry, you'll be the first one I call, Detective Dayton, sir." He gave Dale a toothy grin.

As Dale turned to leave, the bookie stopped him.

"Detective." Pitt extended his hand. "Here's my business card. If you find Calvin, get my money back."

Dale read the inscription on Pitt's card and laughed to himself.

"Donald Pitt and Associates," he said. "Is that the associate I just met?"

CHAPTER 17

He hadn't stayed long at the apartment. Since the cops hadn't yet been there, they would be soon.

Calvin knew he had one major vulnerability. Even though he tried to keep his relationship with Rachel a secret, people had seen them together. If Calvin's guess was right and Pitt had set him up, then Rachel was exposed because Pitt knew of her. But Calvin didn't think that Pitt was smart enough to organize this elaborate setup and was probably working with a partner. If that was the case, then Pitt would surely give this information to whoever was pulling the strings. They'd go after her, even torture Rachel for information. Yet she didn't know anything. The murder had occurred more than twenty hours ago, so there'd been plenty of time for the bastard to already be on Rachel's trail. He had to find her.

He had to watch the cops and watch his enemy, who at this point knew everything about him while Calvin knew nothing about his enemy.

He had double pursuers.

He made a quick stop at a side-street convenience store, found a phone booth and made two calls. First, he called a taxi service he'd never used before. He dialed again.

"Wanda, it's Calvin. I need you to give Rachel a message." He left the message with Rachel's roommate and hung up.

He ran into the store and picked out only the necessities for the first few days. Tomorrow, he'd buy enough to last more than a month if he ended up having to stay in his workshop in a state of siege.

Outside the store, the taxicab was waiting. He exhaled when the driver showed no signs of recognition. As the vehicle pulled out, Calvin scanned for police or a tail.

As the cab wove its way through the busy Vegas streets, he continued to glance out the back window. He had the driver switch lanes the whole way.

He stopped by a clothing store: one suit, street clothes, sportswear. He dropped $3,500, but it was a necessity.

One more stop with the meter ticking.

"Wait here."

He was thankful that the restaurant was open twenty-four hours. He slipped in the back of the almost empty Waffle House. All that he wanted to do now was get Rachel safely to the workshop and keep her under constant guard.

He checked his watch. She was late. He hoped that Wanda had been able to deliver the message. As his concern began to mount, he saw Rachel outside the restaurant. He picked up the phone receiver, using it as a prop to hide from her, and turned his back to the door, watching Rachel out of the corner of his eye. He had specifically warned her not to identify him.

She stepped inside the restaurant carrying two large, overstuffed knapsacks, made her way to the back and passed by him. She turned and entered the bathroom. He looked around a moment and then followed her.

Before she could speak, he put his finger to her lips. He checked the stalls and locked the entrance. When he turned around, Rachel jumped into his arms.

"I missed you so much," she said, smothering him with kisses.

"Easy, Rachel, I missed you too. But we don't have time to talk here."

"Okay." She stepped back.

Just then there were two hard and two soft knocks. Wanda. He unhooked the door.

The waitress stuck her head inside. "All clear, Calvin. Rachel wasn't followed."

"Thanks."

Calvin and Rachel slipped out the back. His taxi driver hadn't deserted him.

They got in the back and didn't say a word to each other. Once in the workshop, he'd tell her everything.

Calvin had the driver drop them two blocks away. "Pick me up here in an hour." He tipped the driver twenty dollars.

He and Rachel dipped in and out of backyards and made several circles before arriving at the workshop. He dropped the bags on the concrete floor and scoped the old building.

He had Rachel shave off his long dreadlocks and shaggy facial hair. After she had removed enough with the electric razor, she used a disposable one to finish.

When the transformation was complete, he looked much as he had in college. But even with a bit of hair loss, Calvin was still too recognizable. He'd need to give the next step some thought.

"What do you think?"

Rachel ran her hand along his now-smooth scalp. "I like it," she said, wiping off the last of the shaving cream.

"Now it's your turn." He helped her dye her hair black and gave her the short version of the situation now. With the hair change, Rachel looked like a different person. He missed her real looks already, but they also cut her long hair into a bob.

The cab was waiting and the driver did a double take at the new looks but said nothing.

They headed toward Cruiser's Bar.

After stopping at a convenience store for a new tin of chew, Dale ran over his interview with Pitt. Why had the bookie given up Watters just like that? If Watters really was the bookie's number-one employee, then why was Pitt so eager to help?

Dale had been expecting lies and deceit but had gotten the complete opposite. It had been too easy, just like Watters' fingerprints in Grant's office. That had him on edge.

He parked in his space at the precinct. When he stepped into the damp, air-conditioned lobby, he felt a chill. He wasn't sure if it was from this case or the weather. He walked past the few others working after-hours and straight to his desk.

After booting up his computer, he ran Watters' name through the Nevada Crime Index (NCI) database and at the national FBI level (NCIC).

Had Watters known Grant or had he been in any direct contact with the casino owner prior to his death? Because of fingerprints, Dale knew that Watters was in Grant's office the morning after Grant was murdered, sent there by his boss. But why the phony disguise and fake name?

When the computer beeped, he searched the website of the USC Trojans. He researched team lists from five years back and clicked on

Calvin Watters' name.

Even though the disguise had been elaborate, the pictures on the USC site made it obvious that the visitor to Grant's private office could have been Watters. By now, Watters could be anywhere—Canada, Mexico or even off the American continent. If he was guilty it was highly unlikely, but a remote possibility, that he was still in Vegas.

Dale ripped off the sheet and left the office. He threw the two color pictures onto the front desk counter and ordered a city-wide APB. All he could do was get the photo across the state, to the FBI and to Canadian and Mexican police. No Interpol stuff—not yet.

He went back to his office to study the crime scene photos again. As he sat back down and removed the magnifying glass from his desk, he was interrupted.

"Excuse me, Detective Dayton?"

"What is it, Craig?"

"I have a copy of the phone records." The young man, the relative rookie he'd taken onto the case, held up a stack of computer printer paper.

The detective waved him into the office. "Just set them on my desk."

The phone records dated to three months back, with the local calls separated from the long-distance calls. Craig had spent hours on this. Short on time, Dale skimmed over the copies.

On first glance, most of Sanders' calls could be accounted for—other casinos, strip clubs, 900 numbers. Dale recognized these from their 702 area code. But there was one unusual call, a 504 area code. He couldn't place it off-hand. He would have to look it up.

He moved Sanders' reports to the side and shuffled the pages to Calvin Watters' phone records. Watters had called L.A. once—his brother?—and that was it. He made few calls of any kind.

From their home, work and cell phones, Doug, Linda and Shawn Grant had only made a handful of calls out of state. Three of the seven calls were to Atlantic City, where Dale assumed calls had been placed to rival casino owners. Two calls were to Boston and another two were made to Memphis, where Linda Grant had been born and raised and still had family.

Then he saw the obvious. One call was made from Grant's private office after his time of death—to Pitt. The scheduled appointment guest list from Grant's office complex indicated that Watters' assumed alias was the only name on the list.

Interesting.

"I believe I've seen that number before. That lyin' son of a bitch!"

He checked the clock at the bottom of the computer screen. Go home to an empty house or follow a lead while it was hot?

Not much of a decision.

He grabbed the stack of papers and left his office.

"Tommy, I need you to cross-reference every single phone number in here."

The man looked at the enormous stack of papers and then looked up at Dale.

Before he could speak, Dale did. "I know, I know. Just think of it as overtime."

CHAPTER 18

Calvin could now only deal with people he trusted—or who were too afraid of him to contact the cops. He needed to make vital decisions about whom he could rely on and who might backstab him by turning him in.

Cruiser's Bar was a local watering hole for bikers and prostitutes. Those who would recognize him there were not likely to help the police.

"Keep the cab running," he told the driver.

"It's your dollar."

Calvin and Rachel walked past the Harleys and beat-up pickup trucks to the door. Inside, he approached the sticky bar. The sounds of chatter, '80s rock music and pool balls clicking together engulfed him. A biker covered in tattoos wiped his hands and walked over.

"What, Mack?"

As the bartender got closer, his eyes widened. "Calvin." He chuckled. "Is that you?"

"Hey, Bernie. I need to talk to Mike."

"Man! I didn't recognized you." The man snorted with delight.

"Yeah, this is a new look for me."

"I'll let Mike know you're here. Hold on." The bulky bartender entered a back room.

Calvin surveyed the bar. No one seemed suspicious or new. Rachel stayed close to him. No one seemed to notice them and no one cared.

The bartender came back with a grin. "He'll see you now. Man, will he get a kick out of you."

Calvin, leading Rachel, walked to the back room.

Mike squeezed out of a wooden chair behind his desk and limped over.

"Hey, Calvin."

If his new appearance surprised the bar owner, he didn't show it.

"Hey, Mike." Calvin shook his hand.

"Rachel." The man nodded toward the silent woman. "Please, have a seat."

Calvin and Rachel sat and waited for Mike to do the same.

"I saw the Chargers signed Jenkins. Wasn't he your backup at USC?"

"Don't remind me."

Mike snorted. "The world works in mysterious ways. What can I do for you?"

"I'm in some trouble."

Mike picked up a note pad, flipped to a fresh page and grabbed a pen. He sat back and listened. When Calvin was through, Mike spoke up. "I thought you went back to your college look for a reason. Man, does that take me back. You didn't know your man back then, did you, Rachel?"

She shook her head.

"He was something. King of the campus."

Calvin shifted in his seat as Mike continued.

"I remember the day my nephew, my sister's only kid, called me here, excitement in his voice. He told me how the great Calvin Watters came and sat at his table in the library with his nerdy computer friends. Andy said they were as nervous as hell. Boy, were they some surprised when you started talking shop with them. What most people didn't know, Rachel, not even his college teammates, is that our boy Calvin here used to hang around with the computer geeks in the library at USC. He asked them to show him some computer stuff, even skipped a football keg party one night to hang out in their dorm room. Andy was fixated on him. The party, booze, drugs, sorority girls, that just wasn't Calvin's style."

Rachel smiled at Calvin as he said, "I think we heard enough, Mike."

"No," Rachel cut in. "Tell me more about Calvin. He never talks about his college days."

Mike ignored Calvin's protests and continued. "All Calvin thought about was the NFL."

Calvin cut him off. "How is Andy?"

"Doin' great. Stuck around California working for some big computer company out there. I still help him out when I can. But don't change the subject. You were a big part of Andy's life back then. You protected him and kept him out of trouble. He was never the kind to make friends easy and you helped him. When you got to Vegas, I was glad to do the same."

"And I owe you for that."

"Nonsense. The first thing I did, before I agreed to help you, was a little digging. Rachel, did you know that Calvin here scored 145 on an IQ test? I knew you were smart, but not that smart. That categorizes him as highly gifted."

Calvin held his breath. No one was supposed to know about that.

As if Mike read his mind, he said, "That's right, I found out about it."

"No one was supposed to know. In my line of work, brilliance isn't an essential attribute. If no one knew, I knew I'd always be underestimated, which gave me an advantage every time."

"I figured that. Modest too. That's why I agreed to help." Mike winked at Rachel. "We've been playing around with computers for three years now. Calvin's almost the hacker that I am. But I have to admit, he's a bit more aggressive, ready to take more risks."

Calvin intervened. "You taught me how to hack into any computer in any protected system in the world, which is going to be an extremely valuable skill now. But you also have underground connections throughout the country. You can get anything for anyone. That's what I need."

Mike turned back to Calvin. "Okay, chitchat over. What do you need?"

"New IDs. The total package and by tomorrow."

"Shouldn't be a problem," he said, checking off items on a list. "Anything else?"

"Some added protection for me and Rachel. We need to secure my hideout. Rachel and I need every corner of that building protected."

Mike thought to himself for a moment.

He opened his desk drawer and pulled out a thick book. Calvin and Rachel pulled their seats closer to the desk.

"This package is just right. Security alarms, motion sensors, fail safes, detectors and cameras inside and outside. Since I helped you set up the computer system there, I already know the place inside and out."

As Mike continued to write, Calvin asked, "What about a secondary emergency exit plan?"

Mike chewed the end of his pen. "I'll have it tomorrow when I come out with all the gear. I'm assuming payment isn't a problem? It's $20,000, cash."

Calvin counted Pitt's money out onto the desk. He could hear Rachel breathe in deeply and hold it.

"Here's ten thousand. You'll get the rest tomorrow."

The bar owner slipped the bills into an envelope, sealed the flap and stuck it into the top drawer of his desk.

As they were leaving, Mike asked, "Do you think Pitt set you up?"

"I'm going to find out."

"I bet you will. Just let me handle your security issues."

He felt better hearing Mike say that and was starting to like his chances.

When the cabbie dropped them off again, Calvin said to Rachel, "I'll walk you to the door and make sure you're safe. Then I have one more stop tonight."

"Where are you going?"

"I'll be back soon."

"What the hell are you doing here? I thought you said we shouldn't be seen together until things blow over." Pitt sat at his desk and eyed the bathroom.

Ace loomed silently in the doorway so the bookie would be even more on edge.

Pitt poured some scotch and twisted the lid back on. He threw the bottle into the bottom drawer of his desk, slamming it shut, and rose, finger-combing what was left of his hair over his bald head.

The bookie wore nothing but a pair of white boxer shorts. His fat, hairy belly hung over the waistband and a cigarette dangled at the side of his mouth. He took a hit off the cigarette and then flicked it on the side of an ashtray.

Obviously, Pitt had been trying to disguise his lifestyle, trying to persuade Ace that he could fit in with the rich and powerful. Now Ace was disgusted.

"Don't get up." He entered the office as Pitt sank back into his desk chair.

"How'd you get in here anyway?"

"You gave me a key, remember?" He twirled the key chain around his index finger.

Pitt swallowed hard. "Want a drink?"

"No, thanks. I just stopped by for an update."

He tucked the key inside his jacket pocket and removed a deck of cards, which he started shuffling.

"Speaking of which," Pitt said, his voice cracking, "what the hell happened to the original plan? I wasn't going to say anything. I knew you had changed your mind about when and where to murder Grant and I didn't think I wanted to know why. But since you're here, why did you change? The cops were supposed to find Watters with Grant's body in the office. Case closed. The plan had been to set up Calvin. I had started to dial your number at the Golden Horseshoe but thought better of it. So I sat back and waited. So?"

"Sometimes plans just change. That's all you need to know. If you want to run with the rich and powerful, you have to learn that."

"I will."

He moved toward Pitt, through a haze of cigarette smoke, all the while shuffling the cards.

Pitt squirmed in his chair and glanced toward the corner of the room, his neck and face damp with sweat. "Don't worry. The cops don't suspect a thing. They were already in here asking about Calvin. They suspect him because he was at the office this morning and now they're searching for him. Poor bastard—in the wrong place at the wrong time." He grinned, raised his glass and drank a silent toast. "Like I asked before, what are you doing here? You only come out of the shadows when something's up."

"What did you tell the cops?"

"Nothing, I swear."

"Does Calvin suspect anything?"

"That boy is as dumb as a stump. Not a thing." Pitt took another hearty swig. "The idiot left his prints all over that office. But it wasn't easy getting him there. Calvin came in here screaming he wanted out, that he was done. But I managed."

"You'll be well compensated, Donald."

Ace's reassurance seemed to relax Pitt.

"But I don't think we should underestimate Watters. He could be a dangerous liability. We don't know where he is, where he's going, or what he's going to do next."

"You worry too much." Pitt ground his cigarette into an ashtray and took another sip. His bleary eyes suggested he'd been sipping on scotch all evening. "We both have much invested in Grant's death. For as long as I've known you, I've learned that you leave no detail out. That's why you're rich and about to get even richer. We have nothing to worry about."

Because Pitt had been talking and drinking continuously, he hadn't noticed that Ace was now standing behind him. He couldn't see Ace pull on a pair of black leather gloves.

But Ace knew the man sensed him. He saw Pitt's back hair rise.

"You are right. I am a rich man because of my attention to detail." He dropped a gloved hand firmly on Pitt's shoulder and kneaded the tight ball. "You're too tense, Donald. Relax a little." He massaged the bookie's fat shoulders and neck.

Pitt tightened up more and gripped the arms of the chair.

"You like poker?"

The question seemed to catch the bookie off guard. "What?"

"Poker. I love it. I know that Texas Hold 'em is all the craze right now, but I've always been a fan of Primero, or as rookies know it, Straight. This was the very first game of poker ever played, the root of the game. This is what they played in the Wild West."

"What's with the gloves?" Pitt asked with a tremble in his voice.

"Oh, you know me. Always the cautious one. Shall we try your luck?"

When Pitt attempted to get up, Ace wrapped an arm tightly around Pitt's throat, squeezed and raised his chin to expose the esophagus. The man struggled to breathe, so Ace tightened his grip, obstructing the air passage. Pitt tried to call out but couldn't.

"Sorry, Donald. No loose ends. Wrong place, wrong time."

The cards were gone. With his right hand, Ace pulled a new hunting knife from his jacket and with precision and speed swiped the blade across the bookie's throat.

Pitt instinctively grabbed at the wound, but it took only seconds for his body to go limp.

In a calm, easy manner Ace cleaned his knife on Pitt's already blood-stained white boxers. As he was about to slide the knife back into its sheath in his pocket, he heard the toilet flush in the office bathroom. A sliver of light showed beneath the door. The light flickered.

Moving with great speed and agility, he flipped the knife from his right hand to his left to get a better angle on the person coming out of the bathroom. He slipped behind the door, waiting for it to open.

A small, thin woman stepped out. He moved in behind and grabbed her around her wiry neck, the knife ready to strike. He flexed his arm, stifling any scream, and breathed in her heavy floral perfume, but the woman tore at his grip. Her nails cut into his bare right wrist.

"You bitch!" he roared. Saliva spit from the corner of his mouth.

He overpowered her with ease. Sliding his arm down to her shoulders, he slashed the blade across her throat. Blood squirted from the gash as he let the woman drop to the floor.

Again he wiped his knife clean on his victim's limited clothing and put it back in its sheath. He looked down at the two bodies and smiled.

Now to get what he came for and make it look like a robbery.

He'd known for years where Pitt's safe was and how to unlock it. That kind of information was always easy to buy, for the right price.

Ace pulled open the cheap framed painting hanging on the back office wall and looked at the hidden safe. As he was about to start spinning the heavy combination lock, he heard a loud thud in the back alley. It might have just been a stray cat, but he couldn't take that chance.

"Shit!"

After making sure he had left no evidence, he quickly surveyed the area and closed the painting. He exited through the front and locked the door on his way out.

CHAPTER 19

Calvin left Rachel in a motel until he could return. He didn't want her to see what might happen when he confronted Pitt.

He couldn't see Pitt pulling off an elaborate scheme to set him up alone and he wasn't leaving the office without a name.

The bookie's Cadillac was parked out front. Calvin used his key and let himself in, locking the door from the inside. Pitt wasn't getting away.

He marched back where he knew he would find Pitt, a good chance screwing one of his working girls. The thought of a sweaty, hairy Pitt on top of a young streetwalker turned Calvin's stomach.

As soon as he entered, he picked up the unmistakable, repugnant odor of blood even through the usual stench of the back office. When he followed the scent and saw them, he grabbed the wall. His torture and cruelty hadn't prepared him for the blood spatter and damage that had occurred in the tiny room. Calvin bent over at the knees.

There was no point checking for pulses—Pitt and the woman were dead. He still had to find out who worked with Pitt to set him up.

As he stepped over the woman's body, he heard something or someone fumbling at the front door lock.

"Fuck!"

He couldn't be found there.

With no time to search the office, Calvin jumped a pool of blood and bolted through the office and out the back door.

The front door was locked, of course, so Pitt could engage in activities Dale didn't want to imagine.

After he picked the cheap lock on Pitt's door, he walked inside. He saw no one in the front office and kept moving to the back room. The faint fluorescent lights were dim and made the corners of the room difficult to see. He couldn't hear any noise so, hoping to do a brief search before Pitt heard him from another area, he used a bright compact flashlight to examine the room.

Pitt's files looked out of order. Drawers were open, magazines lay open, papers were everywhere and opened food wrappers and containers had stained many of the documents. A coffee mug had been overturned and the liquid had absorbed into a sheaf of papers. A bottle of Jack Daniels was still uncapped.

By the looks of it, Pitt hadn't kept his files up to date or in any kind of order. Standing in front of Pitt's disorganized desk, Dale swiftly examined all the scattered papers on top but found no clues in the disarray.

He moved around the side of the desk to search the drawers and saw Pitt's body sprawled on the floor, his face frozen in shock, his throat slashed almost as deep as Grant's had been. The blood had splattered his head, upper body, waist and thighs and pooled around them.

He pulled his gun and crouched behind the desk. Seeing and hearing nothing, he looked again at Pitt's corpse. From the thinness of the pooled blood, the murder had happened not long ago. Old blood would have thickened.

He then saw the woman on the floor just inside the office bathroom. Sidestepping a pool of blood, Dale ran to the girl's side, holstering his weapon. Like Pitt, she had been sliced at the neck and suffered the same massive blood loss.

She was no more than seventeen, a dark-rooted blonde with soft features and freckles over the bridge of her nose. She had a ring in her lower lip and her pupils were severely dilated, pinhole pupils telling Dale she'd been high at the time of her murder. Her overwashed T-shirt and white thong were soaked in blood.

He raised her hands and saw what he thought was skin underneath her fingernails.

Dale did one more search with his gun drawn, turning on every light as he went, but found nothing before calling dispatch for the crime scene teams. Then he called Jimmy.

"I thought I told you I was going home for the night."

"Two people were just murdered, Jimmy."

"I know. I'm sorry. I'm tired, but I'll be there."

"I'm sorry too. Please apologize to Tina for me. Some things are beyond our control. And call Mark and get him down here too."

Dale retrieved his equipment from the trunk of the car. Pulling on gloves and disposable paper boots, he went back inside.

Within minutes, he heard screeching and whining ambulance and police sirens. When the officials burst through the front door, he waved them to the back.

"No disruption. This is now a crime scene."

Jimmy showed up less than ten minutes later and snapped on a pair of gloves. Dale was dusting for prints.

"What we got?" Jimmy asked.

Dale said, "Two dead bodies. One is Pitt and the other is a Jane Doe, maybe a hooker. We'll have to hunt to see who she is. One killer. Both had throats slashed by what appears to be the same knife. Just like the Grant murder. Same killer or a copycat? Not sure on that."

"What do you want me to do?"

"CSI is working over the body, so collect any evidence that you can. I doubt we'll find anything. The murderer was here for something. That's why he called here from Grant's office."

"He did?"

"Sorry, Jimmy. Forgot to tell you. That's why I came back here for a follow-up interview with Pitt. When I was searching through the phone records of calls made from Grant's office, the last number dialed was Pitt's at nine-forty this morning, when Grant had been dead ten or more hours."

"What do you think? Same guy?" Jimmy asked.

Dale nodded. "I think it's our guy. I want to say that the murders are a serial killer profile. We have three—let's expect a fourth to make it official. Knife used every time to cut the victims' throats with one hand, while he has them under complete control with the other arm. Fast, easy, almost impossible to defend against and little or no struggle."

He thought it was also someone Grant and Pitt had known and trusted.

While waiting for McAllister to arrive, he skimmed Pitt's files. He searched through papers, drawers, filing cabinets and any other document container in the front and back offices.

Nothing with Grant's name.

If Grant didn't owe Pitt money, then why send Watters to the suite? Could the Pitt-Grant deal, if real, have been a cash job with no paperwork involved? And what about the anonymous phone call? Had the caller been trying to frame Watters, or was he reporting what he thought was accurate information? Pitt had admitted sending his employee to Grant's suite that morning, but only for collection. Presumably, that meant that neither Pitt nor Watters had known that Grant was already dead.

Mark McAllister walked through the crime scene and over to Dale. "Have you found the safe yet?"

"No. We're leaving that up to you while we do our own work. Okay, do your magic."

It took McAllister two minutes to find the safe and less than three minutes to have it unlocked. Without a word, the safe breaker left.

Together, Dale and Jimmy opened the safe and found more than thirty thousand dollars in cash. Underneath the stack of bills, Dale found and carefully removed a stack of papers.

"What is it?" Jimmy asked over Dale's shoulder.

"Not sure yet, but I'm glad we got them before the killer did. I'm too tired to think straight now, so I'll go through them in the office tomorrow morning."

The whole office would be bagged, brought back to the precinct and sifted. But Dale was sure it would yield little or nothing.

He had three perfect murders.

But if you looked hard enough, even "perfect" killers once in a while made mistakes.

CHAPTER 20

On the bed of his expensive hotel room, he sat cross-legged, naked except for a pair of latex gloves. He stared at the wall and awaited instructions. He had dropped the room temperature, which was now as cold as a meat freezer. Just the way that he liked it. It kept him alert.

The man didn't sleep much. Sleep was for the weak. Every time he closed his eyes he opened himself to a series of vivid flashbacks—POW camps and torture.

He had only been in Vegas for a little over an hour and already he couldn't wait to leave. He just didn't like the town.

He heard footsteps in the hallway and then a knock on the door. Someone slid a manila envelope under it. From the sounds of the footsteps leaving he could tell it was a man.

The name Mr. Scott was printed on the outside of the envelope.

He split open the compact folder and removed its contents. He picked up a black and white photograph and an excited chill climbed his naked skin.

He threw the information on the bed when the phone rang.

"Yeah."

"Did you get the package?"

"Yeah."

"Stay in touch."

He hung up without saying goodbye. He would be checking out and on his way soon enough.

It was late by the time Calvin returned from Pitt's office, picked up Rachel and crossed the city to their hideout. Rachel, exhausted, excused herself and went to bed. When she left, Calvin went to his computer room to update his database.

He hacked into the LVMPD and learned that Detective Dale Dayton had been assigned twelve officers. With Dayton and his partner, there were now fourteen detectives on Calvin's trail.

He had to be the prime suspect.

His search on Dayton told him that the detective was thorough and methodical, with a high success rate. If Calvin could find nothing on his own about the real killer, maybe Dayton could.

There was nothing yet on Pitt or the woman in his office. The murders happened too late to report.

But his DNA was on the scene. That was certain.

He needed to update and expand his database about the victims and possible suspects.

It was almost three when Calvin shut down his computer.

CHAPTER 21

Dale got to the office after eight. He hadn't slept much the last three nights. For almost twenty-four hours now the new homicide investigation had consumed his life. His mind felt sluggish, but he had a team of thirteen people to run.

As he walked to his desk on Thursday morning, he went over in his mind what he thought to be true: Pitt had something or knew something. He might have known who was behind the Grant killing or had been involved and his murder had been a cover-up. Either way, Dale blew it. He hadn't gotten the information out of the bookie.

He found his team huddled around Jimmy, probably telling a tall tale. They quieted down when they saw Dale. Had they been talking about him?

"Craig, fill this up." Dale held his mug out to his youngest and most inexperienced officer. Dale smirked when he saw the cup. The mug, which read "#1Dad", had been a gift from his wife after Sammie's birth.

The kid moved on command, bringing back the mug filled to the brim with steaming coffee.

"All right, folks," Dale started. "What did we find out? Parker?"

The young officer stepped forward. "Pete and I interviewed Grant's first wife and his son and daughter. They were all cooperative. Grant and the ex were having no problems and Grant had been making all his payments on time. She said she still can't believe what's happened."

Officer Duncan took over. "We took your advice and paid particular attention to the son. We hit the whole family with the description of the will right away. Shawn, Melanie and the former Mrs. Grant all said they knew about the terms of the will. Grant had told them about the changes he made after his second marriage."

"By all reports, Shawn and his sister, Melanie, loved their father very much," Parker added.

"Shawn, of course, has been running the Greek with his father for fifteen years," Duncan said, "and told us he was in no hurry to have his father retire and turn full operational control over to him. The mother said Shawn had taken the divorce harder than the girl, but he had always loved his father. He didn't like or trust Linda then and doesn't now. He even thinks she's capable of having been involved in his father's killing."

Dale's brow rose, but he said nothing.

"Shawn despises Sanders, as his father did," Duncan said, "and started hating him more when he kept pressuring his father to sell the Greek. Shawn said he could see how much that was wearing down his dad. He was hesitant at first, but then he mentioned the rumors that most of us have heard that Sanders was having an affair with Linda Grant. Of course, he didn't have proof. He, as well as the women, thinks Sanders may also have been involved in his father's murder."

As Dale listened, he realized Shawn probably didn't know he was a suspect. He gained too much from his father's death.

"Shawn Grant's alibi checked out?"

Duncan nodded. "He was at the casino the night his father was murdered. Melanie is attending med school at Harvard and was seen by many people. All three family members have solid alibis."

Dale nodded. "But any of them, including Linda, could still have hired a killer." He steepled his fingers. "You're next, Ramirez."

The Puerto Rican woman stepped forward. "Smith and I talked with Grant's employees, who had nothing but good things to say about their boss. All of the employees were sad to hear what had happened. We ran background checks on each employee. Not one casino employee has a criminal record. The alibis are being checked, but it doesn't seem like an inside job." She added an endnote. "There was one thing though. The Greek Casino employees knew that Sanders was bidding to purchase Grant's casino. The employees were very happy that Grant wouldn't budge. They didn't want to work for Sanders."

He turned back around. "Lucas."

Derek Lucas sat on the edge of the desk and read his notes with his partner standing behind him. "Lawrence and I hit every competing casino. We have no proof, but no one appeared to be a perfect slasher. Any of them could have paid a killer, of course, and they do seem to hate one another. But nobody slipped up and said something especially bad about Grant. In fact, everyone respected him even though no one liked the competition.

Dale addressed his team. "Right. So now go back and look at who they might have hired—local muscle and out-of-town talent. Check Linda Grant too."

Dale signaled to Lucas to continue.

"Have you ever met Ace Sanders?" Lucas asked.

Dale knew it wasn't really a question, but a dramatic way to set up what Lucas was going to say next.

"He's a piece of work. We weren't able to interview Sanders himself. He wasn't in his office at the Golden Horseshoe or the Midas yesterday afternoon. So we walked around the casinos and spoke with some of his employees. They're terrified of him. A few admitted that at the time of the Grant murder, they were busy working and couldn't know whether Sanders was really in his office or not. When we went to the Midas, his other casino, same story. He wasn't there and no one was talking."

Dale wasn't surprised. Sanders was cautious and smart. He thought Sanders looked good for this, maybe too good.

"Harper and Elliot?"

The team that had been staking out Calvin Watters' apartment had nothing to report. Watters hadn't returned to his home and Dale suspected that he never would.

Watters was the only suspect who had disappeared. That didn't look good.

"Why don't you two go home and catch up on some sleep. I'll call you when I have another assignment. Great job, guys."

Harper and Elliot nodded, their eyes droopy, and left the group.

Before continuing to his next team, Dale turned to his partner. "Jimmy, find Watters."

Jimmy went off to work the phones.

Dale went on. "Officer Morris?"

"We searched and dusted Grant's casino office and I mean we checked everything. Sorry, Dale, but we found nothing. Everything is locked up in evidence with the stuff from Pitt's office."

Dale was about to hand out new assignments when he heard his name being barked out from across the room.

"Dayton!" The sergeant stuck his round bald head out the office door. "Get your scrawny ass in here!"

"Oh, yeah," Craig spoke up. "The sarge wants to see you."

Dale saw the sergeant through a cloud of cigarette smoke in his glass-partitioned office. Even though smoking in public spaces was banned, the sergeant didn't look worried about a complaint. He had just returned to work a week ago from a heart attack. His red face, and by the way that he was pacing about, told Dale that he was on the road to another one. The sergeant had started chain-smoking again and was showing no effort to hide it.

"Okay, people." Dale acknowledged his group. "I know it seems like we have nothing, but we knocked off most of the obvious. Now the real work starts. Good work with your first assignments. I'll be back."

"Sure thing, Terminator," Ramirez said.

Dale walked into his sergeant's office as the boss held the door for him. After he had entered and took a seat, the sergeant slammed the door.

"Dayton, why the hell hasn't Calvin Watters been picked up yet?" He spit as he barked out the words.

"Well, Sarge, we haven't been able to track him down."

The sergeant was smoking, nail chewing and almost ready to explode.

"It seems that Watters has friends on the street willing to protect him. For all we know, he may have already left town. He could be anywhere on the map. What are you doing about it?"

Dale updated his boss on everything that had happened over the last twenty-four hours—a citywide APB on Watters, as well as photos sent out to local, state and federal officials with nothing in return.

"Just get it done, Dayton." The sergeant said.

"Yes, sir. But he may not be our guy."

The sergeant eyed his detective. "What do you mean? I talked to Jimmy and he said that we have all we need on this guy."

Dale thought about turning and leaving, but instead told him about the prenup, the will and his interview with Pitt. He explained why he thought Ace Sanders, Linda Grant, or Shawn Grant could be involved. He had already questioned Sanders' employees under caution, careful not to make waves.

The sergeant nodded as Dale spoke and then said, "I don't want theories or conspiracies. I like Watters as our guy. The mayor—that little puke—has been breathing down my neck on this one. Grant was an important man."

"Yes, sir."

"Don't 'yes sir' me, just do it! I want this guy's ugly mug on every channel and newspaper in the U.S. The more we broaden the investigation and get the word out to local, state and federal law enforcement authorities and the public, the greater the possibility of good information coming in. Let's smoke him out."

Dale was not against searching for tips, but most cases were solved when someone directly involved ratted out a partner in crime. A national publicity campaign would not catch this killer. Dale counted on Jimmy's snitches coming through.

"Yes, sir."

He blew air from his cheeks when he left the office. His partner was waiting with a wide grin.

Dale slumped into his seat. "Please tell me that you have some good news. Any luck at all?"

"Yeah, lots of luck, only it's the bad kind. Sorry, buddy. I used every link. Nothing. My contacts said that Watters was private and cautious. He's been seen at Cruiser's Bar from time to time, but no one knows where he conducted his business and no one dares cross him anyway. He could be out of the country by now."

"Great. Send someone over to Cruiser's Bar just in case."

As a public service to a fellow cop, Dale called Joshua Watters at the LAPD.

"Detective Watters, this is Detective Dayton, LVMPD."

"What can I do for you, Detective?"

"I'm calling about your brother."

"Yeah, I've heard. Have you brought him in?"

"I don't like to admit it, but we hoped you had some idea of how we might find him."

"Under different circumstances I would laugh at a group of detectives who can't find a tall African American built like a truck in a town your size. But Calvin is not dumb and I'm not surprised you haven't flushed him. Sorry, Detective. My brother and I haven't seen or spoken to each other in years. Not since he took that job with Pitt."

"Well, I believe your brother is innocent. I think he's been set up."

"Really?"

Dale heard the shock in the LAPD detective's voice.

"Yes, I do. If you talk to Calvin, tell him that. Tell him to contact me."

"That changes things. I'll see if I can help you find him. Not that I wouldn't have done my job anyway, brother or not. But now I'm going to get creative. But I believe TV is to blame."

"What do you mean?" Dale asked.

"Detective, we both know that in real life, the police treat a suspect who comes forward with respect and assume that only an innocent man would voluntarily turn himself in. TV cop shows indicate that cops try to twist a suspect's story. My brother is probably thinking that."

"Anything you got will help."

"Calvin is a survivor, detective. He doesn't trust too many people. He was only thirteen when our mother died of pancreatic cancer. We didn't have a father. Calvin bounced around the foster care system, moving from house to house, parents to parents. I was more fortunate. I was twenty-one and already enrolled in the Academy. Even though I was legally an adult, I was in no way capable of taking care of Calvin. I did the best I could, but I wasn't the brother I should have been. Calvin used football as his salvation and a way out. As a boy, he overcame all of these obstacles to succeed when most *men* would have quit. So I'll do anything I can to help my brother now."

"No leads?"

"It won't be easy, detective Dayton. Calvin is a U.S. military history buff. He would read up on it any chance he got. I know that he used this knowledge in football to break down team defenses. He showed a special interest in past wars, studying line of defenses, as well as actions taken on the offensive. He had learned every possible tactic used by the military and how the armed forces involved made their decisions. But I'll do my best to help."

"Thanks, Detective Watters. Call me anytime," Dale said over the lump in his throat.

CHAPTER 22

"Jimmy, I'm going downstairs to retrieve the stuff from Pitt's office. We can review it now while I decide in which direction we want the team to run."

Dale skipped down the concrete stairs and into the basement evidence room. "Mornin', Joseph. I need the Pitt stuff."

"You got it, Dale."

The swarthy officer jumped off his stool, dropped the logbook on the counter in front of Dale and walked to the back of the cage. Dale could hear lockers being opened and closed as he signed in. The man returned with two large-sized garbage bags.

Dale eyed him. "That's it?"

The man shrugged. "That's all that was signed in last night."

Dale grabbed the bags and sprinted up the steps. He threw them on his desk. "How many bags did we confiscate from Pitt's office?"

Jimmy shrugged. "I didn't stay all night, but there were at least four when I left."

Dale sizzled with rage and felt a shiver form. Goose bumps sprung on his arms. He marched into his sergeant's office without knocking. "What the fuck is going on here?"

The sergeant was on the phone. A cigar drooped from his lips. "I gotta go," he said into the phone and hung up.

"Excuse me, Dayton? Do you know who I was on the phone with?"

"I don't give a fuck right now. What happened to the Pitt evidence?"

"What Pitt evidence?" His boss seemed genuinely puzzled.

"The evidence we took from the office last night."

"What are you saying?"

"At least two bags are missing. I want to know what's happened to them."

"Dayton, are you accusing me?" The boss did not sound as angry as he should have.

"It's a mighty big fuckin' coincidence that bags of evidence with names of important people vanished overnight."

"Get out of my office! I'll find out what happened to your fuckin' evidence."

"You do that."

Dale slammed his way out of the office and rushed to dump the bags out on his desk. Jimmy didn't say a word.

He and Jimmy skimmed the contents of Pitt's safe, but all the good stuff was gone. What was he going to do about whoever was messing with him from inside the department? He had no clue who it was.

He wanted to make some calls, do some complaining, but he knew his superiors would ignore him and he'd be wasting needed time that they didn't have.

He reviewed the suspects.

Ace Sanders' alibi was confirmed by the scared employees from his casino. The household staff confirmed that Linda Grant was at home at the time in question. Shawn Grant was also at his casino. But all three of them could have hired a killer.

The only suspect without an alibi was Calvin Watters and they couldn't even find him to question.

"Anything?" Jimmy asked.

"No!" His voice was raised. "Sorry, Jimmy. I'm still too pissed to think straight right now. Just give me a few minutes to put my thoughts in order."

He tried to forget about the missing evidence and corrupt cops. He jotted down assignments and grabbed the files on Pitt and the prostitute. As he opened the file, he heard his name called.

"Dale, conclusion on the tread marks. Perfect matches to Grant's vehicle."

"Thanks, Ian."

Confirmed: smart killer. One set of tire tracks.

Dale got up and approached his team. "Neil, you and Tim interview Pitt's family, because your natural sleaziness will win them over."

The men grinned as Dale moved on.

"Amy, you and Smitty talk to Pitt's employees and business associates."

Dale moved to less experienced detectives.

"Lucas and Sanchez, you have the hookers. Actually, scratch that. Amy, you can get more out of the hookers than those fine young men."

He threw a black leather book onto the desk.

He gave Lucas and Sanchez a new task. "That's Pitt's client list. Go through every name. Pay particular attention to those with outstanding debts. That's potential motive. Maybe Pitt was killed by a friend, but it also could have been a client back for revenge for what Pitt had Watters do to collect."

Before Dale turned to go, Lucas asked, "What about Sanders? Derek and I still haven't talked to him."

"Leave him. Jimmy and I will handle that."

Dale went to his last team. "Charles, you and Eddy see if Pitt's business was failing according to other bookies."

Dale and Jimmy returned to the lead detective's desk. Dale punched a number. "Stan, it's Dale. Anything on Linda Grant yet?"

"No, nothing. She spent yesterday expressing her grief by shopping. You want us to shut down surveillance?"

"No, I still don't trust her. Watch her around the clock for at least today. I'll call Harper and Elliot and have them replace you."

"Yes, sir."

Dale hung up.

Jimmy looked at his partner. "What about Sanders? We gonna go see him?"

"Not just yet."

"Dale," someone called out.

He turned and saw Craig, the youngest officer in the department.

"Since her first call to Sanders after your departure, nothing else has been recovered on Linda Grant's taps. What else can I do?"

Dale liked his initiative. "Okay…" He reached into his desk drawer. "Here's the search warrant for Calvin Watters' apartment. Secure the area and wait inside for us to arrive for the full search. Be very careful, Craig. This guy could have already killed three people. Call for backup if you see him."

The young man grabbed the paper and hurried away.

Dale and Jimmy shared a laugh as they watched the excited officer exit the building.

Another folder was then thrown onto Dale's desk. Tommy had been up late going over the phone records.

"Doug Grant's only long-distance calls were to Atlantic City casinos and his daughter in Boston. Locally, he only made a few calls home, to Shawn's house and his ex-wife. Ace Sanders and Linda Grant call each other all the time," Tommy said.

Dale had been sure they had a thing going and maybe a plan too.

"Another interesting thing," Tommy said. "That number you highlighted and wanted me to check into from Sanders' phone? I tracked the out-of-state calls to a public phone booth in a remote area down by the docks in New Orleans."

Dale blinked. "New Orleans? Why would Sanders be calling New Orleans?"

The officer shrugged.

Jimmy had a clueless expression.

"Tommy, call the New Orleans Police Department and see if they'll dust the booth and see if they can place surveillance on it. Don't expect much."

After Tommy left, Dale shook his head and glanced at Jimmy. "We don't have the manpower to deal with this."

Book Three: Circumstantial Evidence

CHAPTER 23

Mike Armstrong arrived at Calvin's hideout almost on time. He'd meant to be there at nine, but he decided overnight to outdo himself with the best system he'd ever assembled.

Calvin watched out the window as Mike circled the neighborhood four times before coming in—caution on the edge of paranoia and overkill that might bring notice instead of safety. Not now, but Mike needed a talking-to. "Did you get everything?"

"Not a problem. You are getting all the extras."

With the aid of a ramp and a trolley, they rolled in a backup generator and a backup for the backup. Calvin did most of the heavy lifting. Mike assured him that the generator was not loud and would not attract attention to the house. It was only for emergencies.

Once they had all of the equipment inside, Mike disappeared up the stairs for a couple of minutes and then returned. "Nothing I can't handle."

He set up monitors and cameras for every inch of the two-story house and motion detectors with camera feeds to multiple viewing screens.

No system had value unless used expertly, so Mike briefed him on how to take out any threat before it became serious. At least that was the plan.

They'd arrived at the bank later than they'd hoped, but Dale hadn't anticipated that there'd be so much to do at the station first. He had obtained the legal authorization from the sergeant through a circuit of phone calls and Jimmy had already called his wife to confirm with her manager. With the key found at Grant's office, Dale and Jimmy entered the Sun West Bank at 5830 West Flamingo Road.

Tina met Dale and Jimmy just inside the door. "The manager said you can go ahead in."

"Thanks, Tina."

Dale had to act before lawyers or the Feds would demand access to Grant's safety deposit box and whatever it contained. He prayed that Linda didn't know anything about the box.

He followed Tina into the back room, gave her the key and waited. He didn't have access to a number or password, so Tina looked it up on the computer, brought the box back and set it on the table.

"If you need anything, let me know." She winked and left the room.

When the key slid in the lock, Dale's heart began to race. He lifted the lid and peeked inside at a stack of black-and-white eight-by-ten-inch photographs. He picked them out and spread the pictures across the oak conference table. The photos were professional and showed Sanders and Linda doing what could only be referred to as the "nasty."

Busted!

As stupid as attempting to grab both things was, he could see why Sanders wanted Grant dead so that he could have both the girl and the casino. Then he remembered the financial motives. With Grant dead, Linda would get much more money than she would as an ex-wife. Unfortunately motive wasn't proof.

The photos alone did not tie them directly to the killing. But now that he knew all the players a bit better, he could not be sure who was really playing whom. Did Linda fool Grant and Sanders? Did Sanders fool Linda?

The detective put all the photos inside his coat pocket, closed the empty box and left.

Ace got to his office after working the casino floors for hours. He was delayed by a bimbo he'd had sex with in a variety of interesting locations in the club. She seemed to need a little flattery to calm her down—every once in a while a girl threatened to sue him before he had one of his beefy security people talk to them in clear terms.

"Excuse me, Mr. Sanders?" The pretty redhead's voice quavered and the glasses on the tray she held clinked.

"Yes," he said, in no mood to talk with this dimwit.

"I just thought you should know." She glanced around the casino.

"What is it…" he looked at her name tag, "Samantha."

"The police were in here yesterday asking about you."

"Really?" Now she had his attention. "What kind of questions?"

"They said they were conducting an investigation on the Doug Grant murder."

He relaxed. "Thank you, Samantha. Don't worry, the police questions are routine procedure because Doug Grant was a local casino owner. I'll look into it further."

"I can't lose this job, Mr. Sanders."

He smiled. "Don't worry, nothing will happen. I promise."

He double-timed it to his office. He couldn't help being a little disturbed. Maybe the cops were not quite as stupid as he assumed.

He was sure that the police must have done the same questioning at his other casino. What bothered him more than the questions was that he'd heard nothing about the cop visit from the Midas and Golden Horseshoe staff. Overpaid idiots! Heads were going to roll! Maybe the redhead wasn't just a good lay. Maybe she had half a brain too.

He brushed past his secretary. "Hold my calls, Sylvia."

The more he thought about it, the madder he got. He had been buying off cops since he was a teenager. What had gotten into them now?

The truth was that he had anticipated such questioning, but he didn't like it and would have stopped the police at both casinos if he'd known. Now, it was time for damage control.

Rather than using his secretary, he dialed a number and a calm female voice answered.

"Mayor Casey's office."

"Yes, I would like to speak with Mayor Casey, please. Tell Paul that it's Ace."

"One moment, Mr. Sanders, while I put you on hold."

The mayor came on the line without making him wait for more than a minute.

"Ace, it's been a long time."

"Hi, Paul. Yes, it has. Too long."

"What can I do for you?"

"I need a favor."

"Shoot."

"Yesterday, the police interrogated all the employees at both the Golden Horseshoe and the Midas. I was away chairing a meeting with the board of directors and none of my miserable executives told me when the cops came in. I just found out this morning. The cops and their questions are making my people think that maybe I'm a murderer and it's shaken them up. It's an outrage and abuse of police authority."

"I'm sorry, Ace. I had no idea. Why would they suspect you, anyway?"

"Oh, it's no deep secret that I did not like Grant and wanted to buy the Greek. Listen, I know you're a very busy man, but this hurts my business. It's a public humiliation."

"I understand," the mayor said. "I'll call the chief of police and make sure that this doesn't happen again."

"Thank you, mayor."

Ace felt calmer. But what if a gung-ho cop didn't know when to quit the investigation?

CHAPTER 24

The detectives hadn't sat down before the sergeant hollered at them.
"Dayton! Get in here now!"
Dale hustled in.
"Shut the door and sit down."
The sergeant sat on the edge of his desk. Dale could smell his coffee and cigarette breath from two feet away. His eyes were red, as though he'd gotten no sleep.
Dale opened his mouth but the sergeant put out his arm. "Don't speak! Just sit there and listen."
Dale sat still. He hadn't grabbed a spit cup and had to swallow the tobacco juice, which was not going to sit well with his stomach.
"Guess who I just got off the phone with?" The boss asked with a sarcastic sneer. "I just had a one-on-one with the lieutenant. He just got off the phone with our dear mayor, not a personal call either. It seems that some members of our department, your team, Dayton, were harassing Ace Sanders' employees yesterday."
"Sir—"
"I'm not finished. You know how much money Sanders contributes to the mayor's campaign? Does that take detective work?"
"No, sir, it doesn't. I told you yesterday that we'd be investigating all the casino owners and what we had on Sanders. I told my team to be

particularly courteous when questioning Sanders' employees at the Golden Horseshoe and the Midas and I'm confident they were. I hope you have that same confidence in them because you assigned them to me."

The sergeant opened and closed his mouth, then picked up his already-lit cigarette and smoked in silence for a few moments.

"Dayton." The sergeant sat back. He pressed his hands together in a triangular position and brought them close to his face. "I'm going to say this one time. You are to leave Sanders alone. Do you understand the phrase 'leave alone'? If I hear about surveillance, indirect questioning, or a whisper in the squad room, you are done. Get that?"

"Yes, sir. But I found something under warrant."

"What? Where?"

"Jimmy has them." Dale opened the sergeant's door, yelled for Jimmy and signaled him to bring the photos.

Dale and Jimmy watched in silence as the sergeant went through the photos one by one, his face reddening by the second. "Jesus H. Christ. What a fuckin' mess," he finally said. "This case is going to kill me. Does anyone else know about these photos?"

"Not yet, sir," Dale said.

"Well, keep it that way for now until I figure out what to do. And Dayton, if this case blows up, I am not the one who will get caught. You're on a very short leash."

Dale and Jimmy weren't surprised that Sanders had used the mayor to take the heat off nor that he had moved so quickly. But he was bound to have made a mistake somewhere.

Dale took some small comfort in knowing that at least all of Sanders' employees had been questioned without direct interference from Sanders himself. Ace was smart enough to know that Dale and his team would still be watching him, even from a distance.

"What do we do now?" Jimmy asked.

"Now," Dale said, leaning back in his chair. "We have to get around Sanders and get around our bosses too."

He went down the team list.

"Has anyone heard from Craig?"

He got a head shake from everyone in the room, even though Craig was late in reporting in. Even Jimmy shrugged.

Dale dialed Craig and got his voicemail. He shot out the door with Jimmy.

They reached Watters' apartment and saw no signs of forced entry.

Dale picked the door lock, careful not to make any noise or alert anyone who might be inside. He unholstered his weapon and popped his head inside. He searched the room and saw nothing.

"Kid?" He called out.

The detectives went in and started a room-by-room check. They found the officer stuffed into the closet.

"Fuck! Man down." Dale whispered to Jimmy.

He knelt next to the body, trembling, as Jimmy confirmed that the rest of the apartment was empty. Tears blurred his vision. Craig's skull had been half blown away.

This was the fourth time he'd had to kneel beside a dead body in a little over twenty-four hours. Four murders in a day and a half, and now there was either a new killer, or the same killer had completely changed his M.O.

Oh, goddamnit!

Jimmy came back and knelt beside Dale. "Rooms are cleared. No sign of anyone."

"Okay. Call it in, Jimmy." The bitterness and anger in Dale's voice was obvious.

Jimmy grabbed his phone and made his man-down report. He looked at the bloody corpse.

Dale knew every murder investigation was given top priority, but a cop-killer made a police force go crazy.

"Good God, Calvin Watters, what have you done?" Jimmy said.

"We don't know Watters did this," Dale said quietly. "Sure, it's his apartment, but it's the last place I'd expect him to return to. We don't even know if he's still in Vegas. Do you think he would kill a cop here? That's the only reason I sent Craig. I thought there'd be no risk at all and he would feel important, but not get into any trouble." He stopped and closed his eyes. "I was wrong. I fucked up."

"Bullshit! It's not your fault, Dale." Jimmy put his hand on Dale's shoulder.

Dale stood up and angrily shook Jimmy's hand away. "Of course it is! It was too dangerous. I should have known that."

"Dale, you gave Craig direct orders to use extreme caution and not make a move without backup. I heard you say it."

"I know I did, Jimmy, but come on, we both know Craig. He was looking for advancement and making his own bust would be the move to put him over the edge. That kid had never even drawn his gun in the line of duty before. He wasn't prepared."

"That's not your call. We need to refocus while the trail is still hot. So, if Calvin Watters didn't do this, then who did?"

Dale nodded. "You're right, sorry. All I know is that we have four murders and no forensics or leads."

Jimmy continued. "We know the killer's strong enough to control victims with one arm and slash their throats with the other."

"Watters could do that and he's got the IQ. But that means he wouldn't be stupid enough to kill a cop and stuff him in his own closet. He knows the police code of honor. His brother's a cop." Dale shook his head. "If he did the first three, this one is not his."

"Sanders and Shawn Grant are strong enough, but too smart for it too. And I never liked Watters for the others: he's an intimidator and maybe a bit of a sadist, but not a killer."

Dale continued in the same breath. "Also, Craig was shot in the back of the head. Anyone who can hold a gun could have done that, including Linda Grant."

"I think someone came here to take out Watters and stumbled on Craig. Maybe Watters knows too much. And except for the gun blast, the scene's clean. Where's the God damn blood and chunks of tissue? Gotta be the work of a pro. That means the investigation has just widened."

Jimmy put his hand on Dale's shoulder again and this time squeezed.

Dale walked outside. He stood at the railing, popped some chew in his mouth and looked out over the city.

He felt guilty about Craig, but something else too. Watters was now a target, a fugitive and maybe innocent.

That someone wanted Watters dead made it even less likely that he'd killed Grant or the others. Dale thought again about how much he wished he could talk to Watters, get his alibis, confirm them, clear his name and now perhaps even try to protect him…if he ever found the man.

Now all Dale had to do was catch two killers, win his family back, outwit the mayor and the other cops, and keep Watters from getting killed before he could find out what was really going on.

The crime scene unit arrived and cleared the scene. As the murders continued and the investigation kept getting much more complicated, seeming to go in all directions, with only suspicion to guide them, all of Dale's veteran instincts after twelve years as a homicide investigator told him that somehow all the murders were connected.

He immediately had officers do a canvas, but the only interesting thing was a neighbor who saw someone trying to boost Watters' car, then give up. How did that fit in?

To make matters worse, the sergeant came by before the lab guys had finished—another chance to parade his authority and ask about Watters, again. He was obsessed with Watters. To Dale, that was tunnel vision. The sergeant's obsession with Watters made him rule out all other suspects, no matter what Dale reported or showed him.

Supervision was bad enough, but the sergeant was basically controlling the investigation and all Dale could do was follow orders. The sarge had moved his way through the ranks from his success as head of the Vice Squad. That meant he had no direct homicide investigation experience of his own and it showed over and over again.

Dale was going to have to do what that lazy desk jockey told him, but find enough time to really solve the case. With the mayor, lieutenant and sergeant watching his every move, he hoped that he'd successfully solve these cases and still be sane.

He watched the sergeant cross the lot, stop at the bottom of the stairs, drop his cigarette and step on it. Dale met him at the top. "The apartment is being processed."

"Good. What do you think?"

"Looks like—"

"Detective." A CSI stuck his head out the door. "You should come and see this. Sarge, if you're coming, put on the paper boots."

"Christ." Dale heard his boss say as they headed inside.

"We found where the murder happened."

Dale followed the tech into the main room. The man turned and hollered, "Wally, hit the lights."

When the room went dark, the techie turned on a handheld ultraviolet light and waved it in front of the wall. Dale could see the trace of a large blood spatter.

"We have the scene pretty well narrowed down."

"Tell me." Dale heard his boss's footsteps enter the room behind him.

"We think the killer was already in here when Craig entered. He might have surprised Craig and got his gun. They moved over to this side of the room." The CSI member moved as he spoke, following the direct line and imitating as best he could how the team discovered it had taken place. "Craig was in the lead with his back turned and the killer was behind him with a weapon with a silencer."

So it was a pro.

"The killer put one round through the back of the head. He dragged Craig's body to the closet and then had the presence of mind to come back, methodically take time to wipe away the blood and chunks of tissue with a disinfectant and dig the slug out of the wall. The only thing he didn't do was plaster over the hole."

"Any chance of identification from just the hole?"

The CSI tech removed a tube of Mikrasil from his kit. "I'll make a mold of the impression and take it back to the lab. Maybe size and internal characteristics will help. But I'm not optimistic."

"What happened next?"

"The killer stuffed the officer in the closet and came back to make everything clean as a whistle."

"Jesus, Jenkins, enough already. You sound like a fuckin' fan," the sergeant chimed in.

Jimmy said, "What's the point of cleaning it all up but leave behind the body?"

"He would never be able to sneak a body out of here in broad daylight. He was probably hoping to come back tonight when it was dark. But we got here first." Dale thought about something else and said, "So let me get this straight," You have never seen an amateur work like that, have you?"

"No."

"This is a seasoned assassin, right?"

"Calvin Watters is no pro. He's a street thug on a mission," the sergeant replied.

Dale ignored him.

"Hey, Sarge!" Officer Simpson came into the apartment from outside. "The boys just found Watters' car in the parking lot. It's been abandoned."

"Impound it. Maybe we'll be lucky and the guy who tried to jack it left something."

There was something at the edge of Dale's mind. He walked out and had to squint even though he wore sunglasses.

As he crossed the lot to his car, he could hear his sergeant following him, wheezing like an asthmatic smoker. The sarge called after him.

Dale waited to be caught and told himself not to fly off the handle.

"So, where's Watters?"

"Not here." He kept his answer short, trying to keep the irritation out of his voice.

"He took out one of our own." The sergeant glanced at the body bag.

"We don't know Watters killed Craig." He resisted saying anything more.

"Listen, Dayton." The sergeant's voice grew louder. "You need to get on the same page with the rest of us. We all feel bad about Craig. He was a good kid. But we need to focus and do our jobs."

"If I'm not conducting this case up to your standards," Dale said, his voice getting louder, "then take me off, but if not, then—" It clicked, midsentence. He turned away from the sergeant and ran across the lot.

He picked up his pace. "Hold on guys. Back away from the car."

The officers looked confused, but they backed away. Dale knelt underneath the car and spotted the casing and detonator. "This is great news. If we have a demolitions expert, this is going to lead us somewhere."

Dale didn't bother to wait around for the bomb squad. They knew their job.

He grabbed Jimmy and got in the car. He had not mouthed off. He had found a bomb and had probably learned as much from the crime scene as they ever would. For a moment he thought he was doing pretty well.

But he was going to have to tell Craig's family before they heard it on the news. He could do little for them, but at least he could tell them in person. He loved being a cop, but delivering the death notification to a family always made him feel like a failure.

CHAPTER 25

Outside the house, Mike had mounted hidden security cameras at each corner. He positioned motion sensors on the surrounding grounds as well as tiny, potent booby traps. Then he hooked up a remote-control joystick before handing the controls over to Calvin, who maneuvered the joystick back and forth. From his seat he could control every mounted camera and motion sensor around the "fortress."

Mike then installed three phones with an unbreakable code that scrambled all communications coming in or going out. He'd also brought two military satellite phones with the same scrambling functions. The phone batteries would provide power for a full year. They were more for backup and when he was on the move. When Calvin was in the computer room, he was to use the landline phones—three instead of one, for double backup.

Also, for backup, Mike had brought military wireless servers that would receive Calvin's signal, boost it and then provide him with continuous internet access and untraceable e-mail.

He performed all of the outside duties while wearing a telephone lineman's suit, to make it look like phone company work.

In four hours, the building and attic inside and outside had the finest defense and security system Mike had ever installed. Calvin felt fully relaxed for the first time in two days.

"That's it," Mike said with a smile. "You're protected almost as well as Fort Knox now."

"Thanks, Mike. A strong defense beats a good offense every time."

Just ask the Nebraska Cornhuskers.

They had a beer in the garage and broke for lunch. Rachel had left the men alone to sort out their details.

"So, Calvin, have you found out anything more about your situation?"

He took a drink. "Yeah, I've been doing some digging." He brought Mike over to a terminal. "I've started updating and collecting everything I could find on Grant in my database, including all the articles I've collected and stored in my file. Check this out. Grant is twenty-eight years older than Linda."

"Yeah, I remember the wedding. That's all the city could talk about." It was Mike's turn to drink.

Calvin pointed to a picture of the bride and groom. "Anything unusual?"

"What about it?"

"The background."

"Is that Grant's son?"

"Yeah. Shawn Grant."

"He doesn't look too happy."

"He looks pretty pissed off to me."

"Angry at dad robbing the cradle?"

"It's only a picture, but a good place to start."

"What else you got?"

"I googled the words 'Las Vegas casino owners' and three names appeared frequently: Doug Grant, Shawn Grant and Ace Sanders."

Mike shrugged. "Sounds about right."

"So I tried to find out as much as I could about the men."

"What did you find?"

"Shawn Grant is the youngest man in Las Vegas to be a part owner of a casino and it's said that he's ready to take over for his father. Sanders—"

"Sanders is a lowlife."

Calvin smiled. "You and I know that, but from the public's perspective, Sanders is popular and respected. He's contributed a lot to the city and has supported other businesses. But we also know the rumors about the hatred between Doug Grant and Sanders. Sanders made consistent attempts to buy the Greek. He has a mean, quick temper. He's a ruthless leader and womanizer—rumor is he's banging Linda Grant. I have first-hand knowledge that he employed Pitt for dirty work he didn't want to be involved in. The work was perfect for Pitt. Dirty knows how to handle dirty."

"What did you find out about Doug Grant?"

"Not much yet. But despite what Pitt told me yesterday, I had never heard Grant's name mentioned for any job during the years I've been collecting. Sanders had been Pitt's biggest and most important client. And anyone who conducted business with Pitt is either crooked or greedy."

"So Sanders has Grant's wife and casino if he kills him?"

"I'm not so sure about the casino. Shawn Grant will be running things now and I doubt he's in any hurry to sell to Sanders."

"Do you think Sanders would actually go that far? Kill a man?"

Calvin shook his head. "I'm not sure yet. I checked to see if the three men had conducted business together but came up empty."

The two men sat in silence for a while. Calvin got up. "Want another beer?"

"No, not until the job is done. Sit down, I've been thinking about your backup emergency plan. When I was outside, I had an idea."

Calvin sat back down as Mike continued.

"I scoped the attic and think my idea is plausible. I'll cut a hole in your roof and set a two-foot-wide board outside that leads across to the roof of the neighboring building. I'll build a secret trap door that covers the hole. The board will be short enough to store in the attic, ready to be used when needed."

Mike and Calvin took a swig of the canned brew.

"It's perfect. Cops never look up when they're surveying a house. We'll set up a smoke screen for them. They'll be so busy with the explosions that they won't see you escaping. I'll plant tiny detonation devices underneath the floorboards. If there ever comes a time when you need to evacuate in a hurry and you don't want the cops nosing around in your equipment, the failsafe will protect your investment."

He paused for a moment and then continued. "When the time is right—and you'll know when that is—all you have to do is activate the program on your system and the timing device will give you an adequate countdown to escape before the massive explosion. Of course, because of the multiple-server backup system that I installed three years ago, all of your data will still be saved, but on a remote terminal where the cops won't have access to it."

Calvin liked it.

"There's more. That's the beauty of this system." Mike said. "Not only is your system protected by a password, an intruder must also get past a retina scanner and fingerprint test. A lot more than you really need, but it's all part of the package."

Mike put Calvin and Rachel through the procedure of having their eyes and fingers scanned.

It was early evening by the time they were finished and everything was set up. Mike packed his tools into the van and slid the side door shut. He shook Calvin's hand, accepted the rest of Calvin's payment and jumped into the vehicle.

Before pulling out, he rolled down his widow. "Oh, yeah, I almost forgot. Here." Mike threw a package to Calvin. "Your new IDs."

Calvin caught the package. "Thanks for everything, Mike. I owe you one."

"You owe me nothing, Calvin. You're a good friend and you took care of Andy." Then Mike's face turned grim. "I heard this morning about your boss. I can't believe that he was killed only hours after we were talking about him."

Crash!

Calvin turned to find Rachel standing behind, the broken beer bottle she had dropped scattered around her feet. She turned and ran into the house.

Calvin turned back to Mike. "Thanks, Mike. Take care and give Andy my best."

"Did I say something?"

Calvin waved as the bar owner pulled out of the parking lot. He checked the neighborhood and pulled down the fortified garage door. Then he sprinted into the house.

He found Rachel sitting on the cot, her face buried in her hands, sobbing. He sat down next to her.

"Just tell me the truth, Calvin." She sniffled.

He wrapped his massive arms around her and pulled Rachel close. Calvin, with the gentle hands of a Swedish masseuse, rubbed her back and shoulders.

"I didn't tell you last night because it was late when I got home and you had enough to think about."

"Did you do it?"

He stared hard into her eyes. "I swear I didn't, Rachel."

"What happened?"

"I'm not sure. I did go to his office, just to talk to Pitt. To get some answers, find out what was going on. But when I got there I found him dead. And not just him, there was a woman with him."

"A woman? Who?"

"I don't know that either. I didn't stick around long enough to find out. I didn't want to be caught there and get framed for that too."

"You promise you didn't do it?"

"Have I ever lied to you before?"

She shook her head.

"I promise. I had nothing to do with it."

"Then who did?"

"I don't know. But I'm going to find out." He got up from the cot but Rachel pulled him back down.

"Promise you'll tell me everything."

He stroked her hair and kissed her forehead. "I promise. Let's go."

He led her to the computer room.

"It's cold in here," Rachel said, rubbing her bare arms.

"Has to be. There is enough processing power here to generate heat and risk damage."

Calvin logged on. News of the Pitt murder was widespread, but because it had only happened last night, little was reported. He read the summaries and thought about the details.

The murders were linked to Grant by MO. Same killer?

"Who would do such a thing?" Rachel asked.

"I don't know. But you know Pitt. Maybe an angry husband or an unpaid client. But I can't think of any clients who hadn't paid up."

It had to connect with the Grant murder.

Three people benefitted from Grant's death—Ace Sanders, Linda Grant and Shawn Grant.

Calvin could see that Sanders had what it took to be a killer, but not Pitt. He could have arranged for a hit man, however. And Linda's affair with Sanders, if real, indirectly connected her with Pitt.

A *bing* from the newsfeed broke his thoughts.

Rachel saw it first. "Oh my God!" She brought her hand to her mouth. "It's you! And that's your apartment!"

Calvin felt a lump in his stomach. His pictures, a current one and an old one from college, appeared on the screen.

"Oh my God, Calvin. That's your apartment! Is that a body bag? What's going on?"

He didn't have an answer. He read the caption: *Cop killed inside his apartment and a bomb found underneath his car.*

The newsfeed triggered by his name meant another frame for another murder. He had to evade the cops—and he now had to keep ahead of whoever was trying to kill him.

Calvin knew that going out to meet people was a risk no matter how careful he was. If he was spotted or didn't detect that he was being tailed, then he was putting at risk not only himself but also the person he was visiting.

He knew he never had to worry about Mike. The man was like a ghost and had select friends who knew what he really did. No one would ever trace him and he never left a trail to follow.

But everyone else was exposed.

Calvin picked up his untraceable phone and punched in the number.

"Hello?" The voice was a raspy smoker's.

"Dixie?"

"Calvin, is that you?" she whispered.

"Can you talk?" He couldn't take any chances.

"For you, always." Her voice regained a normal tone and volume.

"I'm sorry to call, Dixie, but I couldn't think of anyone else. You're the one who persuaded Pitt to take me on when no one else would. You're the only one in the office I trust."

"Thanks. Back then, I could talk Donnie into anything." She grunted. "Boy, can I pick 'em. I have a history of falling for the wrong man. Once Nathan was born, Donnie wanted no part of me."

Dixie was a single mother and Calvin had added her to the long list of reasons he hated Pitt.

"What can I do?" she asked.

"I do need something. But I don't want to put you at risk. If you don't feel comfortable helping me, I understand."

"Don't be silly. I don't believe for a second you're capable of doing what they say."

"Thanks. Listen, I don't want to open up old wounds, but I know that when you were with Pitt, he trusted you with everything."

"A lot changed since then."

"I know, but you might know something and don't realize it."

"You want to know what Donnie was doing at his office that late?"

He knew what Pitt was doing at his office.

"That would have been me last year." Her voice caught. "I can't believe I thought he would leave his wife for me. That poor girl…"

"Did you notice anything peculiar or out of the ordinary at all at the office?"

"Donnie would never change." She almost spit out the words. "He was always the same and even more so since our breakup. I can't think of anything or anyone peculiar except Ace Sanders was in a lot more than usual. But that's no surprise. He and Donnie were just right for each other."

Calvin had never trusted Sanders and had told Pitt that many times. But Pitt only saw the money at the end of the tunnel.

Sanders without a doubt had an opportunity to kill Pitt.

"Did Pitt ever talk about Sanders?"

"Sure, lots of pillow talk. Donnie would open up afterwards."

"So what was their partnership like?"

"Huh, I don't think you could call it a partnership. Not according to Donnie. He didn't trust him. In fact, he was terrified of the man. He had been hesitant about any business deals with him, but like usual, he let his greed win out. He said Ace was unpredictable and Donnie never knew what he was capable of."

Calvin heard her lighting a cigarette. She had quit two years ago when she had learned she was pregnant, but the murder must have sent her spiraling back. "Are you sure you haven't seen anything suspicious at all?"

He heard her take a drag from the cigarette.

"No." She hesitated a moment. "Wait, now that you mention it and since we're talking about Ace, I did hear something one morning last week."

"Go on." Calvin felt lucky.

"I happened to be passing by the office when Ace was inside and I overheard a discussion. He said something about when he took over the Greek, Donnie would be his silent partner. When Donnie saw me, he raced across the room and shut the door."

"Are you sure that he said 'when he took over the Greek'?"

Dixie thought about it for a moment. "Pretty sure. I never thought about it again until I heard about Mr. Grant's death."

"Can you think of anything else?"

"Nah. Not really."

He knew she wanted to talk. Dixie was always either raising her kid or at work with no time for friends. Her life hadn't exactly been a fairy tale.

"So, has that boyfriend of yours proposed yet?"

She spit out a laugh through the phone. "That's done. Once he saw Nathan, he was gone."

Calvin regretted bringing it up. "You know, if I was single…"

"Yeah, yeah, yeah. All you men are alike." She chuckled. "Calvin, you take care of yourself. And if you need anything, promise you won't hesitate to call."

"I promise. Thanks, Dixie."

He hung up. When this was all over, if it ended the way he hoped, then he would have to do something for Dixie and Nathan.

CHAPTER 26

Ace lay on his Golden Horseshoe Casino office sofa. His arm dangled over the side of the couch, his hand grasping a glass of expensive Scotch. He clinked the ice cubes in his drink and closed his eyes. A deck of cards was scattered across his 35K touch-screen, interactive multimedia coffee table.

Ace's sources on the LVMPD had just told him his hit man had failed. Ace would tell the hit man he wasn't the only shooter and it would be easy to hire one to take Watters out. Watters would join Grant and Pitt. The longer Watters was alive and free, the more of a threat he became.

But the setback had been evened out by his latest news. He had just bought a piece of the Greek.

Grant must be rolling over in his grave.

As a rule, a purchase as large as this one took days, sometimes weeks, to transpire. But Ace had the Nevada Gaming Commission expedite their review and give approval that afternoon. The contracts had been fast-tracked for signing and countersigning. He was now preparing for the press conference with Linda on the final sale.

Gaming corruption was so great it was beyond any local or state control, though the constant effort was there to keep it clean. But the Commission could at least make sure that the casinos themselves were being bought and sold with all the legal proprieties observed.

He had expected the Commission's approval to be almost automatic. His purchase of part of the Greek was exactly what it appeared to be: legal, fair and not even close to monopolistic control over all the other Vegas casinos. The competition for gambling customers would be as free and fierce as before.

He had to purchase his portion of the Greek Casino at fair market value, $40 million. That was a Commission requirement. A lot of money, but compared to the $250 million that had been his last offer to Grant for the entire Greek, much more affordable. It all meant smaller mortgage loans on the Golden Horseshoe and Midas and a much smaller cut of his operating cash flow from both casinos to pay it off. Even though the annoying Shawn Grant would have majority control and ownership, Ace's net worth with three casinos would be much higher.

His final purchase of his share of the Greek had not happened as he and Linda had planned, but they'd made it work anyway. With Linda selling him the shares that she already owned, which even Shawn couldn't stop, he was in. No one would be able to stop him from a full takeover. He'd already worked out how to sabotage the other stockholders, gradually forcing them to sell him their shares. Shawn would be the hardest to take down, but Ace had no doubts about the outcome. He'd do whatever it took.

So far, his plan had been flawless. There were only two remaining matters to deal with—Watters and another vulnerability that would need to be eliminated soon. Ace wasn't going to risk what was turning into a fiasco. His top assassin was not able to find and kill Watters, after a day and a half. Killing a Vegas cop and the failed car bomb had only brought more police attention to the search for Calvin and made the hit man's job more difficult. The cops would start a new massive investigation into the murder of one of their own, in addition to looking for Calvin and all other suspects. That meant that the LVMPD was now probably at its highest state of alert, investigative effort and more motivated than they'd ever been, perhaps in decades.

They all assumed that Watters was still in the city. By now, he could be in Europe. Ace's only hope was that Watters would be too proud to let anyone push him out of Vegas. He thought that fit the most successful and terrifying collector that Pitt had ever employed. Watters was hiding, but not outside the city.

Right now, killing Watters was Ace's number one priority

He had hoped the cop killing would make Watters a multiple-murder suspect, but the whole situation enraged him. He was not in control of too many things.

Ace would tell the killer to kill or be killed and if he failed, he'd take out the assassin himself.

Just then his untraceable phone rang. Only two people had the number.

"Hello."

"It's me."

"I know." The assassin was never late with his check-in call. "You failed."

"It won't happen again."

"No, it won't. You've already killed a cop."

"The cop was collateral damage."

"Convince me you'll get this done."

"I found out about Watters' hooker. He's bangin' a local girl. I haven't been able to locate her yet and other whores don't seem to know where she is. I'm pretty sure she's with Watters. If I find one, I find the other."

"So what now?" Ace asked.

"I'm confident Watters is still in the city. I put the word out through my few trusted contacts who know about tracking. They've been working it and they haven't received any data to indicate he's gone. But I'm prepared to go on a long fugitive pursuit that could take me anywhere if it comes to that. Did you get the information I need?"

"I did. It wasn't easy. I found what you need in Pitt's files, but even Pitt didn't know where Watters conducted his business."

"I have my own methods of finding his location. Get it to me," the assassin said.

"I may need one of Pitt's employees eliminated. She had Pitt's personal USB and I don't know if she looked at it. I doubt it though. The files were well hidden. I'll let you know if the situation escalates. Watters is your only priority."

"Got it. It'll be done very soon."

Scott spoke so easily about taking a life that Ace felt a strange, excited chill.

"Mr. Scott, let me be clear. If you fail again, I will find out who you really are and I won't just kill you, I'll have everyone close to you tortured and terminated. You know I have the means to do it."

He hung up, thinking his assassin had an incentive to deliver, and glanced at his watch. He had a conference to attend.

He got up from the couch and moved towards the windows. The soft, Italian leather of the new sofa exhaled as he stood. He opened the curtains and looked down over the Golden Horseshoe lobby to the main floor.

Security was tight at both casinos. He'd buckled down with troops at the Golden Horseshoe because it was larger and easier to defend and protect. He could deploy many more security guards. He was not about to let Watters come in and destroy the place, or the Midas. Ace had doubled the guards to walk the floors. He would keep his ships running tightly until Watters was dead.

As usual, the place was packed and the slot machines were being worn out by the hopeless losers looking to hit the jackpot. Didn't they know the house always won?

As he reached for his suit jacket, he noticed that his right shirtsleeve had turned a dark red. He had treated the scratch marks on his wrist and had changed into fresh bandages, but it hadn't worked. As he pulled up his sleeve and removed the stained wrap, he noticed how deep the gashes were. He knew he couldn't go to the hospital for stitches and explain the wound. Tonight he would call a doctor friend and ask if he could be stitched up at the man's house.

Had his skin flaked in a way that it could be found in Pitt's office, on the floor or under the hooker's nails?

He cursed the woman and even more so himself for being so careless. He had allowed a struggle, a flaw in his perfect plan. Ace was not accustomed to being sloppy.

CHAPTER 27

After coming back from the hardest part of a police investigation, talking to the family of the murdered victim, Dale sat at his desk reading reports. One by one his team members came to check in with almost nothing to show for the day. He had to have something to inspire his aggravated group.

Parker and Duncan had talked with Pitt's wife.

"Mrs. Pitt was cold and distant. She knew he was a cheating dog, but she stayed with Pitt because of the children. Also she shows no signs of being employable herself. Anyway—no help from her. She seemed happy that a hooker died. No surprise."

"So she has a motive?" Dale asked.

"She didn't kill her husband," Parker stated without delay. "She has a solid alibi and is too fragile to do it anyway."

Dale agreed, but like everyone else who gained financially but didn't have the strength for the killings, she could still have hired a killer. She was just playing the good wife and wanted her sleazy man dead.

Smith and Ramirez reported that Pitt's employees all had been hired off the street. Most of them have a criminal record of some sort, but no one seemed to hate Pitt. No one was too sorry he died. They all had solid alibis.

They hadn't seen unusual documents or visitors around the office.

Sanders had made several appearances in the office to talk with Pitt, but that was routine.

Dale thought the $30,000 in the safe was enough for Pitt's employees to kill the boss. The killer was definitely looking for something in Pitt's office.

And again, Sanders' name came up. The biggest problem: Sanders' employees refused to talk while Pitt's couldn't stop.

Lucas and Sanchez reported that many of the prostitutes knew the girl who had been killed and had Pitt as a client themselves. But none had any reason to kill Pitt.

"They called her 'Amber,' but no one seems to know her real name. Just for fun, I flashed Watters' picture around to see what kind of reaction I would get. One prostitute ID'd him. She said Watters has a soft spot for another whore. The streetwalker that I talked with said that he is more than just a client. The two are close. She goes by the name Chloe."

"Any luck finding her?"

"No one had seen her all day, which is unusual."

Dale just went through the motions. He was sure Watters was with Chloe somewhere. Any man would think of his woman first. So why hadn't Dale?

Watters was such a good collector that there were few accounts outstanding—killers who wanted to erase a debt.

"Watters had left his mark on the clients. A few were hobbled in some manner and even though they never admitted it, we assumed the injuries were from Watters. The gamblers were afraid to talk. Watters is more scary than jail. Even the few who still owe money are accounted for."

Edwards and Morris had interviewed private and public bookies. The general consensus was that no one liked Pitt, but no one felt threatened by his business.

Harper and Elliot showed up before their night shift on Linda Grant. The lead officer got right to her report.

"Linda Grant spends her days in high-end boutiques and her evenings in five-star restaurants getting wasted from the top shelf. She's made very few phone calls—a couple to friends and family, her attorney and one to Shawn Grant to discuss the terms of the sale."

Dale wanted more information from this group. "Before I pulled you off the Grant questioning to put you on Watters' stakeout, how far did you get with Grant's attorney?"

"Like we said before, Grant had made an appointment to see his lawyer for Tuesday morning. The attorney wouldn't say what the purpose of the meeting was. When we asked about a divorce, he couldn't say because as Grant's lawyer, he also represents Linda Grant. But I don't think he really knew the purpose of the meeting."

Was Grant going to his attorney for divorce papers? Did the killer know about the meeting and murder him before the papers were filed and served, which would automatically bring the will into play? Grant's death made the prenup null and void, while a divorce would cut Linda out of the will completely. His death, twelve hours or so before the appointment with his lawyer, was more than coincidental.

"Okay, team," said Dale. "Meet back here first thing in the morning. I hope to have something for all of you by then. Good night."

The group nodded and went home.

He turned to Jimmy. "Well, partner. Our surveillance team has nothing to report either. We're goin' nowhere with this one and fast."

"What do you want me to do?"

"You go home too. Spend some time with that pretty wife of yours. You and she both deserve a night together and a family dinner."

"What about you? Maybe you should do the same."

"Don't tell me what I should do," Dale snapped, his pulse quickened, but he caught himself.

Jimmy's wide eyes answered Dale.

"Sorry, I'll be fine. I'm just gonna finish up some paper work and go home too."

"All right, buddy. Have a good night." Jimmy rushed from the office.

Dale was alone in the detective bureau. He needed to get to the "basement." The crew had turned up nothing useful from Watters' car, so he hoped they could retrieve something from the bomb that had been planted underneath. Anything.

He knew that spending excessive amounts of time on the job was one of the reasons why Betty had left. This investigation kept expanding at a dizzying speed. In less than forty-eight hours, four people had been murdered. He thought that more people were going to die soon. Because forty-eight hours had passed, his chance to solve Grant's murder was, by the stats, cut in half. Two weeks without a break came close to a zero rate of success. The clock was ticking very loud. He still suspected two killers. Someone else had killed the police officer with a gun. A knife was close and personal. A gun was remote—it suited another kind of killer.

He had to find a break in the case somewhere. He turned the night lamp off on his and Jimmy's desks and followed the long, musty hallway down to the basement forensics lab.

The tech looked up from a microscope and checked Dale out over the bifocals perched on the end of his nose. The man's hair was greasy and disheveled and his white lab coat grimy. The eraser head of a pencil peeked out of his breast pocket and another was tucked behind his right ear. After a deferential nod, he went back to his microscope.

While Dale waited, he checked the dismantled bomb resting on the countertop. The pieces lay strewn about, each numbered and named.

He was inspecting the blasting cap and C-4 when the lab technician finally looked up again. "I've been waiting for you to come down." He smacked on gum and blew a bubble.

"So, tell me about the bomb. And no mumbo jumbo bullshit. You know that I know squat about bombs."

"Great, another simpleton."

"Just tell me."

The techie got up off his stool and walked over to Dale and the bomb. "All right, in layman's terms. A chunk of plastic explosive had been secured under the driver's seat, because that was the center of the target—the driver. The C4 had a detonator shoved into it and the detonator wires had been attached to the ignition wires. The bomb was to go off when the car was started. Do I need to slow down?"

Dale considered the explanation. In a sense, it would've been the perfect murder—except Watters was long gone and not worried about his car.

The tech continued. "I fed the information through the FBI Bomb Data Center and the ATF's National Repository, but I couldn't find a signature match to our bomb."

"So, what do you think?"

He yawned and removed his glasses to rub the bridge of his nose. "Well, the fact that plastic explosive was used does tell us that the suspect is an expert bomb maker. You can't get this stuff over the counter. The setup was elaborate and the bomb hidden so well that it couldn't have been detected by the naked eye, unless you actually squirmed underneath the car looking for it. It would've taken a pro to design and dismantle the explosive weapon. This car was detonated to explode if someone either started or tampered with the vehicle."

There was nothing in his bio to indicate that Calvin Watters had any special training in the detonation of bombs. Also why would Watters set a bomb under his own car? Someone wanted Watters out of the picture. Why?

"Thanks," Dale said.

"No problem."

He was more convinced than ever that Watters was innocent, but he couldn't prove that any more than he could Sanders' guilt.

Now, along with the three "perfect" murders, he had to deal with a "perfect" attempted murder.

In the basement he pulled out his cell phone. No signal. He began to climb the stairs and as the signal was restored, he called his partner.

"It's Dale."

"Where have you been? I have been trying to reach you."

He heard the tension in his partner's voice. "I've been in the basement with the lab tech. I can't get a signal down there."

"So you haven't heard?"

"What?"

"There was a press conference this evening outside the Greek. Linda Grant just sold her shares of the casino to Sanders. He's now part owner."

"I'm impressed she moved without wasting time. Tomorrow morning check that the deal was legit, but I bet it was."

He paused for a moment. "And I need you to do one more thing before you settle down for the night. Use your network to see if anyone will give up that an assassin has come to town who knows bombs."

"Got it."

Too many questions and not enough answers.

CHAPTER 28

A tiny jingle gave Calvin a start. His head shot up off the desk, a piece of paper stuck to the side of his mouth from drool.

How long had he been out?

He checked the monitor and through fuzzy eyes saw Rachel at the back door, letting herself in. He jumped from his chair and hustled to meet her.

He spoke before she had closed the door. "Where have you been?" He strode to her and lightly grasped her arm.

Rachel shook it away. "I had to get out."

"You know we can't leave. Goddamn it, Rachel! Do you think this is a game? You could have been caught, followed, or even killed."

He peeked out the window.

"Settle down, Calvin. I did what you told me—circled a bunch of times and retraced my steps."

"Where did you go?"

"Relax. You haven't slept for days, so I didn't wake you. I had to see my friends."

"Hookers?" Calvin's eyes grew large.

"My colleagues." Rachel's voice was stern.

"Sorry." He shook his head. "What did you possibly need from them that you would risk leaving here?"

"I can't just sit around and do nothing, Calvin, while, as you say, 'our lives are in danger.' I want to help, but you refuse to let me. I can do stuff. I've been protecting myself for a long time."

He knew that and also realized that Rachel was just being proactive, wanting to do all she could to help him, as well as her. But in his heart, he didn't want anything to happen to her and would do anything to protect her. He respected and admired Rachel all the more now, but he would never tell her. He needed to make sure she knew the consequences of her actions.

"It was Amber."

"Who's Amber?"

Rachel swiped away a single tear. "It was Amber in Pitt's office. She was new and I'd only met her once. No one really knew much about her. But she was sweet."

He wrapped his arms around her. "I'm sorry."

She pushed him away. "That's not all. People are asking about us."

"I know. Once the cops found out about you, your colleagues would be the first ones they'd question."

"I'm not talking about the cops."

Calvin saw fear in her eyes. "Who?"

"I don't know. Wanda said he's pretty creepy though. He asked about me and you. He didn't show any identification and they said he definitely wasn't a cop."

"What did he look like?"

"They all gave me a different description—but all confirmed he was tall and skinny and very strange."

He shook his head. That helped very little. The man could be anyone, working for anyone. "Listen, Rachel. I'm not joking. You're not to leave again."

"Yeah, yeah, yeah."

He was about to say more when he heard the familiar "bing" from his computer—another emergency message alert. He rushed to the computer room and clicked on the blinking icon. He saw two familiar faces on the computer monitor.

Sanders and Linda Grant, hand in hand on a podium set up outside the Greek. He read the writing that scrolled across the bottom. Sanders had just purchased the rights to own a small percentage of the casino.

Bingo! Sanders killed Grant.

Calvin had been sure that there was some connection between Sanders, Linda Grant and Pitt. But he hadn't known exactly what it was.

Seeing the news about the sale, he made the final connection. Pitt, who'd done so much dirty work for Sanders, was involved somehow in making that sale possible. Pitt was probably an accomplice in Grant's murder too.

He closed the document and focused on gathering intelligence that connected Grant's killer and his accomplices. He was sure Sanders had killed Pitt because he had known too much about Sanders' plans and actions and because Sanders, being Sanders, had never intended Pitt to be any kind of partner, silent or otherwise. They'd used Pitt until the deal was done and then killed him. Now it was just Sanders and Linda, which Calvin suspected was their plan all along.

He could have hacked into Pitt's database, but since the cops would have wiped out everything useful by now, he picked up the phone and dialed out. "Please be right. Please be right."

"Hello?"

"Dixie, it's me again. Please tell me that you still have the personal USB key Pitt gave you from his files?"

"No, I gave that to the officer who came to interview me."

"Damn it!" He slammed his fist down on the desk.

"But I saved it on my hard drive."

He took a deep breath. "Thank you, Dixie Miller. Send it to this secure address, please."

He gave her his new email address and hung up.

The file arrived within minutes.

There was nothing obvious in the file folder. But he found a "mislabeled" hidden file in which Pitt had recorded an agreement to work with Sanders to take over the Greek. Pitt had been afraid of Sanders— and the trick with the filename and security opened a new question. Who was helping Pitt? As far as Calvin knew, no friend of Pitt was clever with computers.

Since Dixie had given the USB to the cops, he knew they had the same information and had to see Sanders as a suspect.

Why weren't they acting on that?

Returning to his desk, Dale logged onto the KVVU FOX5 Vegas website to see the press conference with Sanders, staged in the parking lot of the Greek. Dale turned up the volume as Linda Grant, to massive applause, approached a cluster of microphones set up on a podium.

"It is my great pleasure to announce a new member of our team." She read from a prepared statement. "'Because of the passing of my husband and my lack of experience in casino operations, I have decided it is in everyone's best interest for me to sell my share of the casino to someone with experience, someone who can make a real contribution to running the great Greek Hotel and Casino. He is already the owner of two major casinos in our wonderful city and I have the utmost confidence in his future success. My husband would be very proud today. Ladies and gentlemen, it is my honor to present to you the new part owner and team member of the Greek Hotel and Casino—Mr. Ace Sanders.'"

Dale watched as the camera focused on Sanders, who had been seated at a table next to Shawn Grant, the majority shareholder of the casino. Grant's face showed displeasure and a fake smile. Dale didn't see Melanie or her mother.

Sanders approached the microphones—to what Dale considered mixed reviews from the gallery—and shook Linda's hand. Dale thought that Sanders had been born for the spotlight. "Now that's motive," Dale muttered.

"Thank you, Mrs. Grant," Sanders said. "Ladies and gentlemen, I am more than honored to be a new member of the team and I look forward to working with Shawn Grant. I think that together we can create an ever brighter future for the Greek Hotel and Casino."

He smiled, pausing for dramatic effect and waiting for the applause to die down. "I am thrilled that the Grant family has accepted my bid and welcomed me into their family. I hope to do even more for the community now that I'm involved with three casinos. I just wish to do the Grant family justice and make them proud."

Sanders and Linda stood together, hands clasped. Shawn seemed in no hurry to join them, but he finally did. The three members raised their hands in unison as the cameras flashed and reporters yelled questions.

Dale read the article that complemented the video.

There was no public record about the deal, but "informed sources" said that Sanders purchased his share of the casino for an estimated $40 million.

He closed the report and removed the coroner report folders from a drawer.

A single powerful slice from a strong killer, maybe known to the victim, had killed Pitt in seconds, just like Grant. No damage had been done to Pitt's front-door lock, so either the door was unlocked or the killer had a key. But when Dale had arrived at the scene, all the doors had been locked.

This still didn't rule out Watters, an employee, who could have had a key. Sanders could also have had a key if he and Pitt were such tight associates.

Why would Watters kill his boss? To cover up the Grant murder, or, if Dale's assumption was correct, the fact that Pitt had framed Watters? Maybe it was payback.

Dale still wondered about the anonymous phone call. The detective couldn't figure out who would call or why. Why was some of the information right and some wrong? Misinformation to hide the source? Who could have known so much about exactly what Watters was doing that morning, disguised and on his way to Grant's private office?

He had already found nothing in the office or business paper trail. That had only worn down Dale and his team.

How much was he being played by the department heads, who only seemed interested in Watters? Who did Grant, or Sanders, have in his pocket?

He moved on to the death of the prostitute. Her street name was Amber, real name unknown. They had searched the database but no description on an active missing person case had been found. No one seemed to want her—living or dead—except for sex. She was not the killer's target.

Wait.

The slice on Amber's throat had come from right to left. The predator had been behind the victim. That would mean that the killer had held the weapon in his left hand. But Pitt's throat slash had come from left to right, same as Grant's. That killer had been right handed.

Dale called Edgar Perkins at home.

When the medical examiner answered his phone, Dale spoke. "Hey, Edgar, it's Dale. I need some information."

"You want to know about your DOAs from the bookie's shop?"

"Tell me about the throat slash on Amber."

Perkins had been the chief pathologist for the Las Vegas Metropolitan Police Department and Crime Lab for over twenty-five years.

"Well, since we determined there was only one killer, I originally thought that the murderer had been left handed, because of the direction of the wound on Amber's throat. But after a second check on Pitt's wound and substantial consideration, I'd say that the killer is ambidextrous. The slash on Pitt's neck, like Grant's, almost decapitated both victims. But the other one, the woman's wound, was a little more sloppy. The woman had considerable bruising and an abrasion from the pressure of being held, which indicated that the man's right arm was his stronger side. The knife was held in the left hand, but the killer could be trying to throw us off. In my opinion, this attacker can use his left and right hand with the same degree of accuracy."

"Thanks, Edgar."

"No problem, Dale. How's your—"

Dale hung up before Perkins could keep him long. An ambidextrous killer, that had to narrow down the field. He turned the page and read on.

Pitt and Grant were killed with the right hand but the prostitute was not. Dale suspected the rear angle of the attack made it difficult for the killer to control the woman with his left arm and kill with his right, as he'd done twice before. She was weaker than either man, so the killer didn't need the same strength. He controlled her with his right arm, which is why he was scratched.

He assumed that if it had not been for the happenstance of the prostitute, the killer would have slashed both times with his right hand and all the evidence would indicate that the killer was right-handed. But as life happens, she was there and that revealed the ambidexterity of the killer.

They already knew that skin under the prostitute's nails, from fighting her killer, was Caucasian and therefore not from Watters. Even though there had been no scratch marks on Pitt, the trace was still being compared with his DNA.

Dale slid the two medical reports to the side of his desk. He opened up Grant's file and set the report beside the other folders. It made no sense to have more than one killer with wounds this similar.

Sanders was so obviously the person with the strength and will to kill all three. He killed Grant for the Greek. He killed Pitt for cover up. But Dale's sergeant had already put Sanders "off limits." The casino owner was practically untouchable.

Dale compared the wounds. The MO was the same for all three murders, even though two different knives had been used. Any smart killer would change weapons after each killing and destroy the ones used.

Craig's death, shot in the head, was the only wild card. There was a second killer who used a gun.

He did one more search of national and local killings with the same MO, but no dice—nothing to do with this pattern that could not be explained by chance.

But he cross-referenced all of those cases anyway. At the national level, as he suspected because the knife-to-throat MO wasn't unique, he found a total of 124 cases over the last year. But when he dug deeper the suspects were all ruled out for various reasons—they were dead, serving life sentences, paroled or disappeared. The very few who didn't get crossed off and potentially *could* be Dale's killer were very unlikely because the murders happened in Vegas.

He threw the files into his desk and shut down the computer. He was at an investigative dead end.

He looked around the office. The lighting was dim and only a handful of officers remained. He wondered how many of those officers also had empty homes to go to. The divorce rate was high on the force and he didn't want to be just another statistic. But would he ever be able to make it up to Betty and Sammie?

One last thought about the case struck him. He wandered over to his partner's messy desk. He found a DVD resting on top of a bundle of files. The label read, "Sugar Bowl." He popped it into the video player.

He remembered Watters on the football field—graceful and unstoppable. His large frame and long, smooth strides made him the model running back headed for big-league glory. From Jimmy's notes, Dale read that Watters had run the ball sixty-one times that game for the Trojans, a new NCAA record. So finding a sequence of Watters' carries wasn't a challenge.

After the first carry, Dale thought he had picked something out. After the second, he knew for certain. After seven straight carries, it was irrefutable—Watters received the ball from his quarterback the same way each time, cradling the ball with his right arm and using his left to stiff-arm his way through tackles, no matter which side the play was called to run. Watters was as right-handed as right-handed ever got. Someone ambidextrous, at that level of play, would have used that to their advantage.

Why was this department determined to pin this on an innocent man?

CHAPTER 29

Dale took a few more minutes for another search—until he found an article about Sanders in his baseball days at UNLV. Sanders had been an elite pitcher and had to have a glove made just for him because he was an extreme variety: an ambidextrous pitcher who switched arms when he pitched. Dale saved the article and added it to the file.

He was going to nail Sanders somehow without losing his own job and pension.

As he finally strapped his weapon on and turned to go home, he thought he'd grab one more thing, the tape of Linda Grant's phone calls.

A few minutes later, he steered the slow-moving vehicle toward his house. As usual on the ride home, he could feel himself starting to crash after an exhausting investigative day. He summed up where he was with the investigation.

Other than Watters, there were three potential suspects.

Dale thought about the explicit photographs of Linda Grant and Ace Sanders. He put that together with the Grant prenup as well as Linda Grant's twelve-percent portion of the estate that had now been sold to Sanders. Dale knew Linda had a motive to kill her husband.

He cut the headlights and let his car roll into the driveway. He sat and stared at his modest but well-maintained home. His wife had spent hours fussing over the flowers. Would he ever see that again? The yard smelled of fresh-cut grass.

He stepped inside, where the only sounds were his footsteps and breathing. The sights and sounds had changed. No more of Sammie's soft moans on the baby monitor, or Betty on the loveseat, screaming out answers at the TV during Wheel of Fortune. He might never again hear Casper the Dachshund snoring as he slept comfortably on the arm of the couch.

The sounds he had grown accustomed to, that he had taken for granted and had ignored, he might never get back. Those were the things he truly missed, the things that made his house a home.

He flicked on the front hall light, hoping to see Betty standing there, but all that welcomed him was an unfurnished hallway.

Even though his stomach grumbled, he didn't feel like fixing a late-night dinner. He removed his jacket and threw it on the back of the couch.

He used the bathroom sink to rinse the remains of his last pull of tobacco from his mouth and retreated to the living room couch, where he'd been sleeping since Betty had left. He just couldn't sleep in their bed, where so many memories lay—the passionate lovemaking, the meaningful pillow talk, the giggling and playing. Those were happy times early in their relationship, so long ago.

He lay down and closed his eyes, replaying the last argument he'd had with Betty, the conversation that had occurred the last time he'd come home this late.

He had come home late, real late, expecting Betty to be sleeping. He had unlocked the front door and heard his little dachshund growl and bark.

"Shut up, Casper," he whispered, listening for the sounds of footsteps.

He flicked on the front hall light and Betty was standing in the hallway, in her bathrobe, holding the dog.

"Where's Sammy?" he whispered.

"Sleeping, like everyone should be at this time of night. Where have you been?" she said in a clipped tone.

"Work."

"This late?"

Dale let out his breath. "Betty, we've been over this. You know my job isn't nine to five. I'm a Las Vegas detective."

"So you were at the office?"

"Yes, I was at the office."

"Who were you with?"

Dale shook his head. He slid his shoes off and hung his jacket in the closet.

She stepped close to him, stopping him, invading his personal space with a subtle sniff of the air. He was insulted, but he knew what she was smelling for.

"Were you with her?"

"Betty, don't. You know I wasn't. That was a long time ago. I thought we'd moved past this?" For the first time he noticed the lines at the corner of her eyes. The exhaustion set in her expression.

She sighed. "I thought so too." She set the dog on the floor and turned away.

The dog began sniffing at Dale's feet, wagging his tail until Dale scooped him up.

Dale said, "Betty, wait."

But when she turned back, Sammie's cry erupted on the baby monitor.

"Great!" Betty said.

"I'll get him."

Betty put out her hand. "Stop, you've done enough." She walked down the hall toward the baby's room. "And you can sleep on the couch."

He slumped his shoulders. He knew he should go after her, apologize, make it right, but he was too tired and she was in no mood for conversation.

Dale opened his eyes. If he'd only gone after her that night, would it have mattered? Would it have changed things? He didn't think so or at least he told himself that.

Betty's accusations had cut deep.

He closed his eyes again and thought about that one moment in time, that one moment of vulnerability when he had let his guard down and had given in to temptation. That one impulsive, split-second decision had ruined his marriage.

It had been a long time ago—back in his rookie year on the force. Dale and Betty had just been married, already in rocky waters, but that seemed to be the case from day one. Marriage had changed everything.

His first partner, Josie Walker. She had been Dale's vice.

They'd been on a sting, following a load of cocaine flown into the city from Panama. They had the private airfield staked out, awaiting the cargo. But somehow the dealers had been tipped off and were waiting.

All hell broke loose. Lives were lost and more should have been.

Dale and Josie had been taken hostage inside the tiny private jet. If it hadn't been for some quick-thinking and swift-acting SWAT members, Dale and Josie would never have made it out.

After the dust had cleared, rather than going home to his new wife, Dale had gone to the bar with his team to celebrate the arrest. A total of $50 million in cocaine had been confiscated, the largest drug bust in LVMPD history.

Dale still remembered shaking so much that he could barely hold his glass. He and Josie had come that close to death. They'd looked it in the eye and had walked away unscathed. In that moment he had felt a deep connection with his partner—more than just professional.

The sexual tension between them was palpable.

She was a beautiful woman, with all the right curves and a cocky go-get attitude. He knew it was wrong, but Dale rode the moment. He had given in and for that he would be forever regretful. Or was he really?

Josie had felt it too, because she had suggested the motel room.

As much as Dale didn't want to admit it, in his heart he knew that it hadn't been just a one-night stand of meaningless sex with a stranger. It was a night of passionate lovemaking. A deep, heartfelt ride shared between two people who really cared for each other.

The next day he had felt sick at what he'd done. He told Josie they had made a mistake, he could never leave Betty and that he wanted to make it right with his wife. Betty was the one he truly loved. Had that been a lie?

Josie said she could no longer be his partner. She had requested a transfer from the department, claiming mental anguish from the experience Dale and she had been through. Dale never saw Josie again.

He told Betty what had happened, not just to appease his guilty conscience but because he knew it was the right thing to do. Betty didn't deserve that deception.

There were only three people who knew about the incident—Dale, Betty and Jo. Dale had thought that night had been dead and buried, that he and Betty had moved on, but you can't outrun your past.

Dale sat back up and shook his head. Over the last two days, except for her original call to Sanders, Linda had only spoken to her mother and her attorney. She'd followed Sanders' orders and not talked to him.

Dale inserted the first tape. He set the headphones over his ears, lay back on the sofa and pressed play.

He couldn't let the past slow down his investigation.

"Do you see anything?"

Calvin was startled by Rachel's voice coming from the doorway behind him. He turned and looked at her.

He shook his head. "Nothing," he said, looking back at the computer monitor.

"Do you think someone is really out there, hunting us like animals?"
He nodded.

Rachel moved toward him, turned his chair around and sat down on his lap.

"Why are you up?" he asked. "It's three o'clock in the morning."

"I couldn't sleep."

"Me neither."

"Is that your mom?" She reached for a famed photograph on his desk. "She's beautiful."

"Yeah, that's her."

"Why do you never talk about yourself, Calvin? I don't know anything about your family or your childhood. We always talk about me."

"There's not much to say. I'm more interested in you." He smiled.

"I'd like to know."

"It's not much of a story—just another ghetto kid from the streets who had a tough upbringing. Just another sappy story made for Oprah. I'm tired of being just a statistic, another cliché." He smiled again. His childhood had always been a closed book and he wanted to leave it that way. Rachel didn't need to hear about it.

Rachel smiled too. "Maybe we could make a movie."

His grin broadened. "Yeah and Denzel could play me."

She took him by the hand and led him into an adjoining room they were using as their bedroom. They sat down on the cot.

"Tell me about your mother."

He swallowed and took a deep breath. "I was young when she died of cancer. What I do remember of my mother was her voice, how she could soothe me with a whisper. She loved to sing and she would often lullaby me to sleep before leaving for work. She had soft hands and a gentle touch. When she was around, I thought I was invincible. I made a promise to her to someday graduate from college. At that point, I wasn't sure how that would be possible."

"What about your father?"

He grunted. "What father? He left before I was born—just another deadbeat dad with illegitimate children all over the city. He showed up a few years ago after seeing my picture on the cover of *Sports Illustrated*. I was a Heisman finalist and possible first overall draft pick. I told him to get lost."

"So who took care of you?" She rubbed his arm gently.

"Mom and Josh."

"What's your brother like?"

"Pretty successful. My mother would be really proud of him. Josh has made a life for himself. He's the 'good' son, the success story."

Rachel moved in behind Calvin as they both sat on the cot. She spread her legs and moved in close, wrapping her legs and arms around him and pressing her face against his back. He could feel her warm breath.

"Your mother would be proud of you too, Calvin."

He stood up, feeling uncomfortable, and swiped away a tear. "When she died, Josh was already at the Police Academy and I was shipped to an orphanage. It was a rough go, but I survived."

"You didn't have anyone?" Her face showed lines of worry.

"Sure, there were foster families who took me in. I was grateful. Some were good people, others not so much. But no one kept me around long enough to get used to me. It was probably better that way."

"That's not true, Calvin. You're a good person."

He nodded but didn't say anything.

Rachel got off the bed and went to him. "Look how far you've come."

He grinned. "Yeah, look at me—trapped in a shithole, a maniac stalking me and the LVMPD wanting me for murder. What a life!"

"You know what I mean." She scowled. "How did you become a USC legend?"

"Father MacIntosh."

"A priest?" She looked surprised.

Calvin smiled and nodded. "I can't remember how we met. But I do remember Father Mac taking me in and spending time with me at the local YMCA. That's when I found weights. I was always tall, but Father Mac helped me gain twenty pounds of muscle my senior year. He taught me about football and hired a tutor for me. When I graduated high school and was offered a football scholarship to USC, I'd never seen him prouder." His smiled faded. "He died that summer before I had even stepped into my first college classroom." He looked at Rachel and swallowed. "It seems like everyone in my life, the people who really love me, die. You better get away, Rachel. Quick."

"I'm not going anywhere, Calvin. I love you and we're in this together." She took him by the hand and led him to the cot. She smiled. "Let me show you just how much."

Book Four: All Bets are Down

CHAPTER 30

There hadn't been much on the phone taps. Linda Grant had made one call to her mother to argue family matters and then had a lengthy conversation with her attorney to discuss the sale of her share of the casino. The talk was for the most part about numbers and there was no mention of Sanders.

Early on Friday morning, Dale's investigative squad of the homicide division gathered around the detective's desk. The conversation was minimal.

They had exhausted every possible clue and lead and had come up empty. Dale was out of answers and options. He had a lot of motive for Sanders and Linda Grant and a stack of circumstantial evidence, but nothing solid that would stand up in court. That made this current impasse even more frustrating.

The only ghost of a lead was that Pitt's killer had been searching for something in the office and hadn't had time to find it. Perhaps he'd found it, however, and taken it with him.

For Watters, he didn't have motive that made sense for Grant's killing. If Watters hadn't killed Grant, then he had no apparent reason to kill Pitt. All he knew for sure about Watters was that he'd been in Grant's office, but with no body and nothing missing.

Dale was running Craig's murder as a separate investigation. In every case there was a sacred bond between victim and cop and with Craig, it was even more than that.

He still suspected that two different killers were involved, but he couldn't be sure about that either. Even though Grant's death was his major case, finding the killer of his fellow officer was a personal crusade.

If he had nothing more, he could only keep the team doing busy work for a few more hours before they'd be pulled for other things, probably all put on catching Watters.

Jimmy sat down on the edge of Dale's desk. He read from his notepad. "I just got off the phone with a member from the Investigations Unit of the Nevada Gaming Commissions. She said the deal Sanders signed for the Greek was legit. They investigated it thoroughly and found no illegal evidence to deny the agreement."

Dale slapped his partner on the shoulder and got up. His bones felt like they'd aged since the investigation had started. On his way to the break room for a cup of coffee, he was pulled aside by one of his officers.

"Hey, Dale. Dean and I went to Cruiser's Bar last night and questioned the employees and a few patrons. Nobody gave us anything. They like Watters much more than they did us."

"Thanks, Carl." Another dead end. Watters wouldn't show his face.

He got back to his office and saw his partner waiting. He sat back in his seat, took a sip of the strong coffee and immediately felt better, but only a little.

Jimmy frowned. "I found out that a first-class assassin flew in on a red-eye Monday."

Dale sat up. "Got a description?"

"That's why he's top shelf. Never uses the same ID twice. No meetings—all email and cash payment at drop points."

"Great." Dale thought of at least three people who could hire the mystery man to kill Watters.

At least he now knew that there was a hit man in Vegas and he was probably after Watters. But Dale had no idea what the killer looked like or who he was working for. There were too many suspects in this case with legitimate money to afford a high-priced hit man.

"Jimmy, find me anything on Sanders. With the sergeant restricting access, all we can do is go 'under' the law, not break it, but utilize what's down there."

Dale got up. Time to update the sergeant—with nothing. He entered the office where his impatient boss waited.

"Any word on Watters?" The sergeant still had a hard-on for Watters for all four murders.

Dale shook his head.

"Maybe we should change our strategy."

That was the opening that Dale had been waiting for. "That's what I was thinking. I need Watters' participation to help nail Sanders."

"I'm listening."

Dale was taken off guard, but he didn't hesitate. He told his sergeant his new findings: the casino sale and how everything supported his original suspicions. He also told about his suspicions of Sanders hiring an assassin. The sergeant listened, reviewing the mountain of circumstantial evidence they had against Sanders. To Dale, the sergeant seemed to put aside their differences and deliberate.

When Dale stopped, the sergeant spoke. "Take it upstairs to Flannery. See what he says about Sanders. If he says it's a go, make the move."

Dale grabbed Jimmy's arm and said, "We're going upstairs to the DA."

Robert Flannery sat at his desk and read over the case file, shaking his head and mumbling. He was a fashion plate who could be mistaken for a trainer at the gym, even though he had a Harvard Law degree.

With his feet resting on the top of his desk, Flannery chewed the end of a pencil. A 55-inch Panasonic TC-PVT50 television and DVD player were set up in the corner. A blackboard behind Flannery's head showed a pyramid of circled names, with arrows and lines to connect them.

Dale and Jimmy waited anxiously, fidgeting in annoyance in the high-back wooden chairs.

When the DA had finished, he slammed the folder shut and tossed it on his desk. He picked up his cardboard coffee cup—a caramel latte, Dale guessed from the scent which made the whole office smell like Starbucks—and sipped at it like a kid with a hot chocolate. Flannery set it back down, sat back in his seat and steepled his fingers.

"I'm sorry, gentlemen." Flannery scowled and opened the file back up. "But everything that you have brought me is tangential. The casino chip—circumstantial. The photographs—sure, they fucked, but did they kill? The documents—circumstantial. Even the sale of the casino is a tangent. What holds it together? Where's the crime?"

Dale had already known that everything the DA said was true, but he had been hoping that Flannery himself might propose a scenario, because he brought a different and expert perspective. At least point to what they needed to make a case.

Flannery closed the file and handed it to Dale. "This is Ace Sanders we're talking about."

"So what do we do about this?"

"Is this your first day on the job? I need a weapon, a witness, or a fact that connects killer and victim."

"We're working on it."

Flannery looked disgusted, rose and slipped into a jacket that looked as though it had just been removed from the press. "I have a meeting to get to. Good luck, gentlemen."

Dale and Jimmy let themselves out and at their own pace, took the stairs back to the office. When they pushed through the door, Dale heard his name being called. "Dale, phone call. Line one."

He sat at his desk and picked up the phone.

"Detective Dayton, this is Senior Special Agent Stanley Marks from FBI Headquarters in Washington." The man spoke at an auctioneer's pace. "I wanted to update you on your request in the search for one Calvin Watters."

Dale sat up. "Yes."

"Although we don't have a direct line on him, we see no signs that Watters has left Vegas."

The words stunned Dale. Why would Watters, a number-one murder suspect, be hanging around the city? But Dale realized that as good as the FBI's resources were, Watters could have slipped under their radar. Watters had the connections, smarts and money to do it.

"Thank you, Agent Marks."

Watters was still in town, but Dale felt the chances of finding him were even smaller.

Why would a giant, tattooed black man, who was well known throughout the city, state and region as either a notorious bill collector, a former football star, or both, take the risk of staying in the city where he allegedly killed a man and was wanted by the law?

CHAPTER 31

Calvin knew that it was risky, but he had to make the call. He needed an ally.

"Mr. Grant's office."

"Shawn Grant, please."

"Whom may I ask is calling?"

To convince that he was legit, he had to use his real name. Because of his special phone, he knew that it was safe.

"Tell Mr. Grant that Calvin Watters would like to speak with him."

Shawn Grant had just sat down at his desk when his secretary rang. As the new president and chairman of the board for the Greek, he had not wanted to be disturbed. He pressed the intercom button.

"Yes, Maureen?"

"Sir, a Mr. Watters is on line one."

Shawn froze, goose bumps springing on his arms. He only knew of one Mr. Watters—the man at the top of LVMPD's list of murder suspects for his father's investigation.

"Thank you, Maureen, patch him through." Shawn picked up the receiver. "This is Shawn Grant."

"Thank you for taking my call, Mr. Grant. This is Calvin Watters."

"How do I know you are really who you say you are?"

The caller gave a list of the collections he had made for Pitt and said, "I know you can't check them out right away, but you'll have to agree that only Pitt, who is dead, would also know them. If I were an imposter, I would know you wouldn't trust me after you discovered a mistake."

Shawn decided to hear him out. What did he have to lose? "That is a good start, Mr. Watters. Okay, you have me interested. Why call me?"

"First, I had nothing to do with your father's murder, or any of the other three murders."

"So you say."

"You have to trust me. I have a solid alibi for the night he was murdered, but I don't want to involve that person if I don't need to. I'd rather prove it by finding your father's real killer."

"And why should I trust the man who allegedly killed my father?"

"The same reason I'm trusting you right now. We both want to know the truth behind your father's murder and the rest of the unsolved ones. I have already started to investigate and I have some leads. If we work together, maybe we can uncover the truth."

Now Shawn was very interested. "So what do you want from me?"

"The way I see it, we both want something out of this arrangement. We both want to find your father's killer and I want to prove my innocence. Let's share information."

Shawn hesitated, contemplating the pros and cons of the proposal. He didn't know Calvin Watters and wasn't sure how far he could trust him. The man was accused of killing Shawn's father. He would have to tread in slow motion. But he knew he needed help in nailing Sanders. His father had always told Shawn that he was a natural-born deal maker.

"Fine. Let's trade information. If that goes well, then we can continue, but if not, then we stop immediately."

"Fair enough."

"What do you want to know about my dad?"

"What was your relationship like?"

He thought about his answer. "I loved him and he was my best friend. That is why we worked together for so long. He'd been showing me the ropes for the last fifteen years and preparing me my whole life to take over the family business. Nothing would have made my father prouder. It was perfect, until she came along."

"Who?"

"His wife." Again Shawn calculated his every word. "She's a greedy, money-hungry whore. The only reason she married my father was for his money."

"I knew that you and your father were close and I'm sorry for your loss. What I don't see is why your father married Linda?"

Shawn snorted. "Look at her. After being divorced for almost fifteen years from my mom, dad met Linda when we upgraded the casino entertainment. Linda was one of the dancers in the night show. He should have known and I tried to tell him. He told me that he had fallen in love the moment he saw her and they married right after that."

"Okay, but she's not the first beautiful woman who went after your dad, I expect. Did he want children with her?"

"Please. Linda would never do that to her body. It's her most prized possession. And my dad was too old to raise another child. But it was his choice to get married again and we never let her come between us. At least he finally saw through her."

"How is that?"

Shawn smiled. "He made her sign a prenup. In case of a divorce, she was only entitled to six percent of my father's estate and was automatically cut out of the will. She wasn't happy about that."

Money was always a motive in Vegas.

"As for my father's other enemies," Shawn added, without being asked, "as a collector, I know you understand who I mean." Shawn considered how much to say. How much could he trust Watters?

"Ace Sanders?" Watters asked.

Shawn's voice grew cold. "The hatred between them is well known. It's not often that Casino owners get along, but the heated feelings between those two were extreme. It was more than just business. It was personal. And now the bitch just made him my partner. I detest the man! I despise Linda, but I hate Sanders more. I'm going to try to get more information on him."

"Wait a minute, you said other enemies. Do you consider Linda an enemy?"

"What do you think, Mr. Watters? First she cheats on my dad with Sanders and then she sells him his casino."

"You knew about the affair?"

"I had my suspicions. Now I'm sure of it!"

"How are you so sure?"

"My dad told me."

"He knew too?"

"He had heard the rumors, so he hired a private investigator to follow Linda. The PI confirmed the affair and had the photos and documentation to prove it." Shawn knew the cops already had the pictures.

"What did your dad do?"

"He confronted Linda. Of course, she denied everything and claimed the photos were manufactured composites. What an idiot. My dad had expected the denial, but when Linda lied, despite all the evidence, he was amazed. Did she think he was a total fool? She used sex even at that point, but she must have been stupid not to see that he didn't buy the repentant loving wife."

"Why didn't your father just divorce her?"

"He tried." Shawn told Watters about his father's plans to file for divorce the morning after the night he was killed. He was also going to change his will but never had the chance to do it. Linda would have gotten nothing.

"Okay, so what do you have for me?" Shawn asked.

Watters explained the Pitt-Sanders business deals and gave his version of what he found at Pitt's murder scene. This interested Shawn and he wanted to find this so-called evidence.

If anything was discovered by either man, they would talk on a secure line. Otherwise, they each had plans about getting Sanders. They'd just have to try not to duplicate their efforts.

Calvin hung up, satisfied that the primary murder suspect had called the victim's son and offered and received help. He sensed that Shawn was thinking the same thing. Why had Grant agreed to join him without so much as a concerned argument? Calvin couldn't really relax his guard. Was Shawn laying a trap to get him out in the open for the cops?

He made another call. His mind kept picturing the news report of the bomb underneath his car. Was it Sanders tying up loose ends?

If anyone had seen anything at his apartment, it would be his neighbor.

Tim Whitney, an out-of-work actor, spent many days locked up in his tiny apartment awaiting a call from his agent. They had first met when he approached Calvin because he'd been studying a part as a street thug. Whitney was the only member of the complex who didn't have a problem with Calvin's occupation. Almost at once they hit it off and he was home enough to keep an eye on Calvin's apartment.

"Hello?"

"Tim, it's Calvin."

"Hey, I've been worried sick about you, man."

"How are you?"

"Don't worry about me. What about you?"

"I've been better."

"What's going on with the police?"

"I didn't kill anyone."

Whitney blew out his breath. "What are we going to do about this?"

"This isn't one of your movies. *We* are not going to do anything. I just called to ask you a couple of questions."

"What do you need, big man?"

"Have you seen anyone suspicious around there in the last couple of days?"

"Yeah, I saw him." Whitney's voice lowered.

"Who did you see?"

"A guy underneath your car."

The bomb. It had to have been the killer. "Did you tell the cops?"

Tim sighed. "I couldn't. I didn't know if the guy was working for you or what."

"What exactly do you remember?"

"Well, I saw him snooping around your apartment and thought that maybe he was a friend. He had a black canvas bag and went inside. When he came back out, he had changed into grease-stained coveralls, so I thought maybe he was your mechanic. He walked around your car, unlatched and lifted the hood. He studied the engine and parts, then checked both sides of the engine block. He pulled on various wires. After a few minutes, he slammed the hood down and shook his head. Then he crawled underneath the car."

"How long was he under the car?"

"Four or five minutes tops. Then he left."

Although he didn't know much about bomb detonation, Calvin thought four to five minutes to skillfully install a bomb under a car seemed professional.

"Do you remember what this guy looked like?"

"I watched from my window and tried to stay hidden, so I couldn't get a close-up of his face. But he was lean, all muscle and sinew, with long black hair. At one point, I thought that he had stared right at me. Like he knew that I was watching him."

"Any distinguishing features?" Calvin couldn't place the man, who would have stood out among Pitt's associates.

"Nothing I could see. He just looked like a normal guy. Until I saw him squirming underneath the car."

Calvin thanked Tim and hung up.

He called Mike and gave him the vague description. Mike said he might have enough to go on but Calvin knew he was pretending.

"Do you still have those vests I got you?" Mike asked.

"Yeah."

"Good, because you're gonna need them now."

CHAPTER 32

"Wakie, wakie, James." Scott sat with the serenity of a corpse, allowing his captive time to collect his thoughts.

He had stripped Pierce naked and sat him in the middle of the room straddling a chair, legs spread, his hands tied over his head, the rope secured to a ceiling beam and his ankles duct-taped to the chair legs. Duct tape also covered Pierce's mouth.

After his last conversation with Sanders, Scott knew that his time was running out. His reputation was on the line. He wasn't worried about Sanders' threat on his life, but if he failed again, he would not only be fired, but his two failures would be spread worldwide, damaging his perfect record.

"Sorry about the chloroform, James." He knew Pierce's head would be throbbing, not to mention Pierce's increased anxiety once he realized his predicament. "I didn't think I'd need it after you chugged those first two whisky sours at lunch. You made it easy for me. I can't blame you though. Most people are less alert to danger at work than they are at home. I've been reading over your file."

Scott held up a sheaf of papers. "Degenerates like you are creatures of habit. You just can't control yourself. Once I found your place of work, all I had to do was wait. I followed you for a couple of days and just my luck—you followed the same routine every day. You couldn't wait for lunchtime to get on the phone with your bookie and hit the nearest pub. I guess Watters' last message didn't get through."

Scott saw that the mention of Calvin Watters' name had sparked his prisoner. He watched the man's eyes wander around the vacated, gutted building to a crumpled body in the corner.

"Don't worry about him, James. His blood-brain barrier has been crossed by a shit load of heroin." He held up a syringe and tension band. Like a trained registered nurse, Scott pressed the plunger and liquid dripped from the needle. "He won't be bothering us." Scott looked around the room. "It's a shame they'll be demolishing this building in a few days. I was introduced to the site by a local friend. Pity really, it's the perfect location for my work."

Scott watched a rat scamper across the concrete floor, stop at Pierce's foot and then continue across, disappearing into a wall crevasse. Pierce's nostrils flared and his eyes leaked.

"Ignore the smell, James. Our friend has been living here for a while. No functioning toilet and no change of clothes."

Scott rose from his seat and approached Pierce. He circled the victim's limp body. "Do you know much about the Chinese culture, James? I do. I studied it." Scott returned to the table he'd been sitting at, slipped on a pair of rubber surgical gloves and opened a briefcase. "Did you know that at one time in China, they used castration for religious and social reasons? After battles, the winners castrated their captives to symbolize victory."

Urine pooled under Pierce's chair.

Scott picked up a tool from the briefcase. "This is called an emasculator. It's used on livestock, to simultaneously crush and cut the spermatic cord, but I thought, 'what the hell, if it's good enough for a horse, it's good enough for James.'"

He set the tool down. "From my estimation, you have twenty-one minutes before you're expected back at work." He smiled. "A lot can happen in that time. I'm going to ask you a series of questions. If I like your answers, you'll make your deadline. If I don't, then I'll show you how much I learned from the Chinese. All you have to do is blink once for yes and twice for no. Understand?"

Pierce not only blinked once, but also nodded.

"Good. Do you trust I'm a man of my word?"

With wide eyes, Pierce blinked once.

"Now, Calvin Watters. Do you know him?"

One blink.

"Do you know where he is?"

Pierce paused and Scott knew his hesitation meant he was about to conceal something or lie. Scott shook his head. What kind of hold did

Watters have on his victims? It was as if Pierce thought that ratting out Watters was worse than losing his manhood. Scott had to put no doubt in Pierce's mind that what he could do was far worse than any punishment Watters could inflict.

"Don't worry about Watters. Worry about me."

Scott shook his head and went back to the briefcase. He slowly removed the emasculator. He fastened the ends of the clamp over Pierce's testicles and locked it into place.

"Well." Scott smiled. "That fits nice and cozy."

Pierce flinched, probably more from discomfort than pain, but maybe also from the anticipation of the perceived future. Trickles of blood ran down the inside of Pierce's leg and beads of sweat dotted his forehead.

Scott gripped the handle of the tool and squeezed a little. Pierce squirmed but couldn't move.

"Again, do you know where Watters is?"

Low muffled sounds got past the duct tape and Pierce began to sob. He swallowed a large lump in his throat before blinking once.

Dale was still feeling the effects of his meeting with Flannery when he pulled into his empty driveway. He wasn't sure why he was home. It was as if the old cruiser had steered itself.

Actually, he did know why. There was something he wanted to do, something he needed to do. He'd been putting it off, hoping that if he didn't do it, if he didn't see the actual words, then it wouldn't be real— like it was just a horrible dream that he would soon wake up from.

But it was time.

Since his family had left, Dale tried to spend as much time at the office as possible, especially during the day when he'd notice the things he missed the most. It just wasn't right. No noise, no smell of home-cooked food and no toys scattered throughout.

For the first time since Betty's departure, Dale went into their bedroom. He lay on the bed and buried his face in her pillow, where her scent still lingered—lavender vanilla shampoo and coconut lime body wash.

He turned onto his back, propped his head up on two pillows and shoved his hand inside his jacket pocket, where Betty's letter had been for four days. He'd kept it there, close to his heart, refusing to read it, refusing to admit it was over. Now he was facing that fear head-on.

His name was written in black marker on the outside of the white envelope in Betty's handwriting.

Dale,

I hate impersonal letters like this, but for the last little while you haven't been around long enough for us to talk. I think we need some time apart. Sammy and I will be staying at Catherine's place until we figure things out.

We both know this isn't working. I knew who I was marrying. You're a cop and a great one, but you've changed over the years. Now that we have a son you need to adjust your priorities with work and family.

I want to say that your job is the only problem, but it's not...and we both know where I'm going. I know I said I'd gotten over your infidelity—that I had put it behind me and moved on. But the truth is that the thought still lingers. Every time you come home late, I wonder if you were with HER. I just can't live like this anymore.

I still love you and hope we can work this out. I want the Dale I fell in love with and married.

Love,

Betty and Sammie

Dale felt numb.

As he reread the note, he felt a sudden, crushing exhaustion and was brought to a complete halt. How tired he was from too many years on the job, the stress of work and his marital problems.

His throat tightened and he was having trouble breathing. Then Dale did something that he hadn't done in a long time. He cried.

He removed the snuff in his mouth and put it on the bedside table. He lay down and fell asleep, his head on Betty's pillow.

CHAPTER 33

From his conversation with Whitney, Calvin had at least a rough description of his follower, unless he'd already changed his appearance, and he began to watch the video monitors around his fortress all the time.

Did this guy have his own reasons for wanting to kill Calvin or had he been hired to take Calvin out?

Calvin knew the more networks he reached out to, the greater possibility of finding his opponent. So, with Rachel surfing the net, he decided to try Gene Lockhart, a forty-one-year-old bachelor with a gambling problem. Lockhart was also a pit boss at the Golden Horseshoe Casino and someone Calvin had grown to trust. He had collected from him years ago and could get him fired at any time. But Lockhart somehow had convinced him that he would get over his addiction and he had kept the secret. True to his word, Lockhart had been clean since. Lockhart had introduced Calvin and Rachel, so each man was indebted to one another, even though Calvin held all the real cards.

Lockhart knew the streets and had major contacts.

"What?" a sleepy voice barked into the phone.

"Geno, it's me."

"Cal? What do you need?"

Calvin knew the sound of his voice had roused his friend. "I need some answers."

"Sure. Is this about your *situation*?"

"Afraid so."

Both were silent a moment.

"I'll tell you anything you need to know, if I can."

"Great. I need some information on your boss."

"He's a popular guy lately."

"What do you mean?"

"Well, just the other day the police came by asking about Ace."

"About the Grant murder?" Calvin hadn't seen Sanders' name in any "suspect" report.

"Of course."

"What did you tell them?"

"Most of this crew is scared to death of Sanders and I know the execs and employees at the Midas are too."

Calvin sat back in his chair. Why had he thought he'd get information?

"But for *you*, I'll talk. I know you had nothin' to do with this and I owe ya."

He was back in business. "Thanks, Geno. I appreciate that. Now, talk to me. Tell me anything you've seen out of the ordinary or anything you might have overheard."

"Sanders is a very private businessman. He shares almost nothing with anyone. I know he was mixed up with Pitt. But you probably know that. Sanders was said to be sleeping around with Linda Grant, but that wouldn't be the first marriage he'd broken up. I wish I could help you more, Cal."

"This isn't anything I don't already know. I need to prove that someone else committed these murders, but so far, I can't do that. I need something to take to the cops."

Lockhart's voice changed. "I might not have proof, but I can tell you this. Sanders is evil and capable of killing."

"How do you know?"

"Nothing you can use. But remember I told you about that young couple we caught counting cards at the Black Jack table two years ago?"

"I remember."

"They'll never cheat again."

At least Calvin had his thought confirmed by a reliable source. He remained silent.

"Okay, there is one thing. You can't say who told you because I didn't tell the police. On the nights of Grant's and Pitt's murders, Sanders wasn't in his office. The first night I saw for myself that he was gone. On the night that Pitt was killed, same thing. But I could've sworn that I remember seeing his Ferrari parked in his private spot. I talked to my friend at the Midas and he told me that Sanders wasn't in his office there on either night."

Now Calvin knew that Sanders could make the entire staff at the Golden Horseshoe and the Midas lie to the cops. Next, he gave Lockhart the description of the hit man.

"Sorry, Cal, haven't seen anyone like that. I'll ask around and get back to ya."

"Thanks, Geno. That would be great."

The two men said goodbye.

Sanders could have done it and could have hushed everyone up.

Dale woke with red, swollen eyes, a rotten taste in his mouth and dried tobacco juice on his chin. He noticed juice stains on the collar of his dress shirt and changed into a new one.

As he tied his tie, the mirror showed him pronounced lines around his mouth and eyes for the first time.

Cops' wives walked out all the time, but how could he have missed seeing it coming?

He knew that his marriage had serious problems that he had not prioritized or tried to resolve with Betty. He had dedicated himself and almost all of his time to his job instead. Even so, he couldn't believe that it had come to this. He had just assumed that Betty would give him more time to work things out. He and his wife were now physically separated. The two people who mattered the most to him were hundreds of miles away.

Dale checked his watch. He had slept for almost two hours. Now Jimmy would wonder what kept him—and ask.

He went through the rooms and remembered the clothes and the other items they had taken. He felt like he was emptied, not just the house. But the nap had cleared his head a bit...at least enough to push forward. He'd feel better getting back to work.

His cell rang.

"Dayton."

"Dale, it's Jimmy. Where the hell are you, man?"

"At home."

"Somethin's come up. You better get your ass over here now. I'm on my way to pick you up."

Dale shut the phone off, finished tying his tie and hurried down the stairs.

It had been four and a half days since they'd left. That seemed to him enough time for Betty to collect her thoughts. Maybe she would be ready to talk.

He dialed Betty's cell phone number, but it went straight to voice mail. He'd try her sister Catherine.

"Hello."

"Hi, Catherine, it's Dale. Can I speak to Betty?"

He could hear his sister-in-law talking in the background before she came back on the line. "I'm sorry, Dale. Betty isn't ready yet. Maybe in a couple of days."

He appreciated the apologetic tone.

"Okay, thank you, Catherine. Please tell Betty I love and miss her. And give Sammie a big kiss and tell him the same."

"Goodbye, Dale."

He hung up and swiped away a tear. Maybe in two days, with a few lucky breaks, he could tell her he'd cracked both cases. No…that was why she'd left him, or at least part of the reason. What would he be able to say to Betty that she would care about?

Cops had good instincts and as a homicide detective, Dale had to use his intuition and deep understanding of the human psyche to help solve his crimes. He saw his job as a mission and he was a third-generation police officer. Law enforcement was his grandfather's calling, then his father's and now his. He'd been raised with those values.

He sat and thought. For the next few days, until it was time to try to reach Betty again, he would put his personal problems aside and focus solely on getting the job done. Later, he'd know what to do. He hoped.

He heard a honk and looked out the window to find Jimmy in the driveway. Dale checked the gun in his shoulder holster. He rinsed out his mouth, tossed his jacket over his shoulder and walked outside. As he approached the car, Jimmy yelled through the open window.

"You look like shit!"

Dale jumped into the passenger seat and did his best to tuck in his wrinkled shirt and straighten his uncombed hair.

Jimmy handed Dale a covered Styrofoam cup. "I thought you could use this."

"Thanks." He peeled off the lid, sipped and felt a little better. "What did you tell the Sarge?"

"I told him you were working the assignment. He was not impressed and wants to hear about some progress right now."

They walked through the crowded lobby and Dale saw a man in a well-cut suit with the sergeant.

As the detectives entered the office, the mayor turned to them. Another visit meant increased urgency and pressure.

"What do you have now?"

Dale knew that the mayor had a minor background in law

enforcement, so he realized that Grant's murder was scary enough, but when cops were also being murdered, it was even worse—especially with possibly two killers hunting people in the city.

"We have some leads," Dale said. "There's a lot of circumstantial evidence to follow."

"What about this Watters character? The sergeant says that Watters has probably already left the city, maybe even the state and country, while you two go around chasing theories."

"We are following Watters as well as we can, but as you say, he might have fled. We are focusing on those who are here and profited from those deaths. My team is totally dedicated and focused."

What he wanted to say was that Sanders was his prime suspect and they should be concentrating on him.

"Listen," the mayor said in earnest. "I want these cases closed. Pick up Watters, connect him to the murders and find the cop killer. And do it now."

The detectives were silent again. Dale looked at his sergeant, who nodded.

Then the mayor changed his demeanor. "Detective Dayton, whatever you need to help with these investigations is available. Manpower, money—whatever resources you need. I'll make sure you have it at your disposal. I have talked to the lieutenant about this and he has assured me that everything possible will be done to bring down the killers. You name it, Detective and it's yours."

"Yes, sir," Dale and Jimmy said at the same time.

"Go get our killers, gentlemen."

The sergeant escorted the two detectives out. As they left the office, he whispered. "Do whatever it takes."

CHAPTER 34

Calvin sat in his computer room eating Chinese noodles from a Styrofoam container when movement at the corner of the monitor grabbed his attention. The long black hair that had flashed by the screen sent chills through Calvin's body. His gut clenched.

He quickly sat upright and placed the container on the desk beside the monitor. He grabbed the remote and maneuvered the joystick, zooming in from another angle. The man was at a distance and somewhat hidden. Any other time, Calvin wouldn't have warranted a second glance. But Whitney's description and the man's actions—continuing to move, circling out wide and returning at irregular intervals from different angles—showed Calvin the man was scoping the place.

He studied the image on the screen. The hit man was less careful than he should have been. So he didn't know about the camera and thought he was too far away for detection.

All the cameras were set to record in a continued cycle until Calvin changed the digital hard drives. Depending on the hit man's location, distance, speed and angle of movement, at least one and sometimes two or three cameras were recording different views.

Then, as if understanding he was being watched, the hit man moved away in haste, turning from the house and starting to walk down the street, avoiding all of the hidden camera lenses.

Calvin dropped what he was doing. He opened the closet and pulled the larger of the two Kevlar vests out, slipping it on over his upper body.

"Rachel, come on."

"Where are we going?"

He ignored her question and grabbed her by the arm. He pulled out his Harrington & Richardson .32 revolver, the smallest weapon he owned, and raced to the back entrance.

"Make sure to lock up from the inside when I leave."

"Don't go, Calvin." She held his arm.

"I'll be right back. Don't forget the secret knock."

He turned before she said another word. He heard Rachel locking up again from the inside. She'd only open for his knock.

His knee was starting to throb, but Calvin caught up with the assassin and followed him on foot through the streets of Vegas.

It had taken Scott only six minutes to spot Watters and realize that the man had somehow identified him and was coming after him. He could play the hunter being hunted for a few minutes until he led Watters somewhere convenient to finish him.

He used the busy Vegas streets and shop windows as mirrors to position himself for a clear shot. He didn't know the streets as well as his adversary, but Scott had years of killing experience to his advantage.

They ducked and dodged inside buildings, crossed back streets and took shortcuts through backyards. The quiet, unoccupied side streets with abandoned buildings were the perfect locations for a pursuit.

But they had been waltzing for a half hour and neither was able to get a clean shot without risk of being exposed to the other.

This was Watters' turf and some street people might even be watching out for him. Best to retreat and finish the job tomorrow.

At the next corner, Scott turned and started running at top speed, twisting, dodging, changing sides of the streets, turning one corner, then another, making a full circle, then breaking away in a new direction. He knew about Watters' weak knee. Maybe with the sudden change in speed, he could break free.

When he was satisfied he'd lost Watters, he took the service entrance into the hotel and rode the elevator to his suite. He swiped his card to unlock his door and went to the bathroom, shedding his soaked shirt, cursing the whole way, before using a towel to wipe his sweaty face and body. He returned to the bedroom, threw the towel against the wall and without hesitation studied Watters' dossier again.

Watters was a formidable adversary. Not many of Scott's targets could find him, let alone pursue him for a half hour and survive. He was going to like this game—almost as good as taking out an FBI agent.

He wouldn't underestimate Watters again.

Watters had to have spotted him by using cameras at his safe-house.

But killing him at close quarters would be tricky.

Scott knew just what he would do.

Calvin had tried to keep up with the hit man when he started running, but his knee forced him to quit the chase long before he was satisfied he knew how his opponent thought and thereby how to fight him.

It tore him apart inside to watch the hit man disappear. Uncatchable. Untraceable. At least for tonight. Calvin took small comfort in having twice eluded the hit man and some pride in keeping their deadly match even, for now. The impasse was short-lived.

The only difference in the two men's ideas was that Calvin didn't want the man dead. He needed answers.

But this was a true pro and he'd had years of practice. Calvin would be killed and Rachel too if he didn't think of something very clever, very soon.

He got back to his fortress tired, his knee swollen and aching, but he appreciated that his years of hard work staying physically fit had saved his life tonight. He had endured hunting and being hunted and knew that he had given his assassin an impressive battle.

He used the special knock and Rachel opened the door. Her eyes were red and swollen.

"What happened?" He rushed inside and locked the door behind him.

Rachel turned without saying a word and walked into the next room. Calvin could hear her quiet sobs as she distanced herself. He hobbled after her and spun her around.

"Rachel, what is it? What's wrong?"

She held a Kleenex to her nose and mouth and choked out words through the sniffling and sobs. "I didn't know if you were coming back."

Calvin's shoulders relaxed and he let out a breath. He wrapped his arms around her and squeezed.

Rachel shoved him away. "Don't, Calvin. You can't just leave like that without telling me where you're going. I was worried. I was scared."

He could see this wasn't the same woman who had snuck out to talk with her friends just last night. With each minute that passed, with them trapped in this hideout, with each news report about another murder and now the face of a man who was stalking their house, this situation became real and Rachel was finally seeing the big picture. This was serious.

He didn't know what to say. A slight smile crossed his face.

"This isn't funny, Calvin."

Again she turned and walked away, entering their sleeping quarters.

He chased her. "I know. I'm sorry. I've just never seen you worried about me before. It kind of feels good."

Without a word, she sat down on the edge of the cot, staring into dead air. He sat down beside her and again put his arms around her. He could feel her rapid heartbeat pounding against his body. She didn't push away this time. Instead, she nestled her head against his chest.

"I'm scared."

"I know, baby. I won't let anything happen to you."

"But what if something happens to you? What will I do?"

"That won't happen."

She stood up. "You can't guarantee that."

He got up too. "Nothing is a guarantee in life, Rachel. But you have to trust me."

"You know I trust you, Calvin. We have a history. We share secrets—secrets that could someday haunt us. I don't like the violence in your life. I've seen too much of it. But I've seen the good in you and I want to help you change. You promised our lives would change."

"I did make that promise and I intend on keeping it, Rachel. We just have to get through this together. We have to stick together."

He smiled at her and she returned it. He hugged her and kissed her gently on the lips.

"Now let's go see what we're up against."

She followed behind as he went to his computer to scan the surveillance camera monitors for details of the killer's face, body type and style of movement. He cross-referenced the pictures against a database of assassins. When nothing came up, Calvin sat back in frustration.

"Is that the man after us?" She pointed at the screen.

He nodded.

Calvin zoomed in on the suspect. The man wore pants and a long shirt, with no distinguishing features visible. Calvin back-tracked the footage and watched the thirty-second clip from the beginning.

From what he'd seen, his opponent was skilled in tactics and an expert in pursuit, surveillance and evasion. Calvin knew such skills were acquired in the elite military, specifically the Marines or maybe Special Forces.

Add that in with the bomb skills and the tracking ability and Calvin came to a scary conclusion. This guy was trained by the best. Calvin could use that particular training against him. Time for some very serious, highest-level hacking.

He hacked a military database, but after the second layer of protection, he was shut out.

He had a hunch. He called Mike and asked him to hack the Marine Sniper School records. Then he emailed Mike the photos from the surveillance cameras taken today.

Less than two hours later Calvin received an e-mail from Mike. The attached document was a full file on the killer. A high-ranking NCO sniper gone bad named Baxter had been charged with a mob hit, but not convicted. That was who was after him. Now Calvin and Rachel were pinned down for sure. Baxter would have his rifle and scope on the building within hours.

Mike wrote two words in the body of the email. "Fuck me."

At midnight, Ace was still at the Golden Horseshoe office, a rare event, but he was going nuts. His perfect plan was showing signs of weakness. The assassin wasn't late calling in, but Ace was on edge all the same.

At his last check-in, Scott said he had found Watters and that the job would be done without delay. But that was four hours ago and Ace's sources at the police hadn't heard anything.

The phone rang.

"You better have some good news."

"Afraid not, boss."

The hit man told him he had played cat and mouse with Watters for a half-hour. Ace listened, his head throbbing harder, as his overpaid hit man recounted his failed attempt.

He had had enough. These failures had gone on too long. But before he could tell Scott that, the hit man said, "I have an idea."

"Forget it. I'm pulling you off. I'll find someone else, someone more reliable. You will never work in this country again."

"No, don't. Now I know where Watters is and I've scoped the area."

"How did you find him," Ace demanded to know.

"One of Watters' clients held a grudge. After his run-in with Watters, he'd followed the collector for days until he'd found the location."

Ace nodded.

"Tomorrow is the end. And you'd need a day at least to bring someone new in. So what do you have to lose?"

Everything, Ace thought. He didn't like it, but the assassin was right. He needed Watters eliminated *now*.

"Call when it's done."

CHAPTER 35

It was early Saturday morning and Dale sat at his desk.

His group was busy living and breathing the investigation, reviewing crime scene photos, witness interviews, 911 calls and forensic, ballistic and post-mortem reports. This case had everyone on edge. The longer it went unsolved, the more challenging it would be to find the real killer or killers. Dale was still not sure if the killers were working together in some way, but it was a very real possibility, given that one killer had killed Watters' boss and another or the same one was trying to kill Watters.

His head ached from frustration and his eyes burned from fatigue. He knew that basically they still had nothing solid. He hadn't expected that after the three perfect murders, there'd be one more and that the second killer had also left no evidence at all.

Feeling desperate, he pulled the most powerful magnifying glass out of a drawer and used it to study the pictures from the four murders.

Watters had some answers. But he was still not located after three days of searching.

Jimmy, who was usually upbeat, looked grim. He ambled across the room and slumped down in a seat. Loosening his tie, he removed his outer jacket, unfastened his shoulder holster and flung it over the back of the chair.

Dale put away the magnifying glass and dropped the crime scene photos, grabbing the folder titled, "Grant, Douglas—Crime Scene Analysis Report." He read through the information one more time and threw the folder down, papers scattering onto the floor. He spun around in his seat and faced the bulletin board beside his desk.

Brought in for the Grant case, photographs of suspects, evidence, crime scenes and theories had been stapled across the board. With the addition of one new murder, the papers had grown and overlapped each other.

Four perfect murders. So far. That was the hope that Dale clung too—that they were only temporarily perfect and that at some point they'd find something that would actually start cracking one or more of the cases and make them less than perfect.

Paperwork was a part of the investigation that most cops hated. But everyone knew that many investigations had been cracked by one tiny, overlooked detail.

"Where would you find a bomb expert, Jimmy?"

"Military, or a police bomb squad."

Dale stared at the board, though by now he had almost memorized it. "What do you think?"

His partner dropped his paperwork and sighed. "I have nothing."

"Hey, Tommy!" Dale yelled. "Who'd you talk to in New Orleans?"

The man rummaged through his desk before answering. "Detective Hopkins."

"You got a number?"

The cop scurried over and handed Dale a crumpled piece of paper with scribbled handwriting.

Dale made the call, hoping the New Orleans detective kept the same pathetic hours he did. He made his request and was transferred to the homicide department.

"Detective Hopkins." A hoarse voice, all business, came on the phone.

"This is Detective Dale Dayton of the Las Vegas Metropolitan Police Department."

"Ah, I was just going to call you."

"Do you have something for me?"

"That's the thing. After your officer's call, we went down to the docks and dusted the entire booth, inside and out. The phone booth had been wiped down and cleaned by a professional. We couldn't pull one print from the site."

Dale wasn't surprised.

The New Orleans detective continued. "We kept a camera on for two days—no connection to anyone you named."

Dale shook his head. "Thank you, Detective."

He leaned back in the chair and stared at the papers on the desk. Was there anything among this collection that would indicate a path to follow?

Another file was thrown on his desk, this time by an LVMPD intern. "Detective, we got an ID on the prostitute from Pitt's office. Carey Reynolds, nineteen years old, from Bay City, Texas. Guess her picture on the news caught a tip. We're doing a background, but so far nothing in her past suggests she was the intended target."

Dale nodded. "I didn't think she was."

Calvin sat in silence, reviewing every feed. There was nothing he could see that might affect him, but somewhere Baxter was staking out the house and preparing his next move.

Baxter would set up a sniper site beyond the range of Calvin's monitors.

Calvin had left his fortress once when he'd spotted the assassin. He and Rachel weren't leaving again. A Kevlar vest was no protection against a head shot. What the killer didn't know, though, was that Calvin could outwait him. He and Rachel could live without fear, if not in comfort, for a couple of months with their supplies. The killer couldn't risk exposure and arrest that long.

At some point, even two months from now, Calvin would have to emerge or have no life at all. Once Calvin did, he would put himself and Rachel in double jeopardy. The police were still searching for him as the primary suspect in Grant's and perhaps Pitt's murder. And if the cops didn't get Calvin first, he'd always know that the killer would pick up the hunt again until the bastard finally succeeded in killing him..

Did Calvin really want to live looking over his shoulder?

He was in the most challenging, problematic and deadliest position of his life and he had no plan yet. Somehow, he was going to have to figure out a way to end this impasse safely. Capture the killer without leaving the workshop and risking their lives, or be arrested by the cops. It seemed impossible, but he had the confidence of experience. Except for the prideful mistake that had permanently damaged his knee, he knew that it was at times like this, when the stakes and challenges were the greatest, that he was capable of fully focusing.

Before, it had been only about him. Now he had to protect the only woman he had ever loved since his mother and that increased the complexity of the situation enormously. He could never again leave Rachel alone as he had when pursuing the killer. Right now, it was a siege and a stalemate and the clock was ticking.

He left the computer room and went to the most secure part of the safe house, where they kept the cots and air mattresses. Rachel was sleeping. He watched her dream and breathe, deep and slow. A little tremor and cry left her at one point. Calvin thought it was more than a bad dream. He had to focus and finish a plan.

Two hours later, Calvin sat up. He needed to do some final prep, but otherwise he was ready to act and not alone. The irony of whom he'd chosen as a partner made him chuckle. It was his only choice.

He dialed. It took over two minutes for his call to be transferred. He waited patiently, knowing that this call was probably causing all sorts of chaos.

"Detective Dayton."

"I'm Calvin Watters. I'm sure you have your technical people trying to trace this call. Don't waste your time or theirs. My phone is untraceable."

He heard fingers snapping in the background. Dayton would continue trying a trace, because Calvin knew he had no reason to believe him.

"If you are who you say you are, then you know how hard we're looking for you. Why should I believe you?"

He told Dayton, in exact detail, the Pitt crime scene and gave details about what he earned as a leg breaker. It was much more than he needed to say to prove his identity and enough to show the extent to which he would cooperate.

When he finished, Dayton replied. "I believe you are Calvin Watters. So why are you calling me? I doubt you are ready to turn yourself in."

"Should I?" Calvin asked with a smile.

"If you're innocent, yes."

"Do you think I am?"

"Mr. Watters, you have no reason to believe me, but I'm the only person in this department who thinks you are."

That wasn't the response he expected. His intelligence and years of bill collecting had made him almost a human lie detector. Dayton's tone and words sounded like the sincere truth. "How can I know that's really what you think?"

"To be honest, there's no way I can prove that. Only you can decide whether you can trust me or not. From the beginning, you've always been at the bottom of my list of suspects for Grant's murder, even while you're at the top of everyone else's."

"Dayton, for now, I'm going to take you at your word, as you're going to have to take me on mine. I had nothing to do with Grant's murder or any of the others—especially not your dead fellow officer. There's a lot I've done that I'm not proud of, but I'm no killer. And I'm without doubt not stupid enough to blow up my own car and commit suicide. Everyone who knows me knows that I'm the only one who drives my wreck of a car. That means the bomb was meant for me and whoever wants me dead is the same person who killed that cop."

"Maybe so. If you're innocent, come in and prove it. You'll have nothing to worry about."

"I'm an African-American former football star who can be shown to have gone bad. Even if I had rock-solid proof of innocence, which I don't, things wouldn't go my way in court. This isn't OJ all over again."

Dayton laughed. "Okay, point taken. But if you don't want to negotiate surrender, why call?"

"Look, we both want the same thing. Capturing the assassin and removing that death threat is my current number-one priority. I believe that same assassin killed your police officer. So the Vegas Police want to capture and arrest the killer as much as I do. I've done my homework on you, Dayton."

"Ah, classic military principle—know your enemy," Dayton said.

"Are you my enemy?"

"I've already said I believe you're innocent. So where do we go from here? Do you have any evidence or information about Grant's real killer, or who is trying to kill you, if it's a different person?"

"Like you, I have suspicions but no proof about who murdered Grant, Pitt and the prostitute. But I do have some solid information about who's trying to kill me. All I'll say now is that I don't think the person after me is the same person who committed the first three murders, but the two killings may still be connected. If that's true, then capturing and arresting the hit man may lead you to the real Grant killer."

Now it was the detective's turn to stop and think. Calvin was sure that his call had caught him totally unprepared.

"You've given me a lot. I'd appreciate it if you gave me a minute to think about where we are now."

"Take your time," Calvin said.

Dale was thinking as fast as he could to catch up and think ahead.

Watters was desperate.

He could see that the hit man was a bigger threat to Watters than the police. That was understandable self-interest. If Watters did have information about the hit man, he was offering something valuable. What did he want in exchange?

Could he trust Watters? Only to the same point that Watters trusted him, assuming that Watters believed what Dale had said about his innocence.

While he was thinking, one of the phone techs confirmed that the call was untraceable and unrecordable. Now Dale knew just how much trouble it was going to be to bring in Watters.

They had the same goal, even if their motives were different.

He got back on the phone. "Okay, you got my attention. I'm ready to deal. What do you want from me, from us, in exchange for your information about the hit man?"

The call had now gone on for four minutes.

"I've been following the investigations, so I know how little you have. You need me to help you solve this—no offense intended."

"One thing at a time. What's your plan?"

Watters explained it. Dale thought it had a good probability of success, but it risked lives, reputations and careers. The usual.

When Watters finished, Dale said, "I'm going to talk to a few members of my team, the ones who have balls and who I trust. Then I'll see if the bosses will fine me if it fails." Dale paused, then continued. "No, scratch that. I know they would. So screw them. Anyway, call me in an hour and I'll tell you if it's a go."

"Fine." Watters hung up.

Book Five: Collision Course

CHAPTER 36

At exactly 3:00 p.m. the phone rang. Dale and Jimmy, with the sergeant standing in the background, answered separate phones. "Hello?"

"It's me," Watters said.

Dale licked his lips nervously. "Okay, we'll do it."

"You are sure you can do your part?" There was doubt in Watters' voice.

"Watters, don't fuck with me. You need this and so do I, so what choice do you really have? Is someone else going to help you, or do I sit back and let them catch you?"

Watters was silent.

"We've held up our end by agreeing to do it your way," Dale said. "There's still a warrant out for your arrest and I can't get it overturned just yet. But my boss has agreed to give us some leeway and time to execute the plan. Now I need something from you."

"I'll help. But I want something in return."

Dale signaled to the sergeant to pick up another phone and listen in. "What do you want?"

"When this is over, you'll owe me. I don't trust witness protection programs, but you can do a couple of things to get me started on a new life."

Dale turned to the sergeant, who nodded. "Okay."

"Good," Watters said. "Now for what you want to know. Earlier this year, Pitt told me that Sanders had put a substantial bid in for Doug Grant's casino. He declined the offer, which infuriated Sanders. It's my belief that Sanders' greed led him to commit these murders."

"Lots of people can see that scenario, but what's your proof? If you don't have it, there's no real deal here for us."

"Not yet, but I know how to get it."

"How?"

"I also know who killed your officer."

"What?" Dale looked at Jimmy.

"His name is Derek Baxter. He's an ex-Marine. He had to have been hired by Sanders."

"What's the proof?"

"Find Baxter. He'll talk."

Watters told them about the hit man following him and what he thought the sniper's next move would be. Dale listened quietly, not liking the situation one bit.

"Okay," Dale said. "This sounds possible. But I'm not happy. A lot of it is guesswork. You think I should protect you from everyone after your hide because of a guess and an internet search?"

"Detective, how many assassins have you caught in Vegas? How many murders-for-hire have there been in the last ten years, would you say? The newspapers suggest ten or twelve."

"So, smartass, how can we get this guy out into the open?"

They went over details for almost twenty minutes.

When they had hammered out the finer points, Dale said, "Okay. Send his photo and all you have on Baxter."

"Done. One last thing. I need Rachel out of the house."

"The girl's with you?" Dale wasn't really surprised though.

"Yes. I know how we can get her out before Baxter moves in."

Dale agreed.

When he hung up, Jimmy spoke. "I agree Watters is smart, but Baxter is a professional killer and is going to drop him."

"Probably so. Do you have a better plan?" He was getting tired of everyone else's plan—kill Watters and put all the killings on him or try Watters and do the same thing. Jimmy was his old friend, but no saint about justice.

The fax spit out Baxter's picture and the plan of Watters' fortress, including the location of booby traps.

Dale looked at Jimmy. "Call in Parker, Duncan, Smith and Ramirez so we can set it up. In your spare time, try to explain why a guilty killer would give all his best secrets and defenses away? Maybe we have a super-genius here and it is all a crazy trap. But I'm pretty smart too and when you're not lazy or hanging out with street sleaze, so are you."

CHAPTER 37

Clouds dark and heavy with rain poured down on Vegas that evening.

Calvin popped a couple of painkillers. Not a full dose, just enough to reduce the pain. He felt as if he were back in college with pre-game jitters. He started to enjoy the ride from the most powerful drug in the world—adrenaline.

He looked for Baxter on the quiet, unmoving monitor. Out there lurked a high-powered scope set for him and Rachel. Calvin got up to choose his weapons.

He pushed the computer desk against the wall, rolled up the area carpet and grabbed a round metal pin that lifted a trap door.

He followed the stairs into the damp, dark bomb shelter. On one side, there was enough canned food for several months. On the other, an arsenal.

He took down an armful of various weapons and then went to conceal them around his fortress. Then, he got the call.

"Yeah," he answered.

"Everyone's in place. Good luck, kid."

Calvin hung up and checked the monitors again. Silence. Nothing. Although he couldn't see Baxter, he could feel the ex-Marine's presence. Calvin heard Rachel's footsteps behind him. "Are you ready?" he asked.

She gave him a slight, timid nod.

In what felt like a trance, he moved to the emergency generator and switched the power off to the entire house, except for the computer room. Total blackness fell.

Calvin and Rachel moved to the garage.

Baxter had circled the house, rejected the back exit as too obvious and then taken a position on the roof of a building down the street. He had a view of the front right side of Watters' hideout, where he had a shot at anyone emerging from about three quarters of the house. This was his third position in the last forty-five minutes.

He had a 7.62 x 51mm M40 resting on a tripod and was blacked out against the tar and gravel of the roof. He would be hard to spot from another rooftop, let alone a helicopter. A military black-camouflage tarp covered him and was little help against the increasing rain, the drops smacking loudly against the vinyl.

The intensity of the moment took him back to his days in Afghanistan.

As he waited, he replayed the last conversation with his employer. Sanders had nerve. Baxter thought about just killing Sanders for a moment, but decided that was a bad option. Someone else might talk. No, that would ruin his rep.

He put on the thermal-imaging nightscope and was chambering a new round when he heard the first faint wails from police sirens. A row of patrol cars approached Watters' house from both directions and stopped. With the road barricaded by the diagonally parked cars, six officers stood behind the vehicles with their weapons drawn.

Had Sanders decided to use the cops and double-cross him?

If Watters slowed the cops down, or even somehow managed to get away, Baxter would attempt a head shot. Most likely he'd get another one when the cops led Watters out in cuffs.

The shooting started. Glass shattered in the house and cops ducked behind their open cruiser doors as Watters returned fire. As two cops approached the house, a series of bombs detonated. Concrete and metal flew around the neighborhood. The explosions sent the cops scurrying for cover.

Perfect—with this much happening, he could take Watters out and then vanish, unnoticed.

Then he saw something that gave him pause.

A group of cops circled the back of the building and disappeared.

More gunfire ensued. Then quiet. Either Watters was in cuffs or dead.

Baxter couldn't believe when four cops ran from the building, got into cars and rocketed away. They were already gone before Baxter realized that only three cops had gone in.

He had to move. The police had underestimated Watters' security and he didn't have much time before the LVMPD would return with a much larger force, perhaps even SWAT.

He couldn't allow a second raid to happen and Watters get caught. Baxter's job was to kill Watters, period.

That time had come.

"The hit man we are up against seems to be slipping a little," Dale said to Jimmy.

Watters was informed that Rachel was out.

Dale said, "Easy part done. Now, capture a killer, keep a suspected killer alive and hope that a Vegas leg breaker is not setting us up."

He rotated the knots out of his neck and surveyed the area. "Make sure everyone removes their blanks and loads live ammo."

Jimmy made the call.

The observation point was the parked car a block from Watters' workshop. The entire workshop and surrounding area had been under long-distance police surveillance, outside the sniper's perceived area of operations, so he wouldn't detect them. The whole team was sitting on Dale's "go."

"Let's move," he said.

"But we haven't spotted Baxter yet," Jimmy said.

Dale knew Baxter had a plan. But what was it? "I know and I don't like it. Let's proceed with caution, but remain out of sight. Gradually tighten our surveillance circle."

"If we move, Baxter will see us."

He slammed his fist against the dashboard. "Okay, let's wait. But the first sign of Baxter and we're gone."

Dale felt a sharp pain in his chest when the radio squawked again.

"Target B located and identified," came over the radio.

Jimmy smiled. "Baxter's taking the bait."

Dale opened his cell phone and grabbed the door handle when the same voice returned. "We lost him."

"What?" He grabbed the radio. "Team leader, repeat."

"Baxter has disappeared, sir."

Dale looked at Jimmy, who rolled his eyes.

"Baxter has breached the perimeter. They can't see anything through the rain, Dale."

"Bullshit! Baxter is not a ghost."

"No, he's just good at that part." Jimmy hesitated before adding,

"You need to make a decision."

"I know." He checked his gun. "Do we go in and blow our cover, or do we wait and put Watters' life at risk? Check your weapon. Baxter is not going to give himself up."

Calvin could at least exhale when Rachel was driven away and her safety was confirmed. He hadn't heard from Dayton, who was supposed to call when Baxter had been spotted. He'd seen no sign of the killer through his monitors until a motion sensor picked up movement.

He knew Baxter was coming.

He shut off the computer monitor in case the light gave him away. Then he slipped on night-vision goggles and positioned himself behind the computer room door. The door was slotted so he could shoot outward, but low enough to make an incoming shot difficult.

He heard the click of the side door and Baxter stepped through the doorway, equipped with a Beretta 92FS Compact M and night goggles.

Calvin waited as Baxter neared, not risking a shot. He only wanted to disable with a shot to the leg.

When Baxter was within range, Calvin clicked back and aimed low. As he went to pull the trigger, his two-way radio said, "Baxter is in the house!"

Calvin looked down for half a second and consecutive, multiple shots ricocheted off the front of the door, one through the narrow metal slot. One inch to the left and Calvin's head would have exploded.

When he peeked back through the slot, Baxter was gone.

This killer was good and Calvin only had a few minutes before the cops rushed the house.

Now Baxter knew this was a trap. He'd be waiting to pick off cops and escape. It would be a firing zone.

Calvin had to get Baxter first and his odds were low. He grabbed his .45 and checked the single action to make sure he had all eight rounds. Easing open the door, he poked his gun and head through the doorway, slipped in and sidestepped his way through the front room. He heard footsteps upstairs.

He took the steps one at a time, thankful the old, worn-down floorboards didn't creak. When he reached the top and stuck his head up over the last step, two bullets flew past and smashed the wall.

He couldn't risk a wild, blind shot that might kill Baxter. Calvin had to evade him until that one perfect shot.

With a deep breath, he launched himself off the top step and into the next room. Three more bullets hit the wall beside him as he dove head first, arms extended to break his fall.

Calvin had counted eight shots fired by Baxter. Chances were he had to reload his Beretta or at least pull a second weapon. That meant seconds to reach him.

Calvin stayed along the floor, crawling the hallway. When he reached the end, he rose and leaned against the wall outside the room where the bullets had come from. He couldn't hear anything, only his own heavy breathing.

He pivoted and extended his arm into the room. As he inched inside, he was too late to spot Baxter, who kicked Calvin's arm and jolted his weapon to the floor.

Before Calvin could react, Baxter caught him flush on the jaw with hard metal, dislodging the goggles. Calvin was stunned for a moment, but he was able to shake that off before receiving another blow from the butt of Baxter's pistol to the bridge of his nose. He instinctively reached for his nose as his eyes watered.

The taste of warm, metallic blood brought him back to his football days. Adrenaline kicked in—no thinking. He heard a new clip snap into the gun pointed at his head.

From the dark, he heard, "Goodbye, Calvin Watters."

But Calvin swung his body. The bullet hit his right shoulder, where the sleeveless bulletproof vest did not cover, and pain erupted. He rolled into Baxter, dropping the hit man to the floor. Calvin gritted his teeth, got into a three-point stance and exploded off his feet, barreling into Baxter's midsection.

He heard the gun hit the floor, followed by Baxter's night goggles. Now both men were blind. Feeling in the dark, Calvin landed a solid punch to Baxter's throat and the two men wrestled.

Baxter went after Calvin's bad knee with a swinging kick but missed.

Then the lights to the entire workshop came on.

For the first time they looked at each other and both saw their guns at the same time. Both men dove for their weapon.

Calvin, half a second faster, aimed and fired. The bullet hit with precision where he had wanted it to—mid-upper thigh—but hit a major artery and exploded, blowing Baxter's leg off at the femur bone. Enormous clumps of thigh, blood and tissue hit the walls, ceiling and floor. Baxter fell to the floor, grabbing at the open wound and screaming. But he still attempted to crawl to his weapon.

Calvin rose to his feet and kicked the weapon away. Baxter stopped squirming and rolled onto his back, staring up into Calvin's eyes.

Blood leaked from Baxter's cut lip when he spoke. "Finish it!" He said, barely audible from the blood and spit in his mouth.

Baxter rose into a one-knee seated position, moving toward the weapon that hung at Calvin's side. Baxter pressed his head into the muzzle of the gun.

"Hold the gun like a man!"

Calvin nudged the gun against Baxter's temple. He struggled to stay conscious from the mind-numbing pain. His eyes burned, his nose stung and his shoulder throbbed.

Then he heard a voice.

CHAPTER 38

"The bullet was a clean in and out."

Dale was jolted awake by a soft hand shaking his shoulder. He had fallen asleep in an awkward position, scrunched up, legs hanging over the arm of an open-armed, fully upholstered hospital chair bolted to the floor. A nurse stood over him, holding a clipboard to sign. The Las Vegas cops were picking up Watters' medical expenses—somehow. There would have to be some accounting magic for that one.

"No problems?"

"Nope."

Dale got up and wiped sleep from his eyes. He took the pen and signed on the dotted line.

"Is he awake?"

"Room 314."

He headed down the hall. He paused outside room 314 and stretched, his back muscles were in a tight ball. He opened his cell phone.

"Jimmy, Watters is awake."

"Did you talk to him?"

"Not yet, I'm just going in now."

"I've been thinking about this all night. Do you think we did the right thing?"

"I don't know. I understood Watters' logic. He got us Baxter. We would have caught him sooner or later, but Watters took a lot of chances, even if he had his own interests in mind."

"Okay. But he's still a leg breaker too, somebody who has got to enjoy that work. Don't forget that," said Jimmy.

"Where are you now?"

"I'm just leaving the house. Tina cooked me Sunday breakfast."

"I'll meet you back at the office."

"What about Rachel?"

"Tell her Watters is okay. But I think we should keep her where she is. There's no telling what the pushback might be now that we have Baxter in custody. Whoever hired him could counterattack. She's safe where she is."

Dale hung up.

He stood outside and looked through the small glass-paned section of the door at Watters lying in the hospital bed. He saw the face of a hero and was all the more grateful that Watters had survived. He hoped that Watters could see some of Dale's admiration, because saying directly what he thought and felt would only embarrass the man.

He knew, from what Watters had told him, that he was an expert marksman, but he also knew that Watters had never shot at anything but paper targets.

In case someone was looking for Baxter, Dale used false names and told the medical staff at the ER to keep Watters' and Baxter's admissions quiet.

After a light rap on the door, he stepped inside. The fetid smell of sanitizer and unwashed bed sheets greeted Dale. Watters' head had been propped up on two pillows, but his eyes weren't all the way open.

"Detective Dayton, I recognize you from the Vegas website."

"Calvin Watters." Dale smiled. "The man with the plan."

They shook hands.

"How long have I been out?"

"Just the night." Dale pulled a chair close to the bed. "How do you feel?"

"Like I got hit by a bus. How's Rachel?"

"She's in a safe house, like we agreed. When you feel up to it, I'll bring her in, but I don't think the timing is right, yet."

Watters nodded.

"You scared the hell out of us, Calvin. When we heard the gunshots, we took off in a sprint. I'm glad you had given us the layout of the workshop so I knew where to find the generator, but when you weren't in the computer room, I thought the worst. When we found you upstairs, it looked like World War III. We were lucky Baxter didn't die, even with the tourniquet I put on. Thank God we had the paramedics on standby."

"Thanks for staying by my side. You weren't the only one scared."

"You're in better shape than Baxter."

"How is he?"

"He's alive. I don't suppose there's too much work for a one-legged assassin."

Watters grimaced. "Sorry, I wanted him in better shape to stand trial."

"Don't be sorry. You did what you had to do." After a few minutes of awkward silence, he asked. "So why'd you do it? Why'd you leave the computer room? That wasn't part of the plan."

Watters tried to sit up. Dale helped him into a partial seated position.

"I had to have him. I had to win. That's the truth."

"So how did you do that?"

Watters smiled. "I know it's corny. But I tackled that motherfucker like I was back playing ball."

"You really pulled my ass out of the fire, Calvin."

Watters' smile broadened. "No offense, but you know I did it to save myself too. I had to save Rachel and get information about the murders."

A nurse entered. They were going to prep Watters for tests on any hidden damage.

When Watters was done, Dale returned to the room where the doctor was addressing the patient. "I've seen worse—a slight concussion, a couple of head wounds, a cut above your right eye and on your left cheekbone. Your eye will swell up some. We didn't stitch up the bullet wound for fear of infection. The bullet had a clean exit. We'll change the bandages every couple of hours to make sure it's clean and dry. Your shoulder will require some therapy, but you should regain a hundred percent mobility. The nurse will be in with your painkillers."

As if on cue, the door opened and a short, pretty nurse walked in holding a tiny white envelope.

She slipped in between the bed and doctor, shook out three pills and set them on the bedside table. "This is Naproxen, 375mg per pill. Take one every 4-6 hours and don't take more than five a day."

Watters snorted and smiled at the doctor. "Doc, you're gonna have to do better than that. I've been on a steady dose of painkillers for the last three years, from Tylenol to morphine. With all my new injuries and my tolerance for medication over the years, I'm gonna need some serious stuff."

The doctor pulled Dale to the side and whispered. "Is this patient narcotic dependant? Should I be concerned that Mr. Watters will go into narcotic withdrawal after a gunshot? Because that will greatly influence my prescription."

Dale nodded.

"I'll prescribe something stronger." The surgeon smirked and left the room.

The nurse took a couple of quick tests and said, "I'll be back with your new medication."

When the door closed, Dale went over to the bed and grinned. "You keep talking like that and they'll drug you up like a racehorse." He handed Watters a cup of water and asked, "So how did you know Baxter would use the back entrance?"

Watters took a drink and smiled. "I made the lock difficult to break, so Baxter would think that everything was real, but I didn't make it impenetrable like the other entrances. That was the only door Baxter *could* use."

"You have a minute, Dayton?"

Dale turned to see his Sergeant. The sergeant shook Watters' hand.

"What do we know about Baxter?" Watters asked.

"Last night was busy. We haven't grilled him yet," Dale said.

The sergeant grabbed Dale by the sleeve. "Can I have a word with you, Dayton?" he asked and pulled him into the hallway.

The sergeant was talking before the door had even closed behind them. "You almost fucked this one up and don't forget that Watters is a civilian. Should we be divulging information about Baxter?"

He looked at his sergeant. "For one thing, why are you here?"

"I'm checking my men, making sure everyone is okay."

"Bullshit. There's more. And two, I think we owe Watters this much. He just put his life on the line for us. Why don't you go back to the office and I'll let you know when you're needed."

"Who died and gave you guts? Okay. Whatever. I'll see you in a few hours."

After the sergeant turned and stomped off, Dale returned to the room and spoke to Watters. "After we got you and Baxter into the ER last night, I spent the night here in the hospital while Jimmy stayed with Rachel in case I needed to contact her. I got back to the office for a few minutes this morning, while you were in surgery, and brought those files with me. But my team has been working through the night. All we know for sure is that Baxter was born in Biloxi, Mississippi. From Sanders' phone records, we found several phone calls to a phone booth in New Orleans and we expect that's who Sanders was calling. As a rule, assassins like to hang out near home, believe it or not. I'll follow up later."

"So what are you going to do about Sanders?"

"I'm not sure yet. I…"

There was a light rap on the door and a nurse entered with a new envelope. "This is Ketoprofen, 50mg capsules for acute pain. It will act as both a pain killer and anti-inflammatory. Take one every four to six hours."

"Thanks," he said.

The nurse left.

Dale said, "I'm going to the office now to see what my team has found. We have to wait for the doctor's permission to interrogate Baxter and I want to be ready when I do. Calvin, Jimmy and I would like you to watch us interview Baxter. We can check Baxter's information with you. Maybe you'll be able to expand on it or illuminate. What do you say?"

Watters smiled and nodded. "I'd like that."

"Good. You should get some rest now. I'll be back later."

CHAPTER 39

Everyone was in that Sunday, recharged now that Baxter had tried to kill Watters and maybe more. The department was in full operational mode—phones ringing, papers rustling, fingers tapping keyboards and anxious chatter. Dale's team hadn't been this alive since the investigation had started, when Grant's body was found more than four days ago.

Jimmy was already at his desk, looking like he'd gotten even less sleep, when Dale strode through, peeled off his jacket and set it on the back of his chair. A steaming mug of coffee was already sitting on his desk.

"How's Watters?" Jimmy asked.

"Recovering. He seems to be in good spirits, considering the circumstances. Any word on when we can talk with Baxter?"

Jimmy shook his head. "Couple of hours. He had a full amputation and will be lucid by then, or good enough."

Dale sat down at his desk. "What do we know so far?"

"We found a knapsack and a briefcase on the roof of the old Hadley Grocer building down the street from Watters' hideout, jammed underneath the fire-exit staircase. Inside the knapsack we found a camouflaged rain poncho and a tarp. The briefcase contained pieces of a 7.62 x 51mm M40 and a tripod."

"Marine standard-issue sniper rifle."

Jimmy nodded and continued. "We circulated Baxter's picture and got a possible hit. Baxter had checked into a penthouse suite at the Bellagio on Monday night."

After a moment's thought, Dale said, "That's over $500 a night. Who's paying the bill?"

Jimmy shrugged. "The hotel manager said the bill was paid for seven nights, in cash. The bed looked like it hadn't been slept in. No fingerprints. We found a suitcase with some clothes and toiletries and a duffel bag full of weapons in the vent." Jimmy read from a sheet. "A Browning 9 x 19mm Hi-Power, a Taurus Millennium series PT145, a Walther P99 semi-automatic, the list goes on. Ballistics ran them all, but they came up empty on our murders and couldn't connect them to any murders across the country. They also sent the data to ATF, to run through their National Integrated Ballistic Information Network. Again, no match."

"We caught a good one."

"This is interesting but leads nowhere," Jimmy said. "The team found ember remains in the sink. Baxter burned a sheaf of papers and ran it down the drain. We took out the pipes, but we couldn't recover any kind of evidence." He held up a sheaf of papers. "I just printed out Baxter's bio, a textbook on becoming a champion killer."

They divvied up the package and both men read without interruption.

Dale stared at Baxter's Marine Corps boot camp ID photo—chiseled jaw, gleam in his eye—ready to make a difference. Baxter was an ex-Marine of the 2nd MEB, 2nd Battalion, 3rd Marines.

Baxter did two tours and was highly decorated, including two Purple Hearts. He had taken out fifty-three people in one two-hour exploit. Not long after he received a dishonorable discharge under a special warrant that was unexplained and classified.

Jimmy whistled. "Wow! Carlos Hathcock, the most legendary sniper in Marine and American military history, has ninety-three confirmed kills is his whole service time."

"Yeah, but who knows how many they really have? The distances and circumstances make it extremely difficult to confirm. It also says here that Baxter received an early psychological discharge." Dale looked at Jimmy. "I have a hard time believing that someone with Baxter's sniper record and numerous combat medals and decorations would be dishonorably discharged from the Corps."

It was Jimmy's turn. "Look at this. The military has an outstanding, special, high-priority warrant out against Baxter."

"Listen to this quote from one of Baxter's commanding officers. 'In training camp, Derek Baxter showed a rare gift for sharp shooting and I sent him to our Marine Sniper-Scout School, the finest of its kind in the world, where only six of every hundred who enter graduate. Derek graduated at the top of his class and joined one of the military's most elite groups. His subsequent performance as a sniper was among the best I've ever seen.' End quote."

"I wonder what happened."

Jimmy smiled. "The advantages of being a psychopath. No emotion about other people."

Dale knew that the right thing would be to call the military and tell them they had Derek Baxter in custody.

At the end of reading, one thing was clear. Baxter was a military asset, but also an obvious sociopath.

Dale's cell phone rang.

"Dayton."

"We've got a problem, sir."

He listened for a moment, the smile fading from his face. He hung up.

"Fuck!"

The uniform who'd been guarding Baxter's room met Dale and Jimmy at the hospital entrance door.

"I tried to keep them out, Detectives, but they pushed their way through with their credentials. There was nothing I could do."

"Don't worry about it, kid."

They took the elevator to the third floor. Dale and Jimmy strode across the lobby and passed the nurse's station. Dale tried the doorknob to the room, but it had been locked from the inside. He jiggled it hard but it wouldn't budge.

"Jimmy, find someone to open this, will you?"

As Jimmy turned to leave, the door was opened just enough for a large head with a blond crew cut to appear. The man had a square jaw and pronounced cords in his thick neck. "The Colonel will see you guys in a minute."

Dale reached for the knob. "Wait—"

The man shut the door and Dale, raising his eyebrows, turned to Jimmy.

He answered with a shrug.

Less than a minute later, true to his word, the door opened and a man in a green military uniform walked out with a Marine swagger. A pair of tough-looking Army men followed him and stopped outside the door. The leader continued toward Dale and Jimmy, his chest displaying numerous medals and ribbons.

"Gentlemen, I'm Marine Colonel John Hughes." The man didn't extend his arm, his hands intertwined behind his back.

Dale thought Hughes resembled a cartoon character with deeply recessed eyes, a prominent nose and a narrow chin. His scholar accent didn't go unnoticed.

"Detective Dayton, Vegas Police. This is my partner, Detective Mason."

Hughes gave the detectives an antagonistic nod. "Detectives, I'm Derek Baxter's defense attorney and I'll be organizing his court-martial."

"So what is it Baxter did that resulted in that special high-priority warrant?"

Hughes's impassive face never changed. "That's confidential information, Detective. I'll be taking him back to base now." He turned to leave.

"Wait a minute, Colonel." Dale knew the military warrant took legal precedence over Baxter's police custody, but he still didn't like it. He played his highest card right away. "I don't think you comprehend the gravity of the situation. You're not taking him anywhere. Baxter is wanted for questioning in the murder of a police officer."

The colonel didn't flinch. "I'm sorry for your loss, Detective, but this is a matter of national security. Baxter is wanted back on base. The military prefers to handle these situations internally."

"Listen, he killed my officer and there's no way you're taking him." Dale moved closer to the colonel.

"We'll see about that, Detective." In one swift motion, the colonel pulled out a cell phone. He turned his back, made a call and held a short conversation. When he had hung up, he turned back around to face Dale.

"So?" Dale asked.

The colonel only smiled.

As if on cue, Dale's cell phone rang. He answered without taking his eyes off the colonel.

"Dayton."

"Let it go." He heard his sergeant's voice.

"Yeah. But…"

"I said, let it go."

"Yeah. Okay, Sarge." Dale slammed the phone shut and addressed the colonel. "Okay, you seem to have some pull in my department. But we have some questions for your client, questions that are imperative to our investigation."

"He will not be answering questions from your department. I have your answers."

Dale licked his lips. "So what can you tell me?"

"He was hired by a man named Ace Sanders to kill Calvin Watters.

He was paid half upfront and the other half was to be paid on completion of his mission. Of course, that never happened. His employer never used his name, but my client, being a thorough Marine, conducted his research and knew who he was working for."

Before Dale could ask another question, the Colonel continued. "He is no longer in your custody. The Marines will take over from here."

Dale's shoulders sagged.

Baxter would never undergo a civilian court trial for homicide. As bad as it seemed, Dale couldn't help but smile at the poetic justice. Having Watters turn Baxter into a one-legged man, some justice had been served.

Dale and Jimmy watched Hughes turn and leave.

"Wow, he thinks his shit don't stink."

"Yeah, an asshole. But we have to let him take Baxter."

"What do we do now?"

Dale would keep investigating the cop killing in hopes of finding evidence that he could give to the Marines and perhaps make their court-martial and sentencing more severe. But at the same time, he knew that he'd already found the real killer, so there was no cop-killer on the loose to search for, only potential evidence—a very slim hope at best.

"Back to square one, Jimmy. Grant's original murder investigation. At least we have hearsay testimony through the colonel that Sanders hired Baxter. Of course we can't use it because Baxter will be gone. That still doesn't link Sanders to the first three murders, but it does strengthen his motives. Why would he want Watters dead, if it's not because he knows too much about the murders?"

Baxter might have escaped civilian justice, but to Dale, Watters' form of justice had been much greater and much more devastating. And he also realized that the military could be vindictive with those who betray their uniform and country.

"Let's go tell Watters."

"What the fuck do you mean he's leaving?" Calvin squeezed out, his throat constricted from emotion. He couldn't believe what the detectives were telling him. He and Rachel had just spent four days locked up, hiding from both the police and a hired killer. Their lives had changed beyond recall. His body hurt, his girlfriend was in hiding and he had to sit and listen as the dicks on the job let Baxter go.

"I know how you must be feeling, but our hands are tied. The Marines wanted Baxter long before we did and they have dibs on him before the Vegas Police," Dale said.

"This is bullshit!" Calvin tried to stand, but the pain won over.

"Give me a hand, will ya?"

The detectives helped him to sit up on the edge of the bed. He knew that he shouldn't be blaming them. They'd done all they could. But Calvin was feeling the aftereffects of the last four days and he needed someone to take his frustrations out on.

"How are your injuries?" Dale asked.

"Better."

"Want some?" The detective held out a tin of Skoal but he declined. Dale jammed in a chunk. "I thought all you athletes did this?"

Calvin smiled but said nothing. He put his good hand on the bed railing and placed all his weight on it, pushing himself to his feet. He still had trouble with balance.

"I need to get out of this stuffy room."

"How about a walk?" Detective Mason spoke for the first time since the introductions.

Calvin hobbled on stiff legs across the room. The detectives opened the door just as Baxter was being wheeled past. He was uncovered, which revealed his bandaged, shortened left leg.

He wore a hospital-issued, sleeveless gown and Calvin saw a tattoo of two eagles flying head-to-head and the letters USMC printed under them on Baxter's right arm.

Like Calvin, he had substantial bruising and scratches to his face and arms. Calvin's and Baxter's eyes met before Baxter looked away.

Dale spoke. "I think for the first time in his life, he feels defeated."

"Where are they taking him?"

"Marine Corps Base Camp Pendleton, which is the major West Coast base of the United States Marine Corps. It's in San Diego County. Hughes is organizing Baxter's probable court-martial for whatever he did that resulted in that special high-priority warrant. He's Baxter's defense attorney."

The three men watched Baxter being wheeled down the hall and into a cordoned-off wing. They exited the room and walked in the opposite direction.

"What now?" Calvin asked, his eyes shifting between detectives.

"I thought I would have an opportunity to interrogate Baxter. All we can do now is focus on the first three murders. Here's what we have." Dale scratched the stubble on his chin. "Baxter's confession is more evidence against Sanders, but it's only hearsay, not admissible in court."

"Fuck the court. We need to—"

Dale grasped Calvin by the arm. "If you're going to work with Jimmy and me, you have to think like a cop, not a bone breaker."

Calvin nodded, but he didn't like it. "Sorry, go ahead."

"Baxter's direct confession advances the investigation in

understanding the person we're pursuing. Sanders could have done the other murders himself or used another hired hand. Willing to pay to have you killed is only one mental and psychological step away from personally committing homicide. We now know that Sanders fits the profile of the very rare and small number of people who are capable of deliberately committing murder, when the vast majority could never cross that line, even in life or death self-defense."

"What's his next move?"

The detective smiled. "Once Sanders discovers his hit man has failed, he'll worry about what Baxter might say to us. And then what you might say to us. So he has to act fast. But with Sanders' range of contacts, we have to factor in the possibility that he's already learned about Baxter's arrest. That should shake him even more."

"If he knows that, then in all likelihood he knows I'm in custody too," Calvin said.

"That's what we're thinking."

Jimmy cut in. "He's got to be sweating. We're not sure he won't try to get you even while you're in the hospital. At this point, we're not sure what Sanders is capable of."

Calvin added. "I have direct confirmation from Shawn Grant that Sanders and Linda Grant were having an affair. He'll want to squelch that."

"But will they pick up their affair? We're still not allowed to touch Sanders and the order is stronger than ever," Jimmy said.

They continued walking, this time in silence. Each detective cradled an arm to help Calvin move with less discomfort.

They were almost back at Calvin's room when Dale said, "Our only hope is that Sanders' rush to action will force him to make a mistake. We're still not allowed to touch Sanders, but I have an idea." Dale looked Calvin in the eye. "Do you think you feel ready to leave?"

He didn't need to think about it. "Hell, yeah."

"We'll talk with the doctor and make sure it's okay."

They entered the room and Jimmy said. "I'll go see the doc. If we get the green light, I'll sign the release forms."

Calvin saw his blood-stained shirt hanging from the back of a chair. A new, clean one was folded and piled on a pair of pants on the seat.

"Rachel picked them out," Dale said.

The nurse came in to change Calvin's bandages. With his arm in a sling, all movement was awkward, so Dale had to help him get his shirt over his head and pulled down.

Calvin said, "I want to stay on this case."

"What do you mean?"

"Since the 'Baxter' problem has been eliminated, I assumed I would be expendable."

"Calvin, you've already been an essential part of this case. You're the reason we have Baxter and we have confirmation that Sanders is behind these murders. I realize your vested interest in this case."

Calvin just smiled.

Jimmy returned with the forms. "Everything is taken care of." He handed Calvin a piece of paper. "This is your prescription. They said they also added Tylenol 3, a brief, self-limited course of Tylenol and codeine. We're good to go."

"Good, because I know exactly what we're going to do," Dale said.

CHAPTER 40

Ace sat at his desk, staring down at the hand he had dealt himself. He surveyed the other three hands and then turned back to his own, the five cards that lay in front of him, face up.

He poured a generous portion of Evan Williams twenty-three-year-old bourbon and drank it in one swallow. Then he poured himself another.

He knew what it meant. Two pairs, black aces and black eights—the dead man's hand.

His pulse quickened and his breathing slowed. A twitching vein behind his ear pulsated. A deep-seated fear crept into his soul.

Legend had it that on August 2, 1876, in Saloon Number Ten at Deadwood, South Dakota, Wild Bill Hickok had this exact same hand when he was gunned down—murdered in cold blood. Although there were no confirmed accounts of what Hickok's fifth card was, Ace dreaded the hand. It was cursed.

Four days ago everything had been under control. After hiring Scott, Ace thought the Watters situation was handled. But as one attempt after another failed, he was only exposed to more risk.

From his informant on the Las Vegas police, he learned early this morning that Scott had been arrested. The cops would be questioning him and that made Ace sweat.

He had spent the day pondering his next move, making sure that the time was right. He had no choice now. With the dark of night, he decided to make his move.

The situation couldn't be worse. Watters was still alive and his hit man was in police custody. Now Ace had to clean up this mess too. He was working hard to get another top hit man to Vegas but that would take time he didn't have.

Even though he never used his name, paid with cash transfers and had left no paper trail, he knew that someone as experienced as Scott would find it out anyway. The assassin was supposed to be the best and had come from a reliable source. That's why Ace agreed to pay part of his outrageous fee upfront.

He picked up his secure line.

"Hello?"

"It's me. I need to see you now."

"Okay," the voice answered back.

"Are the cops still outside your house?"

There was a momentary silence. Then the caller came back on the line. "Yes."

"Okay. Don't say a word. Just listen."

He made his plan very clear, going into fine detail. He wasn't sure the line was truly secure, so he had to make the conversation as unrevealing as possible.

"Don't be late."

He hung up and stared at the cards on the desk. He swallowed, closed his eyes, shook his head and got up.

He left his office lights on and turned up the stereo. He radioed down and told his pit and slot managers that he had serious work to take care of and didn't want to be interrupted for the remainder of the night. He then slipped out the back way of his office and snuck down the back stairs to the employee staff room.

The minute he walked in, the three employees who had been taking their break jumped up from the table and walked out without making eye contact.

Once they were gone, he lifted a set of keys from an employee's jacket and left the casino through a back entrance, avoiding the cameras.

He marched through the back alley, putting on strong skin-colored surgical gloves. His fingerprints would never be found in the car he'd be driving...or later.

Standing in the employee parking lot, he pushed the disarm button on the key chain until he saw a car in the far corner of the lot light up. After securing the lot, he climbed behind the wheel and sped away. He wasn't worried, just being careful as always. Ace knew his call to the mayor had abolished any ideas the cops might have about following him.

He gripped the steering wheel. It maddened him all over again that Watters was still a problem when he should have been dead days ago.

Having already sold her share of her late husband's casino to Ace, Linda just had to wait a few more days while the bank's substantial check cleared and was deposited into her account.

But she had been promised more than just money. Even if she couldn't trust her lover, she was going to give it a brief try. She had been promised love too. Even if he had experienced a change of heart, Linda had enough money to escape Vegas by herself and start over in another part of the world.

She took the stairs, stumbling, to the mansion's wine cellar to return an empty bottle and choose another. She had also been told to use the wine cellar to make all of her "private" calls.

She shut the door and used the phone he'd given her, dialing the familiar number.

"What is it?"

Just the sound of his voice gave her chills. "Ace just called. He wants to meet me."

"Good, that means he's worried."

"I don't think I should go. You know Ace, he's capable of anything."

"Linda, you have to go. This is the plan we've been working on. We're so close, baby. It's almost over and then we can be together forever."

"Are you sure?"

"Linda, listen to me. This is it. You need to go meet Ace. This is important to me...to us. Keep him happy. Give him what he wants."

She smiled. "I'll be thinking of you like always. I miss you."

"I miss you too. But we can't be seen together. Soon."

"Okay, I'll do it."

"That's my girl."

CHAPTER 41

"Well, that was a fuckin' waste of time!" Watters jammed himself into the narrow booth, looking more than a little uncomfortable.

It was late on a Sunday night and they were at a small diner, having just concluded their six-hour shift staking out Linda Grant.

"I agree," Jimmy said

Although Linda had been quiet, Dale didn't feel the new 24/7 schedule on Linda was a total waste. "Sure, nothing happened today. Linda won't yell to the world that she was a part of a master plan to kill her husband. But the night's not over yet."

"Do you really think, with the buzz she put on at dinner, she'll be leaving the house again tonight?"

Dale shrugged. "I don't know."

"I'd like to see Rachel soon," Watters said.

"We can make that happen. We can—" Dale was cut off by the vibration from his cell phone, which had a familiar caller ID. "It's the department." He flipped open the phone. "Dayton."

"Detective, it's Mitch. Linda Grant just received a phone call."

"From who?"

"Unknown."

"What do you mean unknown?"

"The caller used a voice distorter and scrambler, untraceable."

Dale remembered the 911 call on Wednesday with the same security measures. Whoever set up Watters was calling Linda.

"Thanks, Mitch."

He hung up and made another call. "Charlie, it's Dale. Anything?"

"No. The limo dropped her off a while ago and left. Lights are off. Guess she went to bed."

"No—check that she's really at home. She just got a scrambled call."

"What?"

"Get in there! And keep your cell phone on so I can track what's going on."

Through the phone he could hear movement and a car door slam. He heard the faint sound of heavy panting and a knock on a door.

The cop came back on the line. "No answer, Dale."

"Break it down!"

"Don't I need 'probable cause' to go in?"

"The suspicious call is enough."

He heard them crash through the door and running up stairs, then, "Shit."

He closed his eyes and cursed under his breath. He called the department. "Mitch, it's me again. We lost Linda. Please tell me the GPS is operational?"

He could hear computer keys clicking over the phone.

"It was confirmed that the limo had been parked for the night, but the GPS is indicating that it's moving again."

Dale hung up. "Linda's on the move."

They threw some cash on the table and sprinted from the diner. Dale jumped in the passenger side. "You drive."

With Watters in the back, Jimmy peeled out of the parking lot while Dale stayed on the line with Mitch, who was relaying Linda's coordinates.

"We're getting closer."

"Call for back up," Jimmy said.

With the cell phone still pressed to his ear, Dale grabbed the car radio and had dispatch locate four cars to join the tail. He gave them the exact location and made sure they followed his direct orders.

"She's stopped, Jimmy." Dale gave the coordinates. "Pull over here."

Jimmy slowed the car and killed the lights. "There's Duncan and Smith."

Dale saw two undercover cars parked on a side street. In the rearview mirror, he saw two more cars pull up. "Everyone's in position."

Linda's limo was parked beside a pump of a deserted roadside gas station. The lights were off inside the building and the only light came from the low-watt bulb of the corner streetlight.

"What's she doing out here?" Watters asked.

"I don't know. But I see a set of headlights."

They watched as an unfamiliar car pulled up beside the limo.

Dale picked up the car radio. "Nancy, I need a plate check."

"Go ahead."

"Nevada tags—zero, nine, six, four, apple, brandy."

He continued to watch the scene as the dispatch operator located the information.

"The car is registered to a Mr. Gene Lockhart."

"He's a pit boss at the Golden Horseshoe," Watters interrupted.

Dale eyed Watters in the rearview mirror. "You know him?"

Watters nodded. "He's not a killer, if that's what you're thinking."

"Sanders might have asked him to pick up Linda," Jimmy said.

Dale shook his head. "I don't think so."

"What are you thinking?" Jimmy asked.

"I hadn't expected Sanders to do anything in his Ferrari, known all over Vegas. Linda wouldn't meet a total stranger in a deserted area at night."

"You think that it's Sanders?"

Dale didn't respond.

The limo door opened and Linda stepped out. She approached the idling 2004 Toyota Corolla, opened the door and climbed inside.

When the passenger door opened, the interior light didn't go on, but Dale didn't need confirmation. "She's going with Sanders. Let's move," he said into the two-way radio.

The bumper-lock surveillance was all they could do for now.

"Keep a safe distance, Jimmy." Dale spoke into the radio. "Stand down, everyone and stay back. Follow my lead."

"Whose car?" Linda asked.

"A friend's," Ace replied, checking his rearview mirror before pulling out.

"Kind of paranoid, having my driver pick me up two blocks from my house."

Ace ignored her remark. "Your hit man failed." He sneered. "Where did you find him anyway?"

Linda smiled. "I'm not just another pretty face. I have my connections too."

She winked, reached over the middle compartment and slipped her hand in his lap. She fumbled for his zipper and pulled it down.

"Are you drunk?"

"I had a couple of cocktails with dinner." She slid her hand inside his pants.

"Not yet." He pulled it out.

Linda pouted and folded her arms across her chest.

He had to keep his mind clear. Some overzealous officer might pull him over for something as minor as a broken taillight. He kept discreetly checking for a tail in a way that wouldn't make Linda suspicious of his actions.

"Where are we going?" Linda asked.

"It's a surprise. Just sit back and relax. We'll be there soon."

"What's with you tonight? And what's with the gloves?"

Ace noted the iciness in her voice. He didn't reply. They were nearing the spot and he tightened his grip on the wheel. His breath quickened and his heartbeat amplified. The irony was almost too much.

He felt a charge go up the back of his neck.

When the Toyota pulled over and stopped in a hidden rest area, so did Jimmy. "So what's our next move? We can't see or hear inside that car."

"I'm not sure. Fuck! I was hoping Sanders would take her to a motel, where we could set up some sort of surveillance. We're blind and deaf out here. Does this place look familiar?" Dale asked.

Jimmy's eyes grew wide. "Holy shit!"

"Exactly. He's going to do Linda where he offed Grant."

"We need to stop this."

Dale picked up the radio. "Everyone stand down." Each unit was parked a good distance from the suspect's car and couldn't be seen.

A dark cloud floated away, clearing the sky for a full moon. He started to tense.

"Should we move in?"

"And do what, Jimmy? How do we explain it? We're not supposed to be anywhere near Sanders. We don't have anything yet."

The passenger door of the Toyota opened and Linda stepped out. Then the driver's door inched its way open and a man followed.

Even the full moon wasn't enough to identify him. The man walked around the front of the car to the passenger's side of the vehicle and positioned himself behind Linda, always staying hidden.

All they could do was wait.

The unidentified man slipped his left arm around Linda's waist, little by little working its way under her breasts as he buried his face in her hair. They remained in that position for seconds, swaying their hips together in gentle, sexual rhythm—small circular motion. Linda's facial expression was one of orgasmic pleasure.

"Guess we're in for a show," Jimmy announced, leaning back in his seat.

But something wasn't right. At first glance, Linda seemed to enjoy it, but to Dale, it looked like she then clawed at the arm in panic, trying to tear from its grip. She was fighting to breathe. "That's not consensual. Everyone move in!"

Dale thought of Grant and Pitt and was the first one out of the car, gun pointed, sprinting toward Linda. But even Dale's quickness and the blinding headlight rays could not stop the killer, who was already in full motion.

Dale saw the glint of the blade before it sliced Linda's throat with the viciousness seen in a snuff film. Blood gushed from the wound as Linda's hands grasped for it, the blood spewing between her fingers. Her listless body flopped to the ground.

Sanders stood over Linda, blood dripping from the knife, a sly grin on his face.

Everyone had their weapons drawn. It all happened so fast that it took a few moments for Dale and his team to fully realize what they'd just seen.

Sanders shielded his eyes from the lights with one hand. The other one hung at his side, clutching the bloody murder weapon. Linda's blood spatter had splashed on his clothes and skin. He turned to run, but the squad cars boxed him in.

The bloody knife flew from Sanders' hand and soared deep into the woods. But it didn't matter.

CHAPTER 42

Almost midnight, the precinct was full of cops who came in just to watch Sanders get processed. When word had gotten out, many off-duty officers had left their homes, bars, or wherever they happened to be and returned to the station to watch Sanders, issuing dire threats all the way, as he was guided into the police station.

Earlier, as soon as Sanders had released the knife, four cops, flashlights drawn, had raced into the woods after it. Now Jimmy carried it into the station, sealed in a plastic evidence bag.

The sergeant came out of the office, a large smile, apparent relief, on his face. "Great job, you guys. The lieutenant's on his way."

Dale didn't smile. He was glad he caught Sanders—that's all. Jimmy and Calvin seemed happy too, but not as if they were happy for the Vegas police.

After the long and exhausting frustration of leading double murder investigations that were the most important in the homicide history of Las Vegas and with pressure from the mayor on down and absolutely no hard evidence until tonight, Dale felt it all come to a climax.

But that was short lived.

Linda had gotten killed because his bosses protected Sanders—no other reason. Dale's one regret was that they couldn't have arrested Sanders sooner, which could have prevented her death.

What stopped him? Not only the perfect murders, which were part of the nature of his work, but in this context, most importantly—the interference by the mayor and sergeant, for political reasons. That was the real tragedy. Politics had kept the real murderer free until he could kill his fourth victim.

Politics should never have been part of Dale's investigations, but they were, and that was what he really lamented.

He would never know really if Linda had helped Sanders kill Grant because the only person alive connected to it all was Sanders himself. Even if he admitted that Linda was behind it, would it be the truth or just some last-ditch effort to save himself from the chair? Did she deserve to die?

With Watters following them, Dale and Jimmy took Sanders to the booking counter and transferred custody to two officers. They watched until Sanders disappeared from view down the hallway toward the holding cells.

"He better get used to those living arrangements."

Dale turned to find the mayor and District Attorney Robert Flannery standing behind them, wide smiles on their faces.

"We came as soon as we heard," the mayor said. "Good work."

Flannery spoke. "We have enough on Sanders. His band of lawyers and every legal technique in the book can't save him now. Assuming he pleads down, we'll put him away for two consecutive life sentences, without parole. Sanders will never see the outside of a prison again."

"Not in this lifetime." The mayor smiled again. "Let's go, Robert. We have a press conference tomorrow to plan for."

Dale, Jimmy and Watters looked at each other.

Unable to find words, Dale gestured toward his desk and led the way. He grabbed an empty chair for Watters and sat down. "I'm exhausted."

"I feel the same way," Jimmy said.

"I'm sure it'll hit me soon too, but right now I'm still feeling the rush of seeing you capture and arrest Sanders," Watters added.

"Want a drink?"

"In a second," Dale replied. He removed the chunk of Skoal from his mouth and dropped it into an empty coffee cup next to his computer. He rinsed using old water from a cup that had been on his desk for days.

Watters and Jimmy, still exhilarated by the arrest, joined a group of officers who were enjoying the victory. The precinct was filled with laughter, storytelling and cheering.

Dale opened up his desk drawer, pulled out the overstuffed file marked "Casino Case" and opened it up. He spread everything across his bare desk—photos, reports and even handwritten notes.

Piece by piece, he went over what he had. With a single exception, it was still all circumstantial.

For Linda Grant's murder, they already had all the proof they needed.

Had they sacrificed Linda so that they could arrest Sanders? Dale knew that there was no real answer to that question and that the either/or aspects would haunt him the rest of his life, as he kept second-guessing the decision he had made. And he would never know if Linda had been an accomplice with Sanders in Grant's murder, or just his lover who hadn't known of Sanders' plan to kill her husband. Not knowing if she was innocent or guilty would make the question that would always haunt him even more painful.

He'd seen the bandages on Sanders' wrist. There was no doubt in Dale's mind that when the test came back from the lab in a few days, the skin found underneath the nails of the call girl in Pitt's office would match a DNA sample taken from Sanders.

The other three murders?

How did Sanders murder Grant and Pitt? Baxter saying that Sanders had hired him to kill Watters was hearsay. And they hadn't had the time to try to get Baxter to confess to the cop killing.

Convicting one killer for only two of the five murders and being forced to release the other killer to the military made Dale's brief sense of victory seem hollow. Despite the most massive manhunts in the city's history, both led by Dale, this was what it had come down to.

Two out of five was an incredible batting average, but for a homicide detective who'd dedicated his professional life to protecting all of the city's residents, it was a major defeat, or at least it felt like one.

But this was Nevada. One of thirty-four states that still practiced the death penalty—lethal injection determined by a jury. There was always the chance that Sanders, being as arrogant as he was, would think his fame and fortune could buy a verdict. He might decide to plead not guilty. Even murder by hire in the state of Nevada was punishable by death. But Dale doubted it would come to that. Not with the evidence they had.

Baxter, a hired gun, had suffered his own punishment. The ex-Marine had indeed avoided the legal system, but Watters had made sure that the family members of the deceased attained a certain amount of revenge for their loved ones.

Only indirect punishment.

Dale felt like a failure. He might get promoted for bringing Sanders down, but he hadn't solved the crime, not really. He could only accept the praise if he personally felt he'd earned it. By his own standards, he had not.

He thought about the victims—slimy like Pitt and promising like Craig. He had failed them. What could he say to their family and friends? That's he'd tried, failed and was sorry?

Was that worth neglecting his own family?

If he hung around any longer he'd bring everyone down—so Dale went home.

CHAPTER 43

Calvin had persuaded Rachel into moving into his tiny apartment for the time being. But even though the police had brought in a team that left it spotless, they'd always know that a cop had died there.

When he heard the front door chime at exactly 4:00 p.m., he smiled. He expected the punctuality.

He opened the door wide and spread his arms, wrapping his visitor in a massive, affectionate bear hug, though careful not to tear his stitches.

With his large right arm wrapped around the man's shoulders, Calvin pulled his visitor into the small living room and got him seated. Dragging an armchair close to the man, Calvin sat down, leaned forward and said, "It's really great to see you, Dale. It doesn't matter why you're here. I'm glad you are."

"I feel selfish asking to speak to you alone when you've had so little time with Rachel."

"She understands. You know how we both feel about you. She's meeting friends at a coffee shop."

The detective leaned back in his chair and began to relax. It looked like it had been a while. "Thank you. You really love her, don't you?"

Calvin smiled, feeling flushed. "I do. Her strength and determination make me want to be a better man. You said you needed to talk about something urgent, but you didn't say what it was. Is there a break in one of the other murder cases? New evidence? Something I can help with?"

"I'm sorry I couldn't tell you on the phone. It's going to be hard enough to do it here in person. The answers to your questions are no, no and yes. What I want to talk to you about has nothing to do with the investigations. It's only about me, personally and yes, I think you can help me." Dale shifted uncomfortably in his seat. "Before I get to that, Mike Armstrong called the station this morning and confirmed your alibi for the night Pitt and the prostitute were killed. That, along with Rachel's admission you were with her when Grant was murdered, was persuasive enough that even the chief admitted you are no longer a suspect in those cases."

Dale paused, as if strengthening his resolve. "I've never had a talk like this with anyone in my life, not Jimmy or my wife. You may not know me well enough to know I'm a very private person. I stay focused on the job and try to keep my emotions to myself."

Calvin smiled. "I might know you better than you think. Once Grant's body had been discovered and you were chosen to lead the homicide investigation, I researched and created a file on you and Jimmy. Your proficiency speaks for itself."

Dale grimaced and shook his head. "I wasn't the same way at home, that is, during the very little time I spent there. For too many years with my wife I was all business—ready to talk about work but not feelings and very little love. I knew I was ruining my marriage, but I didn't want to deal with the problems. Every time Betty tried to talk to me about them, I'd avoid her and make a quick escape. I've made some big mistakes in the past—which I'm still paying for."

Dale paused again and Calvin remained silent, giving the detective all the time he needed.

"Last night, when everyone was celebrating the arrest, I was as happy as everyone else that we could prosecute and convict Sanders for double homicide."

"And then I thought about the three other murder victims whose files would go in the cold-case cabinet as unsolved and maybe unsolvable, about the families and friends of those victims and I got very depressed. Three unsolved murder cases for which I, as the lead investigator, have to take full responsibility. I was honest enough with myself to accept the pain of blame and failure."

"On top of that—and nobody else knows this—Betty left me a week ago and took our young son with her to Utah to stay with her sister. All my mistakes as a husband and father, which I'd kept denying, caught up with me and it's my own fault that I'm now alone. When I realized I'd sacrificed my family to be a cop and then failed at that too, I almost broke down."

"Then I thought of you."

Calvin was astonished. "Me? I..."

Dale cut him off. "You were an innocent man who'd been put through hell and almost lost his life because of one man's all-consuming, insatiable desire for power. Look at everything you've been through. Four years ago, in less than a minute, you suffered a knee injury that ended your stellar college and certain pro career. You dropped from the top to the bottom. I checked your arrest record, so I know you were trapped at the bottom for a while. But you were on your way back, ready to go."

Calvin shook his head. "I did nothing. You're the real hero. You were the only one in all of Vegas, except for Rachel, who believed I was innocent. If you hadn't trusted me and worked with me on my plan to capture Baxter, I might be dead now and Rachel too. I owe you our lives. You put your life on the line every day to protect this city."

Dale smiled. "Okay, let's say we're heroes to each other. You also have a true loving relationship with Rachel and I admire it all the more because I sure don't have that with my wife."

"I appreciate that. But how can I possibly help you?"

Dale leaned forward, staring straight into Calvin's eyes, his face, expressions, emotions and heart wide open and said, "Tell me what I should do."

Calvin perceived where the man was in his heart and mind and what advice he needed to start moving forward again. "What do I know? I got very lucky. Not everyone would think an ex-hooker and a leg breaker were the elements of an ideal relationship."

When Dale didn't say anything, Calvin shrugged.

"You've already taken the biggest and most difficult step of all, accepting full responsibility and blame for all that went wrong and all that you didn't do that you should have done. I went through that same step."

Dale still didn't respond.

"Okay." He took a deep breath. "Tell her what you told me. Admit your faults and don't bullshit her about your repentance. Tell her that she is in charge—you'll do what she asks. You need her now more than ever and you're totally committed to changing, to becoming the father and husband you should have been and are determined to be now. It won't be easy for you, but ask her for only a little more patience. Can you do that?"

Dale dropped his head. "Yes."

Calvin smiled. "Don't try to be the whole police department. Share the load and make the right amount of time for loving your family and being with them. All the other cops admire you. The problem isn't that you'll let others down."

Dale started to speak but Calvin put his hand up. "I'm speaking the truth. You don't need to be modest or say anything because that'll just get in the way of the point I want to make." He paused for a moment and then continued. "You feel like a failure because you and your team were only able to get hard evidence on Sanders for two murders, leaving three unsolved. If Jimmy, or any members of your team, had said to you that they felt like failures for the same reasons you do, what would you have said to them?"

The detective sighed. "The only things I could say—the truth. I knew they'd done the very best they could, that homicide investigations are too complicated and difficult to solve and get enough hard evidence on for every case to be broken and every killer arrested and convicted. And that in reality, though rare, there are smart murderers. Therefore, they should feel proud about all they did do and move on with all the value of more experience."

"Then why can't you say it to yourself?"

CHAPTER 44

It had been five days since the arrest.

On the steps of city hall on Stewart Avenue, Dale stared out into the gathered crowd. As Paul Casey, mayor of Las Vegas, acknowledged the large crowd and blaze of flash cameras, Dale enjoyed peace.

He'd been able to put what he, as the team leader, had and hadn't achieved in the right perspective. Take pride in what he and his team accomplished and understand his helplessness in the rest—the perfect murders had been by nature beyond his control and law enforcement mission.

And the big one—Betty promised to talk to him again. There was hope.

Now he, Jimmy and Calvin stood before the people of this great city and awaited their medals. Dale and Jimmy were being given the LVMPD Medal of Honor, the most distinguished award the police department could grant. Calvin, as a civilian, was receiving the Las Vegas Freedom Medal, a seldom-bestowed honor for extraordinary public service.

"Detective Dale Dayton." The voiced boomed from the speakers.

A thunderous applause exploded from the crowd. As Mayor Casey draped the Medal of Honor over Dale's head and the medal came to rest on his chest, near his heart, he sensed that they were feeling the weight, honor and beauty of the medal as he was.

He turned to watch and applaud as the mayor bestowed on Jimmy and Calvin their respective awards, beaming with an almost fatherly pride, then he turned back to face the crowd and media again.

There'd never be any such ceremony honoring what Calvin had done for him. Only the two of them would ever know. That was enough.

His thoughts returned to his family, the wife and son he loved so much. He was now ready to act on that love.

"Maureen, hold all my calls and turn away any reports."

He brushed through the reception area and closed his office door. Ignoring his office desktop, Shawn Grant opened his computer case, pulled out his laptop and logged on.

He opened his secure phone and dialed the memorized number.

"Hello."

Shawn smiled. "Good afternoon, Mr. Baxter."

"It's morning where I am." Baxter's voice was silky.

"How are you?"

"How do you think I am?"

"You'll feel better soon. You kept your end of the bargain, so as we speak I'm transferring three million into your Cayman account." Shawn tapped a few keys and clicked the mouse button.

"Looks like everything worked out for you."

Shawn smiled. "Yes indeed; from beginning to end."

"You're not worried about Watters?"

Shawn shook his head. "Not in the least. Watters and I were working together to find the real killer." He chuckled. "It would be inconceivable to him that I had anything to do with it." He cleared his throat. "Can I trust you, Mr. Baxter?"

Baxter grunted. "I'm not helping the authorities, if that's what you're referring to."

Shawn smiled. He knew as much.

Baxter said, "It shouldn't be long before I'm released. I'm too valuable to them. They can't afford to court-martial me, or leave me to civilian arrest." Baxter said. "I'll be on my own again soon. And if they don't release me, I'll find a way to escape just like last time."

"Goodbye, Mr. Baxter. I'll be in touch when I require your valuable skills again."

"Oh, you'll be seeing me before that. I'm not done with Watters yet."

Shawn hung up. He leaned back in his father's Herman Miller Aeron, graphite-framed chair, rested his feet on his father's Mayline Corsica six-foot office desk and smoked one of his father's Cuban Double Corona cigars.

Linda had been the key. He'd made sure to send her to that Casino

Owner conference in Atlantic City last year to lure in Sanders with their "chance meeting."

Shawn had to admit that Linda was a piece of work and a great piece of ass. He might even miss her...a little. Sanders and his father had no idea that it was actually he and Linda playing them. Sanders, the idiot, thought he was a mastermind. They'd manipulated him in various ways for the fun of it.

In a little more than a week, Shawn had taken out every threat and only Sanders was going to prison.

His dad should have tried to work things out, instead of leaving them for the glitz and glamour and that slut Linda.

It was the changes his father had made in his will that had seriously bothered Shawn, because they meant that if Linda was still married to Doug at the time of his death, her share of his estate would include part ownership of the Greek and the freedom to sell that share to anyone she wanted. Either way, if his father died first, Shawn would be stuck with a partner outside the family and he knew how much disruption such a partner could cause if they chose to, even without having voting stock.

All existing problems had been eliminated and Shawn, with a clear mind, could now focus on the next steps. He would buy the shares from Melanie and his mother, even though he controlled theirs by proxy, giving him one-hundred percent voting control and almost eighty-eight percent ownership. All that was left was the part ownership share that Sanders had bought from Linda.

With Sanders sure to go to prison for the rest of his life, he'd be forced to sell his share and Shawn would make sure he was the final buyer regardless of cost. It was the one-hundred percent ownership that mattered the most. Combined with his total voting control, he'd be able to rule the Greek like an emperor.

Shawn Grant was on top of the world.

EPILOGUE

Monday morning, Calvin woke up rested and happy, having just had the first real, dreamless sleep in a long time.

He'd beaten Baxter just over a week ago and he still couldn't believe that he was able to win over such a competitor. The healing was not complete, but the doctors were amazed at his speedy recovery.

Last night, after taking all the medication he'd been prescribed, he'd gone to bed early with Rachel. They had nothing to fear and few worries, a brand new prelude to making love for them.

For the first time in four years, because of the doctor's strong meds, he'd been able to sleep with little pain. He looked at the alarm clock on the nightstand next to him and turned it off.

He set his head back down on the pillow and closed his eyes. A wide grin appeared on his face. He'd been smiling a lot of late and had a lot to smile about. But he needed to get moving so he wouldn't be late for the start of one of the most important days in his life.

He and Dale lived by the same creed—do your best. After that, whatever happened was what it was and whether he was continuing from the top or near the bottom, Calvin knew he would persevere and never quit again.

Energized with excitement and determination, he sat up on the edge of his bed and stretched his side. He twisted his midsection and rubbed the large scar on his shoulder that was slowly beginning to form. It would always be a physical reminder and memory of that night, but only that.

He rose and checked the stability of his knee. After the way he'd pushed his body from that Wednesday evening when he'd learned of Grant's death, through Saturday night, including that pursuit of Baxter, his knee had a lot of new injuries to recover from. He planned to start physical therapy in a week and when his body was ready, resume his grueling daily exercise regimen in small doses.

He laughed. *I want to be Superman again.*

The bathroom door opened and Rachel stepped out.

His eyes bulged. "Wow, Rachel. You're stunning."

Rachel did a little pirouette and smiled.

She wore a new, dark-colored Armani suit and her hair, dyed back to its natural straw color, was cut short to reveal her high cheekbones and strong jaw. She sported black-framed glasses that gave her an intellectual look. Her face displayed just enough makeup, but not too much.

Calvin had always thought of Rachel as beautiful, in her heart and physically, but he was amazed by how radiantly beautiful she looked now. More than ever, she looked like the All-American beauty she'd always been to him.

"Can you believe this place?" Rachel spread her arms out wide.

He smiled. "Yeah, it is pretty amazing." They had just moved in yesterday, so the apartment was still by no means fully furnished. It wasn't upscale Vegas, but it was a definite upgrade from his last apartment. "You're up early."

"This is a big day for me, for us. Did you ever think, even a few days ago, that we'd be here now?"

"No." It was true. That he and Rachel had come this far together as lovers and were now here, even more together, as they shared their love was still a dream to him. The new lives together he'd envisioned for them before had been realistic, not the dreamlike quality they both felt so strongly now.

Calvin sighed.

"What's wrong?" Rachel asked.

"I'm a bit nervous."

"You've never been nervous about anything in your life."

"But this is all so new for me. What if I fail?"

She put her hands on her hips. "Calvin Watters, have you ever failed at anything in your life?"

He smirked.

"I didn't think so. Now get in that shower."

He saluted with a mock grin. "Yes, ma'am." He started to move, then hesitated. "How about a quickie for good luck?"

Rachel rolled her eyes. "In your dreams. Move!"

He jogged into the bathroom, giving her a flirtatious slap on the backside on the way by.

They left the apartment and jumped into their new vehicle, a second-hand Ford Escape—the vehicle Rachel had picked out since Calvin's car had been confiscated. He followed the directions he'd been given and saw Dale and Jimmy standing outside their parked cruiser.

As he strode toward them, Calvin put his hand out, but Dale batted it away, giving him a hearty hug instead, which Calvin was happy to return. When they separated, Jimmy stepped forward, shaking Calvin's hand.

"Another smooth lookin' suit, Calvin," Jimmy said. "You have great taste, Rachel."

She flashed a grin. "Thank you, Detectives. It's so nice to see you again. Especially here."

Calvin looked at Dale. They shared a special bond, as deep as the one between Dale and Jimmy.

Dale motioned toward the big building. "It's not much, but we knew your budget. The rent's affordable and it's in a decent part of town. We prioritized getting the office ready so you could open for business right away and we've had it somewhat furnished. But I'm sure you and especially Rachel will want to put your own personal touches on it. I'm sorry we couldn't do more for you, Calvin."

"What do you mean?"

"What you put yourself through. I'm sorry the department couldn't compensate you in some way for the work you did."

"I didn't do what I did for money or a reward. You've given me...*us*—" he put his arm around Rachel "—our lives back. The fact that the four of us became friends is a bonus."

Dale didn't say anything. He didn't need to.

"Have you registered for training yet?" Jimmy asked.

Calvin nodded. "I've signed up online and I start next week. I'm taking the complete package—interviewing skills, fraud and insurance investigations, surveillance and criminal investigations. I can have my PI degree in eighteen months. But legally I'm allowed to practice, as long as there's proof I'm in session. I have up to three years to acquire my license."

"That sounds great. I know you'll do it. Like everything else you attempt."

Rachel elbowed Calvin's ribs. "See."

"Well, I'm sure you want to have a look," Dale said. "As promised, once your business is set up and running, we'll send as much work as we can your way. Let us know when you apply for your PI license."

"Good luck to both of you," Jimmy said. "You deserve what you have now and we couldn't be happier for you."

With that, the veteran partners turned and got into their vehicle.

As they drove away, Calvin glanced at Rachel. "Are you ready?"

She took a deep breath. "I'm right behind you, Mr. Calvin Watters, PI. It sounds just right."

He could only smile.

♣

If you enjoyed this book, please consider writing a short review and posting it on Amazon, Goodreads and/or Barnes and Noble. Reviews are very helpful to other readers and are greatly appreciated by authors, especially me. When you post a review, drop me an email and let me know and I may feature part of it on my blog/site. Thank you. ~ Luke

luke@authorlukemurphy.com

Novels by Luke Murphy

CALVIN WATTERS MYSTERIES
Dead Man's Hand
Wild Card
Red Zone (featuring Charlene Taylor)
Finders Keepers

CHARLENE TAYLOR MYSTERIES
Kiss & Tell
Rock-A-Bye Baby
Red Zone (featuring Calvin Watters)

Message from the Author

Dear Reader,

Thank you for picking up a copy of *Dead Man's Hand*. I hope you enjoyed reading this novel as much as I did writing it. My goal was to please anyone who loves thrillers, sports, or a walk on the wilder side of Las Vegas. I hope that I succeeded.

According to Wikipedia, "The dead man's hand is a Two-pair Poker Hand, namely 'aces and eights.' This card combination gets its name from a legend that it was the five-card-draw hand held by Wild Bill Hickok, when he was murdered on August 2, 1876, in Saloon No. 10 at Deadwood, South Dakota."

This is a work of fiction. I did not base the characters or plot on any real people or events. Any familiarities are strictly coincidence.

There is not a single moment in time when this idea came to be, but circumstances over the years that led to this story: my hockey injuries, frequent visits to Las Vegas, my love of football, crime books and movies.

Dead Man's Hand became real from mixing these events, taking advantage of experts in their field and adding my wild imagination. The internet also provides a wealth of information, available at our fingertips with a click of the mouse.

For more information about my books, please visit my website at www.authorlukemurphy.com. You can also "like" my Facebook page www.facebook.com/pages/Author-Luke-Murphy and follow me on Twitter at www.twitter.com/#!/AuthorLMurphy.

I'm always happy to hear from readers. Please be assured that I read each email personally and will respond to them in good time. I'm always happy to give advice to aspiring writers, or answer questions from readers. You can direct your questions/comments to the contact form on my website. Please let me know what you thought of the book. I look forward to hearing from you.

Regards,

Luke

About the Author

Luke Murphy was born in Shawville, a small rural community in Western Quebec.

He played six years of professional hockey before retiring in 2006.

His road to novelist began in the winter of 2000, after sustaining a season ending eye injury. He continued to hobby write through the years, honing his craft, making time between work and family obligations.

He constantly read, from novels in his favorite genres to books written by experts in the writing field. He made friends (published and unpublished authors), learning what it took to become successful.

Feeling that he was finally prepared, in the winter of 2007, Murphy started to write *Dead Man's Hand*. It took him two years to complete the first draft of his novel.

He hired Ms. Jennifer Lyons, of the Jennifer Lyons Literary Agency, and in 2012, signed his first publishing contract with Imajin Books.

Murphy lives in Shawville with his wife, two daughters and a pug. He is a teacher who holds a Bachelor of Science degree in Marketing, and a Bachelor of Education (Magna Cum Laude).

For more information on Luke's books: www.authorlukemurphy.com and join his Facebook page and Twitter account.